Stone and Snow

by Sibella Giorello

Published by Running Girl Productions
Contact the author at sibella@sibellagiorello.com

ISBN-13: 978-0692569054
ISBN-10: 0692569057

Cover and Title Page design by Okay Creations
Edited by Lora Doncea, editsbylora.com

For Chris Welander

There is a reason the ribs
don't reach all the way around—
the heart was never meant
to be locked up and—like
a caged bird—one day
it's just going to stop singing.

—Moriah Pearson

CHAPTER ONE

E INSTEIN'S THEORY OF relativity? All points in the universe are created equal.

But Einstein is wrong.

No way another point in the universe can equal where I'm sitting right now.

"PRIME!" shouts Drew Levinson.

The funeral service stops, dead.

No one makes a sound.

I hold my breath. I am sitting right next to the vocal eruption herself.

Reverend Burkhardt glances up from the pulpit. His dark eyes peer around the church, checking the pews filled with teary-eyed students and weeping parents. When he can't identify the voice, he squints down at his eulogy, probably trying to find his place again.

"We are gathered here today for a solemn occasion," he says.

I take a small breath. The funeral air smells like melting candles and Christmas pine and bitter tears.

"We come together to grieve the passing of this much-loved girl who was taken from us in her pr—"

I cringe.

"Prime!" Drew shouts.

From the third row, my maybe-boyfriend DeMott Fielding turns his head. His blue eyes blaze a trail right to me, sitting in the last pew—the seat closest to the door. His expression asks, *You want to go through with this?*

I shift my gaze to Reverend Burkhardt as he tries one more time.

"Sloane Stillman had everything to live for. She was pretty. She was smart. In her twelve years at St. Catherine's School, she never received any grade below an A." Reverend Burkhardt pauses to look at Mrs. Stillman. She's holding a white handkerchief to her mouth, her head bowed. "Sloane's death seems senseless to us. It leaves us wondering why such a promising young life would be cut down in its . . ."

Too late. He realizes it too late.

"That's what I said," Drew pipes up. "Prime."

I sink down into the pew. The human eruption sitting next to me weighs all of ninety-eight pounds, one-quarter of which surely comes from her oversized brain, which at this moment—in the middle of a really sad funeral for a suicidal classmate—decides it's a good idea to generate numbers, so many numbers that this enormous brain causes Drew to scribble madly in her notebook. Between shouts.

I send up a desperate prayer. *God, please shut her up.*

But God has other plans.

"Did you hear me?" Drew asks the somber silence. "I said, *prime.*"

I jab her in the ribs.

Drew, however, remains oblivious. "I said—"

I whisper, "Shhh."

Reverend Burkhardt raises his voice, trumpeting, "And what about us? What about the people left behind. Her family. Her friends. All you young people, still in your pri—best years. You must have so many questions."

"Oh, yes, we do!"

My lungs start to hyperventilate.

Reverend Burkhardt presses forward. "What would compel Sloane at the tender age of seventeen—"

"Seventeen." Drew doesn't look up from her scribbling. "Seventeen is a prime number."

"—want to die. It seems impossible."

"Because it *is* impossible," she says.

"Please." I can't take any more. I grab her wrist, hissing, "Stop."

"Stop?" She tilts her head. "Stop, what?"

I stare at the thin face of my best friend. My freakazoid best friend with her stiletto-sharp pencil hovering above a notebook page smothered with numbers.

And then I remember why we're here.

This funeral could've just as easily been for Drew.

Despite wanting to clamp my hand over her mouth, I gently whisper, "You need to be quiet."

When I steal a glance forward, DeMott's eyes are locked onto mine again. This morning he pleaded with me not to bring Drew. But she insisted.

"Look at this." Drew stabs the pencil into the page. "It's a sign."

I look. At the people. I look at the people looking at *us* from the other pews. They look perfect, and perfectly annoyed. Right in front of us sit the Pressleys. Mister Pressley is a big-shot lawyer, I've seen him argue cases in my dad's courtroom. Beside him sit their thirteen-year-old triplets, each one dressed in midnight-blue velvet. And with the deepest dread on the planet, I shift my eyes to the next person. Mrs. Pressley. The charcoal veil hanging from her pillbox hat does nothing to conceal her profound disgust. Who can blame her—this is a solemn event.

Three days ago, the smartest senior at St. Catherine's School— the girl unchallenged for valedictorian—started her vintage 1957 Chevy, sped down the road, and smashed into a tree. Sloane also left a note. She didn't want to go on living.

Reverend Burkhardt is almost yelling now. "I'm sure many of you are wondering—how could a loving God let this to happen?"

"That is part of it."

"Drew." My face feels so hot it's going to explode. "Try to—"

She glares up at me. "Raleigh, you're the one who doesn't

believe in coincidences."

Mrs. Pressley squints at me, some kind of nonverbal shaming, before turning her perfectly-coifed head around again.

I'll never measure up, I know that. But today I tried. Instead of the usual messy ponytail, I brushed my long chestnut hair till it shone. I even put on my best black clothes. I admired Sloane. I respected her. And she was somebody who actually seemed to like Drew, too.

Reverend Burkhardt steps away from the pulpit, probably to project his voice even further. "Life is not supposed to work this way."

"Because it doesn't," Drew says.

"When Jesus said—"

"Check this out."

I slap my forehead.

Mrs. Pressley spins around. "Excuse me!"

"Excused." Drew lifts the notebook, placing it right smack under my nose. The numbers race across the page: 1, 3, 5, 7, 11, 13, 17, 19, . . . all prime numbers. They stretch into the hundreds, thousands. Hundred-thousands. A math genius who can comprehend even the most abstract number theories, Drew's also an utter social mess who cannot understand why it's wrong at this very moment to call out "Seventy-three million nine hundred thirty-nine thousand one hundred and thir—"

Mrs. Pressley spins around again. "Is there something wrong with her?"

Lady, you have no idea.

I grab Drew's skinny elbow and yank her from the pew.

"Hey!" she says.

I see DeMott half-rising, coming to help. Always ready to rescue. But I shake my head and drag my best friend toward the sanctuary doors. Reverend Burkhardt's voice barrels down the aisle after us, bouncing off the antique plaster walls, boxing my red-hot ears. "You might be wondering," he says. "Does God even care?"

"He cares!" Drew cries out. "He cares because Sloane didn't kill herself!"

I push open the church door and haul my skinny weird wonderful hurting best friend down the brick steps, gasping for air, begging for help, pleading for something—anything—that will make my heartache go away.

CHAPTER TWO

I LEAN AGAINST the church's white clapboards and measure my breaths. Drew looks up at me, blinking innocently into the morning light. "Don't you get it?"

"Drew." My heart stutters. "It's a funeral."

"I know that." She whips the notebook around. "But if you'd just look at this, you'd realize what I'm saying. The facts don't add up."

For the next twenty-one minutes, the longest minutes in the known universe—hey, Einstein, time to rethink your theory—she argues with me until the wide doors of St. John's Episcopal Church finally open.

Mourners stream out.

Richmond's finest citizens are dabbing red eyes and clutching collars of black coats. December is biting its way toward Christmas. Every face looks sad.

"How can you not see this?" Drew jabs her pen at my face.

I flinch. "I just don't."

The argument has shifted from Sloane-didn't-kill-herself to an abstract number theory that's now some "sign" about what really happened when Sloane's car hit that tree.

"Seventy-three million," she says, for what feels like the seventy-three-millionth time, "nine hundred thirty-nine thousand one hundred and thirty-three." She frowns. "Raleigh, we have a duty to find the order of the universe."

"Sure." My breath condenses the cold air. "I get it."

"No, you don't. Try thinking porterhouse steak. Or filet mignon or—"

My stomach growls. We're hidden off to the side, hopefully out of view, but I can see Reverend Burkhardt and Sloane's family. They stand on the brick entrance, shaking hands with the people leaving. Even at this distance the pain radiating from the Stillmans feels like a stab to my own heart.

I glance back at Drew. She could've been in that coffin instead of Sloane.

But Drew came back.

And Sloane is gone forever.

Mrs. Stillman isn't somebody I'd ever describe as easygoing, but right now she reminds me of those tiny candy canes sealed in plastic. The whole thing can shatter, but nothing falls out because the wrapping's so tight. She extends a black-gloved hand to a passing mourner. "Thank you for coming."

"Raleigh. *Look.*"

The notebook, the jabbing pen.

My ragged heart.

"Drew, I'm really not in the mood." My insides clench. Another uptight candy cane in the land of pain.

"But this is not just any prime number."

My gaze drifts back to the church doors. Mary Vale Stillman, Sloane's younger sister, stands next to her mother. One year behind us at St. Catherine's School for Girls from Very Wealthy Families Who Demand Achievement, Mary Vale is beautiful to the extreme. Sloane was pretty, as Reverend Burkhardt pointed out. But Mary Vale? Once or twice I've caught myself staring at her features, like they're an intriguing puzzle. Separately, each feature is kind of ordinary—blue eyes, pale skin, straight nose. But together they create an extraordinary face. Breathtaking.

Drew shifts into my line of vision. The mass of her curly brown hair blots out Mary Vale. "Why doesn't this number ring any bells?"

"Because I hate math."

She rolls her eyes. "Nobody can hate math."

Here we go again.

As Drew launches into the "poetry" of mathematics, I step to the side. My gaze drifts back to the brick stoop. Mary Vale looks impossibly sad. So does Mrs. Stillman, until she glances at the man at her side. Tall and lean, with white hair that almost glows, he looks down at Mrs. Stillman. Her whole face changes. Like all the ravaged grief melts into some kind of almost-peace. Another pang squeezes my heart. My mom's face does this same thing when she looks at my dad. Like they're speaking some silent language, meaning beyond words, with an invisible comfort that's only available to them.

But the moment Mrs. Stillman turns to the next mourner, that peace evaporates. The pain comes back in. "Thank you for coming."

"Raleigh." Drew slaps her hand on the notebook page. "The answer is staring you in the face."

Reluctantly, I take another read of the number-riddled page. And feel another pang. Here I have all this sympathy for Sloane's family, but none for my best friend. Drew, who almost died. Drew, who's been through hell and is trying to climb out the best way she knows how.

I smile. "I need another clue."

"Take away the last digit."

"What?"

"Seventy-three million," she breathes out her exasperation, creating a condensation cloud that appears and disappears with each number, "nine hundred thirty-nine thousand one hundred and thirty-three."

"So if I take away the last digit, the number ends in . . . thirty?"

"Raleigh!"

The sound of my name shoots over the brick courtyard. Swirls around the front stoop. Jerks every face toward us. And instantly freezes all the polite murmurs into another troubled silence.

Perfect.

And Drew remains oblivious. She yells, "You still don't get it?!"

"Drew." I force another smile. "Do you remember what Dr. Armstrong said?"

"Think, Raleigh, think."

"Dr. Armstrong," I speak through clenched teeth, "said there was a time and place for everything. Remember? And this is not the time or the—"

"You heard what that priest said."

"He's not a priest."

"What is he?" She scrunches up her face. Not much confuses Drew.

"He's a minister." I feel hopeful. We are going off the number topic. "This is an Episcopal church. Catholics have priests."

"One more reason to be Jewish. Just say 'rabbi' and be done with it."

"You don't even go to temple."

"His own words, Raleigh. 'Sloane was cut down in her *prime*.' "

Right back to prime. Because the map drawn by obsessive-compulsives has no alternate routes. One express lane. To a single destination.

"He meant that her life ended too soon."

"Not on purpose."

"Drew."

"The priest—"

"Minister."

"—it's a sign."

"It's not."

She crosses her skinny arms. "Sloane did not kill herself."

"She did."

"Did not."

"Did."

Her dark brows furrow in frustration and, ladies and gentlemen, we've reached a stalemate. Not for any logical reason. Not because Drew's finally woken up and smelled reality and realizes that Sloane Stillman did indeed kill herself and left a note explaining her tragic decision. No, Drew's fighting the urge to utter another "did not." Because if I don't respond with "did," that will leave an uneven number. Right now her two "did nots" versus my two "dids." That's four. One more will equal five and five isn't an even number. However, five is a prime number, so I watch the intricate cogs grinding inside her beautiful troubled brain and wonder whether this sudden passion for prime numbers will override her obsessive compulsive dictum for even numbers.

Unfortunately patience isn't my virtue.

"When's your next appointment with Dr. Armstrong?"

"You're in trouble."

"*Me?*"

She aims the sharpened pencil over my shoulder. I turn to see a girl walking across the brick courtyard, heading right toward us, looking like a model ripped from a fashion magazine.

Tinsley Teager. Also known as Satan's handmaiden.

I turn frantically to Drew. "Promise me. Don't say one word. You got it?"

She nods, four times—two up, two down—her wild long brown hair waving in agreement.

"Hello, Drew," says Satan's beloved.

Drew nods. Two up, two down.

"Tinsley," I answer for Drew. "What do you want?"

"Drew, it was so very kind of you to come to cousin Sloane's service."

Tinsley is the most powerful girl at St. Catherine's—maybe even the most powerful girl in all of Richmond. Skinny as guitar string and meaner than a stepped-on rattlesnake, Tinsley is proof positive that DNA plays some mean tricks. Sloane Stillman was her cousin.

My voice is ice. "We're not here for you, Tinsley."

Drew says, "Sloane was my friend."

I grip her arm. "Drew, don't—"

"Of course she was your friend." Tinsley gazes at Drew with enough pity to smother to death every single insane person in America. Her smile glitters diamond-white, all the better to match the real stones stuck her tiny ears. Both match the pale blonde hair washing over the fitted shoulders of her immaculate black wool suit.

Evil has to look this good. Otherwise people would recognize it.

"Drew," she purrs. "I'd like to talk to you about what you said during the service."

"She's sorry, okay?" I grab Drew's wrist. "Come on."

"Drew, you said—"

"Goodbye, Tinsley." I pull Drew behind me.

"Raleigh."

Against every wise instinct, I turn around. Her smile drips even more pity.

"Drew can speak for herself," she says. "You really need to step away for a moment—or a lifetime—and let me talk to her."

"No, you need to go away."

Not my best comeback. Maybe even my worst of all time. But it does offer me one more reason to despise this perfectly attractive animus from hell. Taking Drew's arm once more, I pull her toward the wrought iron gate that runs alongside Broad Street. A crowd's gathered there, and DeMott is among them.

"Drew!" Tinsley calls out. "You'll be hearing from me!"

The crowd looks over. Of course. What a set-up. Tinsley's demonstrating how she's taking care of these inconsiderate rubes who crashed cousin Sloane's funeral.

And once again, I've stumbled into her trap.

Play with snakes, you get bit.

The pages of Drew's notebook flutter behind me with a *tsk-tsk-tsk* sound. But maybe I'm just reading the thoughts of the crowd staring at us. I keep my line of sight fixed on DeMott. This morning I told him I'd handle Drew, leaving him to mingle with the other mourners—the people he belongs with. And yet, he's never stopped glancing over at me and Drew.

Now, seeing us coming, he steps through the crowd. I can't tell which part makes my heart stop—how good he looks in a black suit or the profound sadness in his blue eyes. Maybe both.

The crowd falls silent.

"Ready?" I ask, as if nothing utterly embarrassing has happened.

"Sure." DeMott's eyes are the same blue as gas flames. But now, bloodshot. "You ready, Drew?"

He gently takes her arm. His other hand takes mine and suddenly a wave of relief washes over me. Maybe it's like that peace my mom feels with my dad. What Mrs. Stillman feels with that white-haired man beside her.

Whatever it is, I lean into it and let DeMott lead us away.

CHAPTER THREE

"S O, YOUR MOM'S . . . *drunk?*"

DeMott is driving us in his truck down East Broad Street, away from the church. We sit three-across on the bench seat, me wedged between them.

"Medically speaking, the correct term is *veisalgia*," Drew says. "More commonly known as *hungover*." Drew taps the passenger window, counting something we are passing. "But the general probability theory says she will be drunk by four o'clock."

I can feel DeMott's gaze on my face. But I say nothing.

"I'm sorry, Drew." And being DeMott, he sounds really truly sorry.

The silence swallows the truck cab, sad and reverent as this old neighborhood we're passing through. Once upon a time, Church Hill's high overlook was home to everyone from Patrick Henry to Edgar Allen Poe. Now the storied brick row houses are boarded up and orange rust furs the forged-iron fences.

"Once she quit drinking." Drew taps the window three times. "That abstinence lasted thirty-seven days. Odd."

"That is odd." DeMott's voice sounds gentle.

"Thirty-seven." Tap-tap-tap. "Odd number."

Once again, I can feel his glance on my face. When I turn, there are so many questions in his blue-blue eyes.

"Odd," I clarify, "as in, not even."

He nods. "Oh. Okay."

In the six weeks we've been dating, I've figured out this gesture of his. Most people nod in agreement. But DeMott nods because he's avoiding asking the next question, especially if it's rude or even semi-rude. A southern gentleman to his core.

"Yes, thirty-seven is an odd number," he says.

She taps the window, regular as a metronome. "I would appreciate not being home right now."

He looks at me, while addressing Drew. "But you just asked me to drive you home. Didn't you?"

"I would like to change into clean clothing." She swivels toward me, the unruly brown hair swinging over her narrow shoulders. "Nobody's drunk at your house?"

I sigh. "Not unless Helen's home."

"DeMott," she says, "you will put my bike in the back of your truck."

I feel his glance. But I wonder what's bothering him—the way I referred to my sister Helen, or Drew's impolite order to get her bike? I should apologize for her. But I just spent a funeral babysitting and had to deal with Tinsley and both destroyed whatever remains of my Virginia manners.

DeMott keeps glancing at me, but I stare straight ahead as we cross into downtown. Also I'm studiously avoiding whatever Drew's counting—cars with even numbered license plates, street lights, no-parking signs, who knows.

But as we're coming into the Fan district, I catch DeMott's scent. Clean and warm as fresh laundry, it makes my skin tingle. I scoot closer, breathing him in, resisting the urge to bury my face in his collar.

Drew sighs with relief. "Twenty-two."

"Flags," I explain automatically. Drew always counts the house flags. A Richmond tradition, the flags wave beside the front doors and change seasonally. Right now, they flaunt Christmas trees and candles and angels we have heard on high, flapping as if they're trying to get the bare elms to dance.

"I get it." DeMott smiles. "Twenty-two is an even number."

"No." I shake my head. "Twenty-two is two twos."

He says nothing more. When we reach Drew's house off Westhampton Road, she jumps out and runs toward the butter-colored house—with no flag—that is much too big for only two people and one nasty cat.

I tell him, "She meant to say *thank you*."

He nods.

We watch her run up the stairs. Up, down. Then one humongous lunge for the ceramic turtle that holds the house key. She opens the sunroom door that never used to be locked but now is always locked.

"Just curious—"

"The stoop has three steps, so she can't go up them once."

"Three being an odd number."

"That, and six is the first perfect number."

"Six is perfect?" he asks.

"Do you really want to know?"

"Maybe . . ." He half-smiles. And the thing about DeMott, he will listen. Because he cares. About Drew and her weird compulsions. But mostly about me, and I'm not sure why. I'm not rich or gorgeous or society-savvy, all the things he should want, given who he is in Richmond. In fact, I'm sort of the exact opposite of all that.

"Six is mathematically perfect," I explain, "because its divisors are 1-2-3."

"Divisors?"

"Numbers it can be divided by. Six can be divided by one, two, and three."

"I see."

"*Also* one, two, and, three add up to six."

"Okay."

"But there's more."

"I'm good, thanks." He chuckles and combs a hand through his brown hair, pushing it off his forehead. "Actually, my question was about her saying she needs 'clean clothing.' "

My face starts to redden. "She didn't wear dirty clothes to the

service, if that's what you're thinking." I can hear the defensive-
ness in my voice. I pause. Maybe he was just curious, not
condemning. "Once she wears something, it's 'contaminated.' "

He waits, but I don't have the energy to explain the whole
clothes-changing compulsion that started about a month ago. This
whole morning has drained me, like I donated ten pints of blood,
and now I'm looking at *hours* with Drew. At my house. Which is
another kind of circus torture. I stare out the window.

He takes my hand. "Nice service, don't you think?"

"If you're not babysitting."

"Well, you know." DeMott lets out a deep sigh.

"What's that supposed to mean?" I pull my hand away. The
most gorgeous guy ever, but right now his good looks somehow
annoy me even more. "*Well, you know?*"

"Raleigh, I told you she would react badly."

"And I told you—Drew insisted on going."

"But after what she just went through?"

"She *insisted*."

"Nobody's blaming you."

My eyes narrow. "Tell that to Tinsley."

He says nothing. He knows Tinsley. Because not so long ago,
Tinsley was his girlfriend. Tinsley is everything DeMott should
want in a girlfriend. And I hate myself for even invoking the name
of Satan's darling.

"You noticed I had us sit in back," I add.

"Don't get defensi—"

"Then don't attack me." I turn away, glaring out the window.
Under the cloud-darkened sky, this day feels much older than it
actually is. Two lights burn inside Drew's house. One in her
upstairs bedroom, where undoubtedly she is segregating "contaminated" clothes. The other light is in the kitchen, where Jayne's
probably popping a cork from another wine bottle. Drew's mom
used to drink two bottles of red on Friday and Saturday nights
only, so she could seem sober by Monday for her job at Reynolds
Aluminum. The foil people. But after her thirty-seven-day dry-out,

Jayne got worse. Now she drinks every night. She drinks a lot.

"That was a good idea to sit in back," he says, softly.

"But you still think I should've stopped her from going."

"Raleigh, I just don't like to see you get hurt."

"Here's the thing." I sit up and look him in the eye. "I can't stop Drew. From anything. Nobody can. It's like telling the sky not to rain."

"Maybe if—"

"You don't know her." My head snaps back to her house.

"But I know you. And I might say the same thing about you."

I want to turn, want to see the expression on his face. Because he sounds almost proud of my stubbornness. But I can't look. Not now. I can't bear to see his teasing smile when this day just hung a *No Vacancy* sign over my heart. So I stare at Jayne's red Volvo wagon packed with boxes of aluminum foil and Saran Wrap to help the public relations executive pretend she's not a total secret drunk.

"Raleigh."

He's got a good voice, filled with Virginia. And when he says my name it sounds like music. My throat's tightening, like some rope tied itself to that *No Vacancy* sign, tugging. I stare at the Volvo's bumper.

He touches my arm.

I jump.

"Sorry, I didn't mean to scare you."

"You didn't."

But I am scared. The expression on his face tells me the very next words out of his mouth will weigh 200 tons and all I can think is *No. Don't. I can't handle it.*

So when he opens his mouth, I lean waaaay over to the passenger side and fling open the door. Drew comes down-up-lunge-down the stairs, wearing a clean white turtleneck that glows under a clean purple jean jacket. She grabs the purple Schwinn bike leaning on a tree and pushes it toward the truck.

Mr. Manners climbs out and places the bike in the truck bed, closing the gate. Drew climbs in chattering about something Jayne did that I don't even listen to because as soon as DeMott starts driving down Westhampton Road, she's counting again. Christmas lights, sign posts, it doesn't matter. The only thing I can focus on is DeMott.

You're going to lose him.

"Five?" Drew says as we're driving down Monument Avenue. Her voice is rising. "General Lee is five? No. Wait. His horse." She sighs. "Traveller makes six."

Counting the statues that run down the middle of this wide historic road. Confederate General Robert E. Lee and his horse Traveller stand across the street from my house. In this faint December light, their bronzed bodies look almost black.

DeMott eases his truck down the cobblestone alley behind our house. The alley divides these huge historic houses from their carriage-houses-turned-garages. When he stops at our high stone wall, Drew leaps out. He gets out, walks to the truck bed.

I do not want to get out.

But Drew's already heading for our back gate.

I hop out, swing her around.

"Carriage house," I point. "Count the bricks."

And she's off. Like a compulsive arrow.

DeMott watches her slide open the wide door that used to re-lease horses and buggies for carrying southern ladies to afternoon tea. Drew's already got one finger raised, slipping past my parents' cars, counting the bricks.

"I should get going," he says. "I promised to make the burial."

"Right." No way am I risking *that* event with Drew.

"So," he says, waiting. "Any plans over Christmas break?"

"Not really." My family doesn't make plans. Not anymore. I take Drew's bike from him. "Thanks for driving."

I should say something more. I know this.

But right now, words are failing me.

CHAPTER FOUR

WHILE DREW'S OCCUPIED in the carriage house with thousands of bricks, I fumble open our back gate and try to cross the patio without being seen. I glance at the French doors. Nobody's in the kitchen. So I tiptoe across the blue slate and slide along the side of the house. More bricks, because Richmond was built from baked clay.

At the cellar door, I look up. The Christmas carol rattles through the window above me. *The angels did say . . .* The window's so old the silica molecules have dripped, leaving that wavy surface where everything looks like a mirage. Only what I'm looking at is all too real. Last week, my dad moved our ancient phonograph into the dining room so my mom can play songs while he's in his office in the next room. She stands over the record playing the song, her curly black hair hanging forward.

I wait for the chorus.

Noel . . .

I lift the cellar door.

No-ellll . . .

I step into the black hole and quietly close the door behind me.

No-ooo-elll . . .

Born is the king of Israel as my heart bangs into my ribs. I stick out my left hand, into the dark, trying to ward off whatever's going to jump out at me. My other hand gropes the damp stone wall. My ego wants to insist I'm not afraid of the dark anymore, but my banging heart says that's a big fat lie.

What it comes down to is, some things just scare me more than the dark.

Like my mom.

The song dies. I tiptoe down the steps, still waving my hand around until I feel the string. I snap on the light, fingers tingling with adrenaline.

Above me, the carol starts again. I walk across the uneven stone foundation that somebody laid back when the Harmons built this huge house in 1902. Back when nobody in the Harmon's high strata of society washed their own laundry. Modernity finally caught up, sort of, with a washer and dryer installed down here, where servants washed loads for another decade.

Now the servants are gone.

Reaching behind the washing machine, I pull out my backpack and remove my school uniform. The blue plaid skirt is wrinkled, but my sweater with the St. Cat's crest hangs far enough down to cover most of the evidence. I yank on thick blue tights for warmth and slip my feet into penny loafers, and stuff the black funeral clothes into the backpack, which I sling over my shoulder.

I listen for the refrain, one hand on the light's string.

Noel . . .

I snap off the light, run blindly for the stairs.

No-ellll . . .

I trip and slam into the cellar door, swallow the ugly words that want to bolt from my mouth, and massage my knee, siting in the dark on the cold steps listening to yet another run-through of the same carol.

How long will it take Drew to count all those bricks? I press the light on my digital watch.

The song begins again. I tiptoe out of the cellar and saunter to the kitchen doors like any other girl coming home from school.

I walk through the kitchen, and the now-servantless-useless butler's pantry, and into the grand dining room where my mother looks up from the antique phonograph.

Her eyes are beautiful and strange and remind me of green

jasper.

"They let us out early," I say.

She gazes at me a long moment. The song tells us to sing prais-
es to the Lord with one accord.

"Is Dad home?"

"Yes, David is home, Ray."

Ray?

Why is she calling *me* "Ray"?

Great. More weirdness. *Just what I need.*

I walk down the wide hall, trailed by the *King of Is-ra-el.* My
heart clangs like I'm still inside that dark cellar.

I knock on my dad's office, but he never expects me to wait.
When I slide back the twelve-foot pocket door, I taste a familiar
scent of cured tobacco. It steeped into the wood floor, from when
this room was the men's smoking parlor. When the Harmons
entertained mayors and governors.

"Raleigh, how was school?" he asks, loud enough to be over-
heard by my mom.

"Great!" I try to sound cheerful. It sounds as false as a tin-foil
Christmas tree. "They let us out early!"

"Nice!"

"Yeah. Can I go bike riding?"

"Just be home by dinner!"

"Will do!"

I slide the door closed.

Sometimes these conversations feel like we're playing some
version of charades, where the words we use are the exact opposite
of what we mean.

I FIND DREW in the carriage house, way in back. By the wall with
the dusty hooks still holding horse bridles and buggy whips.

"Four thousand two hundred forty-eight." Her face lights up.
"Even. Even. Even."

Even I would like to believe she'll come back. The girl who

got all my jokes. The girl who made even better ones. The best friend who listened to my problems. And understood.

But life doesn't always work that way.

Just ask my dad.

"Very cool." I grab my bike and push it into the alley.

"What about the bricks upstairs?" she asks.

Upstairs. The carriage house has a small apartment. Once upon a time, a chauffeur lived there.

"Save those bricks for another time, okay?"

She follows me outside, blinking in the soft gray light.

"Cheeseburgers?" I ask. "Titus' place is probably open."

Titus Williams makes the best cheeseburgers in town. Just the thought of biting into one makes my mouth water.

But Drew shakes her head, the wild mane of hair agreeing with her. Drew's rarely hungry these days. Her already-tiny frame is skeletal. And Dr. Armstrong's medication isn't helping.

"Then where do you want to bike to?"

She picks up her purple Schwinn. "Downtown."

"What's downtown?"

"If I tell you, you won't go."

"Just tell me."

She taps her finger on the brick wall, then keeps it there, like somebody holding their place in a book. "You promise you'll go?"

"Cross my heart." I don't say the last part.

"I'm going to show you where Sloane died."

CHAPTER FIVE

A S IF WE didn't already have enough going against us, we ride bikes.

Drew's reason is legitimate. She's only fourteen years old—and in St. Cat's sophomore class with me because her dad put his foot down and wouldn't let the school put her in the senior class. Which is amazing because Rusty Levinson has the backbone of my mother's overcooked spaghetti. Rusty said he didn't want Drew to turn out weird.

Which really means—weirder than she already is.

My excuse for bike riding is much more lame. I'm old enough for a learner's permit but my dad's overwhelmed, and with my mom's serious mental issues—well, I just don't ask. The only time I get behind the wheel is when my sister Helen needs a designated driver. Yeah, I know. Not the smartest move, but the penalty for drunk driving is way worse than the Class 2 misdemeanor for a first-time offense driving without a license. I know this stuff. The way other kids know state capitols, I know Virginia's statutes.

So here we are, riding our bikes down Cary Street into the city. Drew's in front and I'm squeezing my brakes to keep from passing her and making her feel bad. On my right, the James River cuts through downtown. The rippling surface looks a lot like her wild hair.

"You okay?" I call out.

She stands on the pedals, her skinny legs pumping like levers to make the short rise to Main Street. I squeeze my brakes tighter and follow her onto Williamsburg Road. A city bus groans by, heading toward Fulton Hill. Then a white panel truck. Drew cuts across the street and stops at Libbie Park.

I pull up beside her. "You okay?"

Her olive skin shines with perspiration. She pants, "Here."

"What?"

She points.

I don't want to look. But what else can I do?

Just above us, where the road curves upward, yellow tape flutters. Crime scene tape.

I feel sick.

"Sloane's car." She wipes her damp forehead. "Left the road. Hit that tree."

I glance over my shoulder, pretending to be interested in the passing traffic. An old station wagon slows down. The elderly black man driving throws us a skeptical look.

"Her route." Drew climbs off the purple Schwinn, unsteady. "She came down New Market Road from her house. Then Williamsburg Road. She was traveling eighty-eight miles an hour."

"You can't know how fast—"

"Yes, I can." She drops her bike. The purple paint sparkles against the dull winter grass. "Newton's third law."

Slowly, very slowly, I climb off my bike. "What about it?"

"For every action there is an equal and opposite reaction." She points to the tree. "Point of impact."

"So." The tree bark is peeled back like an open wound.

"So, the laws of physics and the rules of engineering, including conservation of linear momentum, say this was not a suicide."

"Drew." How many times will I need to say this? "Her note said—"

She waves me off.

I know how many times: seventy-three million nine hundred thirty-nine thousand one hundred and thirty-three times. Because Drew is not listening.

With her arms wrapped around her notebook like a rabbi

clutching the Torah, she picks her way purposefully across the winter grass and dirt. Another wave of nausea hits me as I drop my bike and follow her over the cold-hardened mud. Footprints are frozen in the mud. Footprints of people who carried Sloane Stillman away in a body bag.

"The newspaper reported debris found three hundred feet from the crash site."

"Drew, she wanted to die."

"You're wrong."

The heat in her voice warns me. *Back off.*

I watch her walk to the damaged tree, scribbling in her note-book, but can't keep looking. I stare at the James River below, silver under the clouds. The water looks peaceful, almost eternal. Like I can see how Richmond got its name from this very spot, when the early settlers stood here and saw their home in England, Richmond-on-Thames.

"Raleigh, come look at this."

Dutifully, I walk over. My eyes sting. It's like witnessing a second suicide.

She flips the notebook and shows me a diagram.

"The x-axis represents Sloane's car traveling at eighty-eight miles an hour."

"How do you know that?"

"The weight of Sloane's car calculated with its collision point, combined with the distance to where the debris landed. That gives a very close approximation of velocity."

"It does?"

"Simple trigonometry"

"That must be an oxymoron."

"Raleigh, someday you will need math for geology. Which is why you're here." She points the pencil behind me. "Take some soil samples."

I look back at the frozen muddy footprints. And tire tracks. One set of tracks ends suddenly. Because that car became airborne.

I feel sick again.

"We know the weight of the vehicle because we know what car she was driving."

"The Cherrymobile," I mumble, staring at those abbreviated tread marks.

Sloane Stillman's Cherrymobile was the coolest car ever driven to St. Cat's. Being an exclusive private school, we see plenty of Benzes and Mercedes, even Bentleys. But Sloane drove a 1957 Chevy Bel Air. The car oozed cool. Which really didn't fit Sloane. She was quiet and studious and that vintage red car was a giant flashing Look-At-Me sign. That's not why she drove it. Her dad collected classic cars. When we were in grade school, Mr. Stillman died.

"A fully restored '57 Chevy Bel Air weighs roughly thirty-five hundred pounds. I calculated the distance from initial impact to final location of debris. And this suicide makes no logical sense."

"Drew, suicide isn't logical. It's not some trig problem."

"Williamsburg Road has several extreme curves." She gestures to the two lanes cuddling the river's edge. Those lanes merge into New Market Road, where all the historic plantations are, like Sloane's family estate known as Still Waters. And DeMott's estate, Weyanoke. You could say their houses were just down the road from each other, as long as you consider "just down the road" to be several thousand acres.

"Sloane had plenty of places to crash on that road if she wanted to die," Drew says.

"But she drove her car into this freaking tree. The. End."

"Let me ask you something." She's still hugging that sacred notebook, but she doesn't look at me. She stares out at the river. "Would you take that chance?"

"What?"

"If you wanted to die upon impact, would you drive a car weighing seven tons? No. You would drive a tiny sports car. The Stillmans have a whole collection of cars, Raleigh. She picked this one?"

"I told you, suicide isn't logical."

"But there is such a thing as an inefficient suicide. I should know."

Her last statement freezes me. After her parents' divorce, Drew started researching the most efficient ways to die.

"And she had just got admission to Harvard," Drew continues. "Sloane was doing even better than Helen."

My sister got into Yale early admission. Now in her freshman year, Helen is threatening to come home for Christmas. This very weekend. I'm looking forward to her arrival like a triple root canal without anesthesia.

"Furthermore," she continues, "Sloane was a scientist. She was much too smart to die in such a dumb way. That means the facts demand we investigate."

"No, they don't."

She stomps away. Her legs look blade-thin as the grass.

I follow her up the hill. "Drew."

"Nineteen, twenty," she's counting her steps, "twenty-one . . ."

"Drew, her note said she didn't want to go on living."

"Don't care."

"I don't care if you don't care. It's *evidence*."

"Soil!" she calls out. "Now!"

I exhale every last molecule of oxygen in my lungs. I want my old friend back, the kooky genius. Not this genius kook.

"Thirty-nine . . . Raleigh!"

I walk over to the tire tracks. Dropping to my knees, I throw my backpack on the ground. Drew knows I keep all my geology stuff in here so my paranoid-schizophrenic mom doesn't find it. My mom who is now calling me "Ray." I dig under the funeral clothes and snag the box of Ziploc bags. At the edge of the rickrack line of tire tracks, I pinch the soil and rub it between my thumb and forefinger. The ice melts. The soil feels a little sticky. Clay, I'm guessing. But there's grit, too. Sand. The color's a weird yellowish-red, almost orange.

"Fifty-four, fifty-five . . ."

I stare at the soil. It's stained my fingertips a color like iodine.

"Sixty-one, sixty-two . . ."

There's a prayer I've whispered for years for my mother. Maybe God's totally sick of hearing it. But right now I'm praying it for Drew.

Help her.

I whisper it over and over and over.

"Eighty-eight!" she cries.

I look up. She reaches down into the hillside grass and comes up with an object. She holds it up against the gray clouds. Light spears red plastic.

"That's a brake light cover," I tell her. "This idea might be too scientific for you, but Sloane wasn't using her brakes."

"Eighty-eight steps from point of impact to here. Incidentally, your carriage house bricks also ended in eighty-eight."

"Only the first floor," I mutter.

"Do you understand how fast she was going? This piece of plastic probably landed here in a jiffy."

Here's what you learn hanging around Drew. *Jiffy* is an actual unit of time, 1/100th of a second.

"Drew, she was stepping on the gas pedal *hard.*"

"You do not know that," she says.

"Now you're a conspiracy theorist?"

"Facts, Raleigh. This case is solely based on facts. And the facts do not add up."

I let a loud sigh fizz out. "Because life isn't a math problem."

"Wrong. Math describes the entire universe. Every corner of it. And when the description doesn't add up, we're supposed to solve the riddle."

I pinch more soil, toss it into the baggie, and zip it closed. *Riddle?* My tongue wants to blurt, *You want a riddle? Look in the mirror.*

"And let's remember all the so-called experts," she continues. "The experts who insist it was suicide. Meanwhile, you and I know that science is the belief in the ignorance of experts."

She's quoting her most cherished physicist, Richard P. Feynman. I wait a moment, hoping my voice will soften. Hoping I will sound more like my dad when he's talking to my crazy mom. Behind her, the breeze lifts the scraps of yellow crime tape, waving it softly like old ladies saying goodbye with faded handkerchiefs. "Dr. Armstrong talked to you about letting things go."

"I am not letting go of this."

"But it has nothing to do with you."

"How can you say that." Her brown eyes flash. "This has everything to do with me!"

"Why?"

"*Why?*" She glares. "Why didn't *you* believe them?"

"Who?"

"The people who said I ran away. You didn't believe them."

I shift my eyes to the yellow tape, watching it lift and fall, rising on hope, falling on sorrow, then rising again. When I glance back at Drew, she looks elfin. But she is here. She is still alive. Only because I ignored the so-called experts.

"So, what happens to that prime number," I ask her, "when I take off that last digit?"

Her brown eyes glisten. "Then you take away the next digit."

"Seventy-three million. Nine-hundred thirty-nine thousand. And one hundred?"

"Yes." She smiles. But her eyes still shine. "Now take off the next number."

"Seventy-three million nine hundred and thirty-nine?"

Her smile widens.

"Drew, I still don't get it."

She walks toward me, eyes still lit up like there's a fire burning inside. Only now it's excitement burning instead of anger. "Think about it," she says. "Every time that last digit's taken away, the number remains prime. Do you see? It's like with Sloane's death. No matter what anybody says, the facts keep saying she didn't kill herself. That number is a sign."

I blink, try to smile back. "Really."

"Really," she says. "Really and truly. *Prime.*"

CHAPTER SIX

After biking Drew all the way to her house to make sure she's okay, I head for home, and then straight to my dad's office.

This time, I close the door.

"How was the service?" he asks, dropping his voice.

"Packed." I sink into the empty chair facing his desk and tuck my freezing hands under my arms. Here's another dumb thing about riding bikes—in December, your fingers freeze. "Every pew was packed."

He winces.

"Dad, you couldn't go."

As if underlining my point, the carol comes lilting in from the next room, reminding us that three wise men fell on their knees. My dad has known the Stillmans for most of his life—Upper Richmond is only so big—but attending Sloane's funeral wasn't an option. We've got enough problems right here, right now, without adding suicide to the hurricane that rages under our roof.

"How was Mrs. Stillwater?"

"Brittle."

He frowns.

"Seriously, Dad, it's better you didn't go. And after the way Drew behaved during the service, you're going to need to find me a new school."

"She couldn't have been that bad."

"No. Worse."

He gives me an odd smile. Sad, sympathetic, I can't tell. Maybe it's just fatigue. On his big desk, yellow legal notepads spread out next to subpoenas and newspaper articles. For the past week, my dad's courtroom has been ground zero for a trial that's split Richmond down its racial divide: A white cop shot a black teenager and now every shade of gray has appeared in the witness stand. Today was a recess because the defense dropped some bomb of information and my dad got to work at home. I've tried to keep track of everything in the newspaper, but it's difficult to tell who's telling the truth.

The carol tells us, *So it continues both day and night . . .*

We listen a moment.

"Cold out?" he asks, changing the subject.

"Freezing. Can I ask you a question?"

"Only until forever."

His standard reply. Times like this, his attitude takes on even more weight. Six days before Christmas and he's pushing through this murder case, holding down the fort at home, and making sure everything's holiday-ready for Helen. And me. The best dad. Ever.

"How do I convince Drew that Sloane Stillman committed suicide?"

"Oh, boy." He lifts his reading glasses from his face, sets them on the desk. "Drew doesn't believe Sloane's dead?"

"That might be next." I explain the current crazy idea, leaving out the funeral outbursts to spare him the embarrassment. I describe the crash site and the trigonometry involving the beloved Cherrymobile.

"I see." He draws a deep breath. "That's where you went bike riding."

"Dad, I didn't know that's where she wanted to go. Honest."

"I believe you."

"Thank you."

Lately I've vowed not to keep secrets from him. But my mom? That's whole 'nother ball of wax and I'm not melting it.

"You do realize it's her OCD talking," he says.

"Yeah. But she asked me what would've happened if I believed everyone who said *she* ran away."

He shifts his gaze. My dad thought Drew ran away. "I'm sorry."

In October, Drew didn't show up for our regular Friday night dinner. We eat—or used to, before trauma and medication stole her appetite—at Titus' burger joint. But when Drew didn't show up for the first time ever, I went searching. Problem was, she'd run away from home before, and even her parents believed she'd done it again, which left everyone assuming that's what happened. But the truth was worse. Much worse, warping Drew's already-punctual personality into classic obsessive-compulsive disorder. Depending on your perspective, it's a good thing I'm so well-acquainted with crazy behavior.

"I was hoping you had some advice," I tell him, "since you're so good at dealing with mom."

"Thanks." His sad expression deepens. "Thanks for telling me that."

"You're welcome. So, how do you deal with mom's crazy ideas?"

"I agree with her."

"What?"

"Raleigh."

"Okay, *pardon*." He keeps trying to get me to lose my habit of saying *what*. He claims only Yankees say that word. "You *agree* with her?"

He leans forward, resting his elbows on the desk. "You find Drew's ideas hard to listen to, is that correct?"

"Yes."

"Then try to imagine what it's like *believing* those ideas. Having them live inside your mind. Horrible, don't you agree?"

"Yes, but—"

"But is this idea of Drew's harming anyone?"

"Yes. Me."

"Raleigh." He smiles, kindly. "You're uncomfortable with her thinking. But is she out to hurt anyone?"

I fidget and sigh. "Drew doesn't know *how* to hurt anyone. Not on purpose."

"Alright. Then be her friend. And when there's an opportunity, speak some truth to her. In love."

"Dad, I am so not patient enough." Right then, the carol leaks through the wall, starting all over again. I let out a groan. *"That's* what I'm talking about. How can you *deal* with this?"

"Raleigh."

"Is she going to play that song a million times?"

"Let's get some dinner." He stands. "You'll feel better."

We both know that's unlikely. But we both know there's no way out of dinner.

I follow him out of his office, into the repeating words of Noel. The Noel with no end.

AT THE KITCHEN table, my dad bows his head and thanks God for his wife and daughters, for bringing Helen home safely tomorrow, and—pure man that he is—for the food we're about to eat.

What am I praying? That we don't die from this meal.

"Amen."

When I look up, my mom's placed one hand on the side of her beautiful head. Like she's trying to stop her brain from falling out her ear.

My dad leans toward her. "Honey, are you alright?"

"We need music."

The Noel song died while we were praying—maybe God's even sick of hearing it—but my dad practically jumps out of his chair. "I'll find something."

Moments later, Bing Crosby croons about being home for Christmas, as my mother wedges a serving spoon into yet another of her notorious casseroles. My dad comes back into the room, singing along, and accepts her hearty serving of epicurean hell.

Then she looks at me.

"Would you like some, Ray?"

I glance at my dad. *Ray?*

He is snapping open his creased napkin, but frowning. A frown gone so fast most people would've missed it.

I stare at him. *You agree with her calling me this bizarre name?*

"Ray of sunshine," he says. "Perfect nickname for you." I let it go, and hold out my plate. She gives me a small serving—hey, A-OK by me—and thank her. She smiles, politely.

As usual, my dad serves her, then kisses her cheek. For several excruciating sentences he compliments her on everything, from the Christmas decorations in the dining room to this casserole—which, as usual, is awful. And personally, I think the dining room looks like it was barfed up from the entire Victorian era. Every decoration we own is going on the tree. All because Helen's coming home.

When Bing repeats how he'll home for Christmas, my mother dabs her eyes. Helen is her favorite. No contest.

I stick my fork in whatever this stuff is, and my dad drops a hydrogen bomb.

"We've been invited to a Christmas party."

The hope in his voice. I can hear it clearly. *Maybe this year,* it says, *Christmas will be normal.*

"That's great," I chirp. He deserves something normal. "When?"

"Tomorrow night."

"But—Helen," my mother protests. "She comes home tomorrow night."

"Her train arrives at five thirty. The party doesn't start until seven thirty. We'll surprise her."

Something kicks in. Call it an inkling. Or an omen. "Where's this party at?"

"You don't know?" he asks.

I shake my head.

"Weyanoke."

My fork drops. *"What?"*

"Raleigh—"

"Pardon?"

"The Fieldings. They invited us to their Christmas party."

"And we can't possibly go because—" I stare into his sparkling blue eyes. *Mom cannot go!*

But she gets there before me. "That beautiful home on the river?"

"The very same one." He winks at me. "I believe DeMott Fielding's quite fond of Raleigh."

"And we can't go because—" I keep sending the signal.

My mother says, "I've always wanted to see the inside of Weyanoke."

Oh, crap.

My dad looks back and forth between us. He does this in the courtroom, too, evaluating the opposing parties. Poor guy. Even at home he's got to be a judge.

"Okay," I say woodenly. "Sure. It'll be fun."

"Excellent." He smiles wider than ever. "Helen'll be so surprised."

I stare at my plate. Something grips my heart. Not adrenaline. Not even fear. It's some slow steady march, matching the next song on Bing's album. The beat of the little drummer boy. *Par-ruh-puh-puh-pum.*

I pick up my fork again. Take a bite. The food tastes like first-grade's glue.

But I clean my plate.

Not for my sake.

Not even for my mom.

It's for my dad.

I have no other gift to bring.

CHAPTER SEVEN

E VERY OTHER SCHOOL kid in Richmond's already on Christmas break.

But not St. Catherine's.

No, our girls get into Harvard and Yale—early admission, no less—and even our dummies get into second-tier universities. St. Cat's college admissions rate is nearly 100 percent. "Nearly" only because of Callum McCallister, a debutante so individualistic that after graduation she changed her name to Calliope—one word, like Pink or Sting—and moved into a commune in New Mexico. Calliope was Helen's friend.

Tells you something about both of them.

So, even with yesterday's funeral for a suicidal classmate, St. Cat's returns to its regularly-scheduled programming Friday morning. I'm still stuffy headed from yesterday's drama, and barely shuffle through History, Latin, and Biology before making it to lunch.

I toss my entire lunch bag into the cafeteria's trashcan, because it's leftovers from last night's Elmer's glue casserole. With money from my Dad, I buy the school's not-great hamburger and fries, add a carton of chocolate milk, and snag a fistful of mayonnaise packets. I carry my full tray over to where Drew's sitting, in the back by the windows. We've sat here since seventh grade. Just the two of us.

"Hey."

"Two percent." Drew stares at a pile of M&Ms spread out on

the table. "Two percent is unacceptable."

"No argument from me." I lift my milk carton. "I always say, more fat, more flavor."

She looks up at me, her eyebrows quirked.

I sit down, feeling bad already because another joke escaped her. I point to the carton of milk. "Statistically speaking, two-percent means ninety-eight percent of the flavor is gone."

She seems this-close to getting my joke. But her gaze drifts back to the M&Ms. She's segregated each color into its own pile. Red, orange, yellow, green, blue, brown—like with like. I shake the milk carton and groan inside. Time to take my dad's advice, even though I'm totally sick of spending every single lunch watching Drew count M&Ms before she bar-graphs the percent-ages. Worse, she never lets me eat any of the candy.

"Which color's two percent?" I ask.

"Brown. But red is sixteen percent!"

"How do these candy people live with themselves?"

"Maybe they don't."

Wonderful. Right back to suicide.

I push my tray toward her, careful to avoid the segregated can-dy. "Eat some fries. I'm about to open the mayo."

She gazes at my food. Not even a trace of hunger in her dark eyes. "Why must you do that?"

"Because mayonnaise is the perfect condiment. It goes with everything."

"You're the only person who believes that."

"More mayo for me."

She pinches a fry, nibbles one end. That will be her whole lunch.

"Drew, you need to eat."

"I ate breakfast."

"Today?"

She doesn't answer.

I tear open the tubes of beloved mayo and squirt them into a beautiful glowing mound. Then I close my eyes and utter silent thanks for . . . what? Well, right now, mayo and fries.

But when I open my eyes, I almost gag.

Tinsley sits at the cool-girl's table, naturally, in the middle of the lunchroom. So she can see and be seen. But for the first time ever, Mary Vale Stillman sits there, too. Several things are wrong with this picture. One, Mary Vale should be allowed to skip school the day after her sister's funeral. But this is St. Cat's, where the ethos is power—power up, power through, power matters—and, two, Tinsley's sick plan suddenly becomes obvious as she pats Mary Vale's shoulder. Yes, a veritable mother hen. But I know what she's doing. Grooming Mary Vale. Not only will Tinsley gain another sycophant, she will guide the indisputably beautiful but painfully shy Mary Vale all the way to the social heights, thus blotting out the dishonor cousin Sloane foisted on their family tree when she decided to off herself.

Reputation, appearances. That's all Tinsley cares about.

But she risks both by getting up and walking toward our table.

"Oh, crap." I mutter.

"Bad mayo?—ten, eleven—bacteria, you know, be careful—twelve—"

"Drew, this time I mean it. Do not say one word."

"What?"

Tinsley purrs, "Hellooooo, Drew."

I glare at her. "Tinsley, go away."

Her glacial green eyes try to freeze me into cryogenics. But when she looks at Drew, those same eyes turn velvety soft.

"This looks so interesting." Tinsley's manicured finger nail hovers over the pile of red M&Ms. "I've been meaning to ask what you're doing over here."

I point a fry at her. "Go awa—"

"I'm checking the packaging of M&Ms," Drew says. "Each bag is supposed to contain twenty-four percent blue, fourteen percent brown, sixteen percent green, twenty percent orange, thirteen percent red, and fourteen percent yellow."

"Why, bless your heart." Tinsley almost laughs, but all that good grooming holds it back. "How do you know that?"

I kick Drew under the table.

"Ow," she says. "Mars told me."

"The planet?"

"The company. Mars. They make M&Ms."

"How very interesting." Tinsley's smile widens. "I've only ever cared about the green ones."

"Green." Drew gazes at the pile of green. "Why green?"

"Because Tinsley's a moron." I really don't need Drew studying why people think green M&Ms make them horny. "Tinsley, don't you have a broom that needs riding?"

"Raleigh." The icicle eyes stab me. "This matter only concerns me and Drew."

Drew looks at me. "Did I miss something?"

"Yes."

"Not at all," Tinsley purrs. "I simply wanted to continue our conversation from yesterday."

"Drew." I point at the clock on the wall. What I'm about to do is cruel, but for her own good. "In less than three minutes, the bell is going to ring."

Drew sucks in a breath, snatches her notebook, and starts scribbling down percentages. An entire section of that notebook is dedicated to this M&M percentage topic, complete with color graphs revealing how the stated packaging percentages are not matching reality. Drew has contacted the company about the discrepancy. They said they'll get back to her.

"Raleigh." That fine manicured fingernail is pointing at me. "Do you mind?"

"Yes."

"No, Raleigh doesn't mind, she saw the evidence."

"Evidence." Tinsley looks at me, confused.

"Nothing," I say.

But Drew says, "The evidence showing how Sloane didn't commit suicide."

There's a sudden silence. So heavy that Drew looks up. "Isn't that what you're here for, Tinsley?"

If every choice looks bad, you have to pick the least-bad one and run with it. Right now my choice means conspiring with the enemy. So as Drew's gaze returns to the bar graphs, I surreptitiously draw my index finger across my throat, telling Tinsley to kill this conversation. *Now.*

"Drew," she says, "what evidence?"

I grit my teeth.

"We examined the crash site," Drew says. "Sloane was driving the Cherrymobile."

"*That's* your evidence?" Tinsley looks back at me, like it's my fault she just walked over here risking her precious reputation. "Hello, earth to Drew? Everyone knows Sloane was driving her car."

Drew stops writing, looks up, and blinks at Tinsley. "But she got accepted early admission to Harvard. Why would she kill herself?"

"Oh! My! God!" Tinsley yells. "That's *exactly* what I said!"

"See?" Drew looks at me.

I feel like yelling *Oh my God*, too, because what are the chances that the smartest person I know and the dumbest person in the universe would reach the exact same delusional conclusion?

As if to answer, the bell rings.

Drew goes into overdrive.

Time has always been important to her. But now? Sheer terror.

"Raleigh, hurry!" She tries to put all the candy back in the bags—in order, color by color—but her hands are shaking.

I reach over to help. But my eyes flick back to Tinsley. She is tapping her foot, which somehow reminds me of my dad's compass theory. He says every person is born with a compass, buried deep inside their soul. The goal is to keep the needle pointed True North. But Tinsley's tapping foot is like seeing the compass needle spinning around, around and around, because it has no idea where True North is. All Tinsley's needle cares about is the quickest route to whatever she wants. And everything—and everyone—is expendable.

"Drew," she purrs. "I really do need to talk with you."

"Not now!" Drew's frantic shout blows Tinsley around.

She whirls, striding back to the cool-girl table.

"Come on!" Drew is sifting through the colors, meticulous about how they go into the bag. I want to point out that once inside the bag, all the colors will get jumbled. But it'd be cruel.

"There!" The last M&M goes in. She grabs her notebook and leaps over the picnic seat bench. "Raleigh, what are you waiting for?!"

I dip an almost-cold French fry in the mayo. "I need to finish my lunch."

"But you'll be *late*!" Like being late is death.

Then again, in the OCD world, tardiness probably *is* next to deadliness.

"It's okay, Drew. I'll catch up. Promise."

She races for the door, her brown hair flying behind her, the skinny legs clumsy in that awkward nerd-run of hers.

But the second she's gone, I grab my tray and march over to Tinsley. She daintily replaces her bottled water and sliced celery into a sterilized lunchbox.

I want to punch her. "Leave Drew alone."

"Oh, please."

"You're using her."

Tinsley glances around the table. Mary Vale sits wide-eyed, like Bambi suddenly finding herself standing in the highway's express lane. The other "cool" girls appear eager to leave, purses on shoulders, but nobody dares make a move before the cult's leader says so.

"I'm helping Drew," Tinsley tells me. "Right, girls?"

"Right," they reply, nodding.

"Helping?" I ask. "How are you helping?"

"Drew likes experiments, theories. Whatever you call them. So I'm obliging, to help her."

"You're using her for your own reputation."

"Raleigh." She zips her lunch box. "I have no idea what you're talking about."

"Suicide." I pause, letting the word land hard. A thick silence fall over the table. So I say it again. "Suicide. What an ugly word. And only ugly crazy people commit suicide. But Sloane, she was a blood relative of yours. Better watch out, Tinsley. People are going to realize your family isn't so great after all."

"Thank you for your concern." She glares evilly at me and hoists a tiny black leather purse onto her tiny shoulder. "But you have a real problem."

"I'll say," chimes in Norwood Godwin. Norwood is like the cult's lieutenant. "If you're talking about crazy, Raleigh's mom takes the blue ribbon."

Tinsley laughs.

I squeeze the tray. My knuckles turn white.

"I know," Norwood continues, unable to resist the attention she craves, "maybe Raleigh even likes Drew better like this. You know, now everything is just like home. Nutsville."

Tinsley throws back her head, shaking her long hair with a good laugh, before heading for the door. Norwood rushes ahead, pushing it open for Tinsley but then steps in front of Mary Vale and the other hangers-on.

I am still standing there, teeth gritted, fingers aching, when Tinsley turns. Everyone stops.

"Raleigh, *you're* the one using her."

I can barely move my jaw. "What?"

"Don't be coy. We all know you can't fix your mother." She throws me one last icy stare. "So you're trying to fix Drew instead."

CHAPTER EIGHT

Because things can always get worse, Mr. Sandberg announces a "Christmas treat."

The world's most tedious English teacher, better known as Sandbag, waltzes back and forth in front of the classroom. Spittle scatters as he enunciates every syllable.

"Today, as we venture into the Christmas season, we will endeavor to light up this rather dreary room with an oratorical presentation of *A Christmas Carol*. You will each be given a part to read."

"You mean, like, out loud?" Tinsley asks.

"Not 'like,' Miss Teager," he says. "Not even 'as in.' This performance is no simulation. It is authentic. Live! And I will play Ebeneezer." His wrinkled old eyes gaze around the room. "I trust that no paradoxical need shall arise which forces me to draft 'volunteers.'"

The dutiful raise their hands.

Hollis Templeton asks to be Tiny Tim.

"Ah," he says. "The diminutive doppleganger of despair."

"Alliteration," Hollis says.

"Correct, Miss Templeton. But for that part, I'm casting another inspiring ingenue."

"Assonance," Hollis mumbles.

"The role of Tiny Tim," Sandbag bloviates toward the back of the room, "goes to Miss Drew Levinson."

Curled like a barnacle over her notebook, Drew lifts her head.

"Did you say something?"

Sandbag glares at her, waiting. His favorite shaming devise is the pregnant pause. Even from across the room, I can hear wall clock *tick-tick-ticking.*

"Indeed, Miss Levinson. I vocalized your Christian name."

Wow, a dig at her Judaism. Just in time for the holidays!

Sandbag raises the book in his hands, shaking it above his head until the pages rattle like Marley's chains. "It appears to have eluded Miss Levinson's notice, but we are endeavoring to bring to life Mr. Dicken's dramatic tale of redemption."

"Allusion?" Hollis asks.

Sandbag, pleased with all the brown-nosing, turns to Hollis and offers an expression of profound appreciation, which looks a lot like he's about to pass gas.

Then he doles out the other parts.

Tinsley is cast as Mrs. Cratchit. She looks upset until Norwood, clapping like a trained seal, gets cast as Mr. Cratchit. The rest of the rich-girl coven becomes the Cratchit children. I wonder what Dickens would think, discovering the Cratchits' net worth just ballooned to more than $100 million.

"Miss Harmon." Sandbag gives me a wolfish grin. "You are Marley's Ghost."

Terrific.

He hands out copies of the play, casting the other ghosts, along with Belle, and Ebenezer's sister.

Drew raises her hand.

"Miss Levinson, does your query pertain to the topic at hand?"

"Yes."

"Then proceed."

"I know which part is mine."

He raises a gray eyebrow. "You're acquainted with the roles?"

"All fifteen."

He stares at her, another pregnant pause. Then he licks his finger and runs it down the page, counting the parts. "Incorrect, Miss Levinson," he says haughtily. "The play has only fourteen parts."

"Did you count the turkey?" Drew asks.

"The . . . turkey?"

"The turkey Scrooge buys. For the Cratchits."

Sandbag shakes his head, offering her a condescending smile.

"Miss Levinson, the turkey is not a role in the play."

"Then why did Dickens write twelve lines about it?"

Now the pregnant pause falls on him. I bite my cheek, holding back a smile.

Sandbag just stares at her. His face seems a lot redder. "The turkey does not speak."

"So what," she says. "Tiny Tim only says five words. But you handed out his role first."

"Miss Levinson. What is your point?"

"That turkey is a key component to this play. And I want to play the turkey."

Laughter explodes. Sandbag snorts. It takes him several moments to even compose himself.

"Congratulations, Miss Levinson." He wipes tears from his old eyes. "You are the turkey."

And with that, he lifts the pages and begins reading the lines like he's auditioning for Broadway. " 'Marley was dead: to begin with.' "

I glance over at Drew, four rows over. She's scribbling in her notebook. Normally Sandbag would reprimand her for it, but he's too absorbed by his own performance.

" 'You will therefore permit me to repeat, emphatically, that Marley was as dead as a door-nail!' "

His booming tenor crashes into the walls. Everyone is following along, line by line. But I can't take my eyes off Drew. Totally in her own world, like nobody else is here.

Yet she knew there were fourteen parts—fifteen, counting the turkey.

And why did she want to be the turkey?

The ache in my chest has nothing to do with Dickens, or Marley being as dead a door-nail, or even stupid Sandbag's bloated performance.

It's the words. Spoken at lunch.

The words that rattle like chains in my mind.

Raleigh, you're the one using her.

CHAPTER NINE

W HEN THE FINAL bell finally rings, I open my locker and stuff
all my books into my backpack. Of course we have
homework over Christmas break—this is St. Catherine's. But my
mind's already mapping an afternoon run. Down the hill, to the
trail along the river, then pound out miles as the water rolls away
on my right. Just the thought of it fills me with peace.

"Ready?" Drew's face appears at my locker door, brimming
with manic energy.

"Ready for what?"

"The reenactment."

"Of . . .?"

"Sloane's accident."

Oh, God. No.

"Drew, we're officially on break now. Why don't we take a
break?"

"Raleigh, what we cannot create, we cannot understand."

More Feynman. When she gets like this, no discussion is possible. As my dad would say, *There is only agreement.*

So I walk down the hall beside her, moving through the giddy
atmosphere, the whistling energy that only comes right before
Christmas break. I feel only sadness.

"Caymans?" shrieks Norwood. "We'll be in Bermuda!"

Standing beside the lockers, Tinsley's got her skinny arm
linked through Mary Vale's elbow, like brand-new besties. Except
Sloane's little sister still looks sort of shell-shocked. Who could

blame her.

"Dedicated time," Drew says over the slamming lockers and more shrieks about vacations. "That's how we get answers."

"Uh-huh."

Tinsley's green eyes follow us, but she leans into Norwood, whispering. Whatever she says causes Norwood to snicker and stare at us, too. I feel a sudden deep regret. The missed opportunity. I should've performed a public service at lunch and clonked that cafeteria tray into Tinsley's head.

"It's all about the laws of the universe," Drew is saying. "Everything in the universe obeys those laws. Otherwise everything would be impossible."

Impossible. I swallow a bitter taste. *Impossible.* That's what this feels like, searching for my best friend, trying to help her function again. *Impossible.*

"Pythagoras said there was geometry even in the humming of strings."

Impossible.

But every day my dad does the impossible.

So I follow Drew into the Earth Sciences lab, ready to warn my geology teacher. But one look at Teddy Chastain and I know he knows.

"Thanks for letting us use the lab," I tell him.

"Ditch them niceties and git it done," he says. "Ellis was just in here, all bealed up about me not getting outta here on time."

Mr. Ellis, our headmaster, has one unstated mission in life—fire Teddy. Unfortunately for Ellis, Teddy uses a wheelchair. And it's not easy to get rid of a cripple—Teddy's word—who also happens to be a brilliant teacher. But that doesn't stop Ellis from compiling quite the dossier on Teddy. But Drew used to work in the Physics lab, staying after school for hours to figure out experiments with vectors and velocity and even what force a thrown baseball exerts on a swinging bat. But that was then. Now she refuses to enter the physics lab. So Teddy lets her come in here, adding to his infractions . . . which also include giving us school supplies for personal use and letting us take reference books home from the science library.

"Due to supply constraints," Drew rushes to the back counter, "I'm forced to use rocks for authentic objects. You'll need to use your imagination."

"Got that right," Teddy mutters, rolling up beside me.

His eyes are a peridot kind of green. Not murky. But not that glass-green like Tinsley either. More like a mossy green but crystallized. With his unruly red hair and bushy beard, Teddy looks like somebody whose ancestors got kicked out of Scotland for spitting on the queen.

He looks up at me and waggles the bushy eyebrows. "Drewsky says you got soil samples. That right?"

"Don't encourage her," I whisper.

"I'm not. I'm encouraging you."

Without a trace of enthusiasm, I dig to the bottom of my backpack, where I'd hoped that bag of soil would remain.

"Tell me again." Drew holds up a pale brown specimen. "What is this specimen?"

"Petrified wood," Teddy says. "Thought it could stand in for that yonder tree."

"Brilliant!"

I narrow my eyes at him. "Not helping."

"Where's the soil?"

I hold up the bag.

He takes it, holding it up to the light. Then shakes it. Holds it up again. Then opens the top and smells the dirt. "Yerp."

"What?"

"Reckon so."

He won't tell me. Everything I know about rocks and minerals, he's made me work for. I take the bag from his hand, suppressing the nasty mutter in my mouth, and walk over to the microscopes. Teddy rolls right beside me.

"Got yer next steps figured out?"

"Weigh it. Wash it. Whatever."

"Yerp." Teddy hails from West Virginia. He's not interested in sounding from anywhere else, probably because the hillbilly accent sends Ellis into grammatical fits.

Shoving back one wheel on his chair, he spins until the rubber squeals on the polished floor. "Drewsky."

She's bent over her "reenactment," holding a slab of ironstone in one hand. The red hue tells me that'll be the Cherrymobile. She doesn't respond to Teddy.

"Y'alright over there?" he asks.

"Actually." She straightens. "Pythagoras said there's geometry in the humming of strings. Do you understand that?"

I freeze. She knows I was patronizing her. My face flushes.

"Rightly so," Teddy says.

"How?"

" 'Cause even our chaos's got order."

She looks over at me.

Teddy does another spin—toward me—green eyes doused with concern. Seeing that expression makes my own eyes sting. So I turn away and pour the soil from baggie onto the small scale next to the microscopes. Soft brown soil, almost crumbly. I write down the weight, blinking back the heat in my eyes.

"Pythagoras," Teddy says loudly. "That reminds me of a dude back home in the hollers."

Here it comes. I move most of the grains to a flat-bottomed beaker, add distilled water, and swirl the mixture to dissolve any organics, so that when the soil dries, only minerals will remain.

"He was a snake handlin' preacher. Like all them jokes about West Virginnie. Only this one was real."

I pinch the rest of the dry grains that didn't go into the wash and dust them over a glass slide. Then I slip that under the microscope. And not just any microscope—these puppies polarize light. Sent directly to St. Cat's from the manufacturer, donated after Teddy won "Science Teacher of the Year." Nationally. For the second time in five years. Ellis probably lost half his hair that day.

I adjust the scope's focus knob. "What does a snake-handling preacher have to do with Pythagoras?"

"Ain't you listening? The dude used pythons for his sermons."

I glance over my shoulder. But Drew's consulting her notebook. Probably making sure the reenactment is done to scale. Once upon a time, she would've looked back at me and rolled her eyes.

"For years and years that preacher done wrapped that snake 'round his arm, calling out to the Lord. *Oh, The Lord! The Lord!*" Teddy lifts his arms, shaking them. "*The Lord who controls all things*. And how do I know? Because my momma hauled me in there to hear that man every Sunday. And then, on Christmas Eve, nineteen seventy-nine, he took that snake and."

He stops.

I look up.

Drew looks up too.

Teddy rolls away, heading for his messy desk at the front of the room.

"You can't stop the story there," I tell him. "What happened?"

He starts whistling.

"Teddy, what happened?"

He whistles louder.

"Hey!"

He picks up an eraser, starts wiping down the whiteboard.

Now I'm mad. "Aren't you going to tell us?"

"No." Drew shakes her head, the hair wafting. "No, leave it. That's perfect."

"What?"

"Raleigh, he just proved it."

Teddy looks over. "Atta girl."

"Proved what?"

"What Pythagoras said. You could tell that story's incomplete. Only the story's nothing more than words spoken into the air. The humming of strings. But you sensed its geometry, the missing parts. Pythagoras was right."

A hillbilly grin splits his red beard. "Drewsky, you're the real deal."

I return to the scope, fiddling with the knobs. I take my time, pushing away something that feels like resentment. "This stuff's a weird color." I keep my eyes on the scope. "And lots of rounded edges on the grains. So, I'm guessing river soil?"

"Gittin' warm," Teddy says.

"Okay, so rock eroded from the Blue Ridge Mountains was carried to the foothills through rain and gravity, and then carried here by the James River." I look up. There's more, I can sense it. Like that humming of strings. "Only it's not just eroded rock, because it's also loamy."

Loam refers to a soil's mixture—sand, silt, clay, plus organic matter, such as leaves and dead organisms.

But Teddy's watching Drew. And she is counting. Of course.

When he looks over at me, there's a certain gravity in his green eyes.

"I really didn't want more homework over break," I mutter.

He must really feel something big. Because instead of pestering me, he tosses the eraser onto his desk and rolls over to the microscope. The lab's tables and counters all sit low, adjusted for the height of his chair, so he slides up and peers through the scope's eyepiece. Fiddling with the knobs, he turns the specimen on its axis. But he has to ply the focus knob with his palm. Whatever tragedy snapped his spine also stole the dexterity in his thumbs.

"Not that I believe that whole Christmas story," he says, "but it is your holiday. So I'm givin' you a gift."

I smile. Maybe he should get sad more often. "Please."

"First clue."

"Clue? How about the answer?"

"That ain't no gift. Least, not one you'd appreciate."

"Says you."

"You want the first clue or not?"

"Hit me."

"Most fertile soil in the entire state of Virginnie."

I roll my eyes. "Do I look like a farmer?"

"Second clue. Name comes from an Indian tribe."

"Chickahominy."

He shakes his head. "Think. This stuff is the oldest tilled soil in the entire United States."

"How old is that?" Drew walks over. "Specifically."

He glances at me, one split-second, but it speaks volumes. "Specifically. You mean, what year?"

"Of course what year."

"Drewsky, we're talking geology. Years are like split-seconds of time."

She taps her pencil on the counter. "So you can't pinpoint the year?"

"Darlin', I can barely name this year."

She walks back to her model crash site. The ironstone is pointed at the petrified wood which is tilted on a piece of slate. Simulating that rise in the landscape that launched the Cherrymobile into the tree.

I feel sick.

"This being Christmas," Teddy says, apparently seeing something in my face. "I am gonna give you the answer."

The sting comes back in my eyes. I nod. I can't even speak.

"Way, way back when, the Pamunkey Indians figured out this soil could grow anything. And I mean, anything. If I planted Ellis in this soil, he might even grow a spine."

"Good to know." I push out the words. "So what's it called?"

"I just told you! Pamunkey soil."

Drew pipes up. "That doesn't sound very scientific."

But I can only stare at him. Teddy's never, ever, *ever* given me an answer.

"Thank you," I tell him.

"Yer welcome." He wheels away. "Now do me a favor. Don't be forgettin' that information, just 'cause it was free."

CHAPTER TEN

RICHMOND ALWAYS ACTS like Christmas is never coming back. Every tree strung with lights. Every window flickering with electric candles. And the flags? Christmas flags flap for *weeks*.

But nothing could've prepared me for seeing Weyanoke dressed up for the holidays.

"Oh my—" my mother gasps. "Oh my lands!"

During our thirty-minute drive out here to DeMott's family estate, my dad has kept one hand on the wheel and the other holding my mom's hand.

"David," she asks him, as we drive down the long-long-long driveway. "Is it real?"

Not a bad question, actually. Weyanoke is fabled estate. First for the visits from Jefferson and Washington and every governor of the Old Dominion. Then during the Civil War, Union troops camped here while General McClellan burned the neighboring plantations.

"No, it's not real," Helen says.

She sits in the back seat with me. Snarky as ever, she arrived this evening burned out from finals and reeking of cigarettes. "Nothing out here is real."

"Helen . . ."

"Dad, this plantation is one giant historical lie."

"We're guests," he warns her. "We have been invited."

"Raleigh was invited. We're just being allowed to tag along because DeMott's got the hots for her. He must like slumming."

She looks at me. "No offense."

Nobody disputes her point. Which only encourages her.

She asks, "Why don't we throw a party for winter solstice?"

"Because we're not pagans," replies my dad.

"The Fieldings are."

"Pagans?" My mother looks stricken. "The Fieldings are pagans?"

"No, honey." My dad glares into the rearview mirror, warning Helen with his eyes. "The Fieldings are most certainly *not* pagans."

"Oh, really?" Helen says. "So if some unwed pregnant teenager shows up here on Christmas Eve, the Fieldings are going to help her? I don't think so. These people wouldn't recognize the mother of God if she bit them."

My dad turns, smiling at my mom. "Honey, you look so lovely tonight."

"Uh-huh." Helen persists. "Maybe the Fieldings would let Mary camp in the old slave quarters and pop out a baby."

"Helen, that's enough."

I crack my window for air.

Up ahead, at the end of the driveway, a flashlight swings through the dark, signaling us to stop.

Helen peers forward. "Black valets. What a surprise."

"That's quite enough from you, Helen." My dad brakes the car, cranks down his window, and smiles at the valet. "Good evening."

"Evening." The valet leans down. His parka carries a name tag, but I can't read it from here. He shines the flashlight at a clipboard in his other hand. "May I get your name?"

"Harmon. Party of four."

I close my eyes. On my list of Things To Do Tonight, the very last item would be Go To This Party. With My Parents. And My Sister. At the top would be Throw High Heels Out Window and Run Way Home, Twenty-Five Miles, In the Cold, In the Dark.

"Right. Harmon." The valet looks at each of us, but freezes on Helen.

She offers him the fisted symbol for Black Power.

The valet smirks, then looks at me. His gaze lingers even longer, then he nods, like he knows me. "Just a second, please." He pulls a radio from his parka and turns his back, talking into it.

"Why is he doing that?" My mother's southern accent sounds tight, anxious. "Who's he talking to?"

Paranoia. Kicking in already.

I sigh. *Long night ahead.*

Helen says, "He's just making sure riff-raff like us actually should be here."

"Helen—"

"Or maybe he's calling the bank. Checking our net worth."

My dad shifts in his seat, fully facing my mom. "Honey, you won't believe the interior of this home. Hasn't changed since the seventeen hundreds."

"Correct," Helen says. "This place is a complete and total refutation of social progress."

"Alright." My dad sounds ready to snap. "Helen, we love you, and we understand your feelings, but please keep them to yourself tonight."

My mother looks over the back seat. Her jasper eyes take in my sister for a long moment. "You must be so tired. Would you rather we go home?"

"I'd rather get drunk." Helen opens the car door and steps out. The valet turns. "Bar," she tells him. "Now."

Her hippie tie-dye skirt paired with black engineer boots— ideal for a solstice party—cross in front of the headlights.

The valet leans down to speak to my dad. "I'm sorry, we had orders to let the house know when you arrived. I can park the car for you."

My dad steps out, explains how our car works. Because it's not like most cars.

"The gears are those buttons on the dashboard," he tells the valet.

"Serious?" The valet stares at the old black Mercedes. "What year?"

"Sixty-three."

"Wow. And mint condition."

Our car's nothing fancy, especially among the Weyanoke crowd, but the '63 Mercedes sedan is cherished by my dad, who inherited it from his dad.

But as I follow my parents down the brick path toward the mansion, I have a disturbing thought.

Sloane.

She probably would've been here tonight, since it's her neighborhood, her kind of people.

I glance over at my dad. And I realize why Sloane drove that Cherrymobile. If my dad died, I'd drive that Mercedes.

"David," my mom slows, cautious. "Do I look alright?"

"No," he says.

She stops. I almost crash into her.

"Nadine," he tells her, "you look like God fulfilled my every wish in one woman." He wraps his arm around her tiny waist, pulling her close. "I love you."

My mom beams, suddenly looking like a woman who belongs in this mansion. My dad, once again doing the impossible.

We walk up the wide brick steps. Glass-lantern candles hang from the banister and above the gargantuan front door decorated with fresh pine boughs. The door opens before we get there, and a butler wearing a white-tailed tuxedo welcomes us into the foyer. He offers to take our coats. My mother hands him her red velvet cape and I watch the man's eyes sweep over her bare shoulders. My mom's stunning. Her skin looks like she bathes in pure cream, eyes glittering like jewels, raven hair that curls and shines. Sometimes I wonder if God made her outside so beautiful for protection, so people wouldn't immediately judge her for being crazy.

I'm handing the butler my old raggedy coat when DeMott appears in the foyer.

I've seen him wearing a tuxedo before, so that can't be it. But something turns me into a deaf-mute. I know, I'm supposed to say something. But I can't. He finally extends his hand to my dad, telling him how much he appreciates our coming tonight. Then he compliments my mother, who actually blushes, but the whole sweet moment abruptly clangs like a really horrible brass gong when he says, "I think I just saw Helen walking into the ballroom."

None of us says a word. My dad and I are probably both wondering the same thing: which bomb goes off first—Helen or my mom?

"Well." DeMott lifts his elbow, offering it to me. "May I escort you?"

I try not to latch on too forcefully. But it feels like I'm drowning and he's my life preserver. He leads me through the grand foyer past the antique sconces with candles, flames flickering against the gilt-framed family portraits—every Fielding, every DeMott, every MacKenna who's ever lived here, ever since King Charles got his head chopped off.

My parents walk behind us. But I hear my mom say, "He has such beautiful manners."

True.

But even better is the rock-hard bicep I can feel in his arm. It's making my stomach do weird things as we move down another huge hallway.

Up ahead a band is playing at just the right volume, so you can still pick up the cultured voices and refined laughter of the crowd. I brace myself as we make the final turn.

I see them. All the Names of Richmond. They're here.

"David Harmon!" Someone in the crowd signals for my dad to come over. "It's been a long time!"

The Harmon heritage doesn't stretch back as far as the Fieldings, but my dad's still an FFV. That stands for First Family of Virginia. If you think that's not important, you're not paying attention.

DeMott leans into me. "By the way, you look great."

"So my nervousness shows?"

He tilts his head. "Why do you say that?"

Because my dad compliments my mom when she's nervous. "Nothing." Then I remember my manners. "Thanks."

Yessiree. Off to a smashing start.

I steal another look at him. He's smiling at me. Now I really can't breathe. Not just because Christmas music winds through the air like ribbons. Not because candles warm the pine boughs and the air smells like a forest full of sunlight. Or because George and Martha Washington once waltzed on this very same parquet-oak dance floor.

No. Nothing as deep as that. Because, turns out, I'm shallow.

The women in this room sparkle. The men are flushed with self-confidence and success. And the girls my age are not sweating through their dresses.

I can't measure up.

DeMott takes my hand—clammy with sweat, I'm sure—and leads me through the crowd. I feel the sidelong glances, calculating my invisible score and deciding that, yes, I come up short. I look around for Helen, just to feel better about myself.

"Dad," DeMott says.

My head snaps forward.

The middle-aged man looking down at me has that handsome, gray-at-the-temples look going. He smiles at me.

DeMott says, "I'd like you to meet Raleigh Harmon."

The smile falters. After a moment he extends his hand. His palm feels cold. Maybe from the ice in his glass. "How do you do, Raleigh, is it?"

"Yes, sir. Thank you for inviting us."

He glances over my head. "Your father's here?"

No, I walked twenty-five miles. In heels.

"Yes sir." I search the crowd. The cocktail chatter around us hurts my ears. Probably because my ears are also burning. "There he is."

My dad's arm is still wrapped around my mother's tiny waist. But she holds herself stiffly, almost frozen. In this crowd, that posture probably looks normal. But I know what it means. Fear.

"I'll go say hello." Mr. Fielding barely glances at me again.

DeMott watches him leave. Maybe I'm imagining it, but he seems a little taken aback.

"Something to drink?" he asks.

"Coke. No crushed ice."

"Be right back." He gives my hand a squeeze then walks over to one of the waiters in white tails.

My eyes follow Harrison Fielding. Every week in church, the whole family sits three pews away from us. But me and my mom are probably mostly invisible to Harrison Fielding. He clasps my dad's hand. My dad isn't holding a drink. Because if he was, he couldn't shake hands with people without letting go of my mom. And he won't do that. I feel a weird ache in my chest, watching him make small talk. What would his life be like if he didn't have to worry all the time? If he could just relax and enjoy a party now and then?

"Here you go." DeMott hands me my drink.

"Thanks." I take a sip and look at him over the rim. "How much did it cost you to get your dad to invite us?"

"Raleigh—"

"You can tell me."

"You're insinuating we wouldn't—"

"The truth." I lower my glass. "Please, DeMott."

In those blue-blue eyes, I see another kind of fear. Different from my mom's. Different from mine. But it shocks me even more. DeMott's afraid to speak the truth.

"Here's something you should know about me," I tell him. "I find cold hard facts really comforting."

It takes him a moment. "I wanted to see you. I didn't think you'd come by yourself. So, yes, I asked my dad to invite your whole family. Feel better?"

"Much." I smile. Really smile. "And thanks for the invitation. I think."

"You *think*?"

I take another sip, watching my parents. Now my dad's talking to—*Oh, God*—Mrs. Stillman. Her face looks like a white mask above her coal-black clothing. And something about that stark contrast reminds me of the damaged tree, with its bark ripped away by Sloane's car. My dad's eyes are so somber. So knowing. Meanwhile, my mom just looks confused. My heart clutches. How will my dad convey condolences without revealing to my mom there was a funeral?

Impossible.

But then that white-haired man appears—the one who stood next to Mrs. Stillman after the funeral. Once again, Mrs. Stillman looks at him with relief. It transforms her face. And when the man glances at my dad, something passes between then. Not just sympathy. Or compassion. It's empathy. Two men who are bearing the weight of wrecked women. My eyes sting so badly I start blinking really fast. One part of me is happy for my dad, glad that somebody understands what he goes through with my mom. But another part is just plain sad. Sad for all this brokenness and death and hurting.

I gulp my Coke, trying to drown my feelings, and scan the room for my sister. Instead—ugh—I get an eyeful of Tinsley and Company. They're all looking like fashion models. But Mary Vale's among them, still looking lost. Who wants to be at a Christmas party after your sister's funeral? Nothing holds these people back, I decide. Not even death.

Helen is near the stage, by the band. She sips an amber liquid from a crystal glass. Whisky. Works on her like a countdown on a bomb. Four . . . three . . . two . . .

"Want to dance?" DeMott asks.

I jump. Then I smile to cover my fears. "Actually, can I get my coat back?"

DeMott laughs. "You mean, ever?"

"No. Like, now."

He pauses, confused. "What for?"

"So I don't freeze. Outside."

"You're leaving?" He frowns. "Raleigh, you just got here."

"Exactly."

CHAPTER ELEVEN

T HE COLD AIR burns my lungs, and yet I can't stop breathing it in, holding the freeze deep down inside, hoping to kill my fear, my shame.

"You don't like parties?" DeMott walks beside me. Light flows from the high windows of the house, making the brick path look golden. But further out, across the wide lawn, darkness stretches forever.

"Parties are okay."

"Just not your thing."

I step off the path. Frozen grass crunches under his dress shoes, while my mind paws for the right words. The polite words. Because dad's advice rings loud and clear. *You're here as a guest.* I glance back, trying to see into those old six-over-six windows, find out how my parents are doing. My sister. Do I really want to know?

"Strange," he says.

"We can't help it."

He stops walking. I look over. Lights from the house bathe the ground, forming a kind of halo around him. Just enough light to see the smile on his face.

"What?" I ask.

"I didn't mean *y'all* were strange."

"Oh."

"I just think it's strange you don't feel comfortable in there."

I start walking again. But every step forward is darker than the last. My heart starts pounding. Which fear will win—my freak-out attitude about parties or my panic about the dark?

"Do you want to know why I think it's strange," he says.

"Not really." I get plenty of that that at school, from girls like Tinsley. "I really don't want to kno—"

"Because you're perfect. That's why it's strange."

I glance over again. Still only silhouetted by the house lights, still looking like he's glowing. But I can't read his face. "I know it's dark out here, but you're talking about me—Raleigh?"

"And you make me laugh."

"Give me one second." I snap my fingers, over and over. "I promise, I can break this spell."

He laughs and grabs my hand, pulling me into him. *Oh, man.* His warmth. It seeps into me at the same time a laugh tumbles from my mouth. We stand like that for a long moment. I can't hear the party noise anymore. But his face. I can see it now. And see that he's going to kiss me.

But he steps back.

Still holding my hand, he walks through the dark. I take a deep breath, holding the cold against my pounding heart.

"Watch your step." He glances over. "Tree roots everywhere."

I look down. Gnarly roots push through the ground. DeMott moves to a wooden bench beside the tree's trunk.

I sit down next to him.

"Now look up," he says.

Tree limbs knit the air, a tapestry of gray lace. I stare up into it and suddenly see tiny white lights, glistening in the black sky beyond, as if God strung this tree with his own Christmas lights. I lift my hand because the stars seem close enough to touch. They sparkle at my fingertips. I shiver.

"Cold?"

No. "Yes."

He shakes off his tuxedo jacket and wraps it around me. Across the wide estate lawn, the party falls away, a distant murmur. For several minutes, we stare up at the starry lace, breaths vibrating between us. I watch one soft cloud stream across the black sky, followed by another. They disappear into the dark.

I shiver again.

"I've got a better idea." He opens his arms, pulls me into him. "Body heat, that'll keep you warm."

"You probably say that to all the strange girls who can't handle a nice party."

"No." He whispers. "Just you."

I lean into him, wrapped in the cocoon of his warmth, and close my eyes. We don't move for a few minutes, and I relax listening to his solid heartbeat.

"Speaking of strange," he says, "how're things with Drew?"

I draw my head back, trying to read his face again.

"Sorry," he says. "Did I just ruin a moment?"

"That was a moment?"

"I sure hope so." He squeezes my shoulder.

My heart pounds so hard I'm afraid he can feel it. Which, of course, makes it pound harder. I draw in another cold breath, tasting frost, and try to read his expression. All I can see is his profile, looking up at the stars. Which is pretty darn great.

He says, "I'll bet you're glad she's back."

"Yes." I pause. "But it'd be even better if the real Drew came back."

"Officially, this is *not* a moment because I'm going to ask you to explain that."

I'd rather bury my head in his arms. "Drew physically came back. But sometimes it feels like I don't know her anymore."

When he says nothing more, I tuck my face into his chest. That scent of aftershave makes me want to leave my entire life behind.

"Give her time," he says.

I speak into his starched tuxedo shirt. "That's what everyone says."

"Everyone's right. She's been through a lot."

"Problem is, I'm not good at waiting."

He shifts positions. I look up.

"I'm excellent at waiting," he says.

"You are?"

"Yes," he says. "I've been known to wait a very long time."

"How long?"

"Forever."

"That is impressive."

"Enough for both of us."

I stare into his blue eyes. My heart's trying to kill me. "How well did you know Sloane Stillman?"

He holds my gaze. "Raleigh."

"What."

"That was a moment."

"You sure?"

"Definitely. And you knew it."

"Possibly."

"And yet you brought up Sloane?"

I fidget.

He sighs, drops his head back and gazes at the stars. "Okay, let's talk about Sloane. How well did I know her? We practically grew up together, what with their place down the road and our mothers being close friends."

Couple things jump out at me. First, "their place" sounds cozy, but these historic Virginia estates are anything but. And two, which might be part of one, is "down the road." That's really miles apart. But three, and most importantly, he answered my question, despite my really bad timing.

"DeMott, I brought up Sloane because you brought up Drew."

"How's that work?"

"Drew doesn't believe Sloane killed herself."

"Excuse me?"

"She thinks the crash was an accident."

"Even with a suicide note?"

"I've tried reasoning with her, but it gets me nowhere."

The sound of the band comes across the lawn. Playing that carol about the things that came upon a midnight clear. That glorious song of old. I watch our breath, silvery against the black night.

"Drew's not stupid," he says.

"You're agreeing with her?"

"Not at all. I'm just saying she's not stupid. But she has some odd ideas." He smiles. "As in, not even."

His smile makes my heart thump against my ribcage, hard enough to crack it. And since I've already killed one moment, maybe two, and since I'm really bad at waiting, I toss my next words into the dark, reversing any charm that's supposed to be in that proverbial third-time.

"Tinsley's pushing Drew to look into Sloane's suicide."

I watch his face. What is he thinking about Tinsley, his old girlfriend? Probably that Tinsley would *never* make him have this kind of conversation, at this kind of moment.

But I need to know. I need to know how he feels about her.

"What does 'look into it' mean, exactly?"

"I think that's Tinsley-speak."

"For?" he asks.

"Save my family's reputation."

He clears his throat.

"Alright." I drop my head, tucking in my chin. "That was mean."

"How's Drew supposed to look into Sloane's death?"

There are many things I like about DeMott. But among the best is he doesn't make me grovel with an apology.

Pressing closer, feeling his pulse beat steady and strong, I tell him about yesterday's bike ride to the crash site. And how Drew built a simulated model of the crash in the earth sciences lab. "She had me take soil samples, like geology can solve this like it did with her disappearance. It's her OCD taking over. And Tinsley's manipulating Drew, turning her into my—"

I clamp my mouth shut.

No way can I say the next words.

My mother.

Party laughter trickles across the dark. The band continues to play. I tuck my chin deeper, feeling a nasty undertow ready to carry me out to sea.

DeMott points up at the sky. "Can you see Venus?"

I look up through the web of limbs. The night sky is a black velvet curtain dusted with tiny diamonds. But one light shines brighter than the rest, burning through the curtain like the fabric's torn, like all the light from the other world is leaking through to ours.

"How do you know that's Venus?" I ask.

"It's December."

"Officially, this is not a moment, too, because I'm going to ask you to explain."

"Great. It'll keep you here." He hugs me to his chest. "In December, at our latitude, Venus starts setting about three hours after sunset."

"And you know that because . . .?"

"Because I notice things." He turns, whispering in my ear. "And I notice you're not running away."

His words close around my throat. I can't breathe. Can't move. I can only close my eyes and feel that strange hum in the air. Yes, the geometry of it.

He asks, "Would it help if Drew saw Sloane's car—in person?"

I open my eyes. "What?"

He lifts my chin, kisses my mouth. So softly my eyes want to never open again.

He draws back. "I know where the car is."

I keep my eyes closed. "The Cherrymobile?"

"Yes. I'll show her, if it'll change her mind. But it's going to cost you."

"How much?"

"Another kiss."

"My kinda bribery."

"Mine, too," he says. "And I'll thank Venus later."

CHAPTER TWELVE

RUE TO HIS word, the next day DeMott picks up me and Drew
and drives us to see the Cherrymobile. He says it's in a
junkyard in Charles City, seven miles from Weyanoke.

Only this part of Charles City doesn't look anything like the
historic plantations. More like the sharecroppers live here.

And my first inkling that something's wrong comes as we pass
the junkyard's chain link fence. Rusting gas pumps stand in long
unmowed grass like discarded metal soldiers.

Drew makes a hiccupy kind of sound.

I look at her worried face. "DeMott, this place is safe, right?"

"My dad owns it."

"Your dad. He owns a *junkyard*?"

"He owns the land." DeMott navigates his truck over a rutted
dirt road. More junks on either side. Old iron plows. "Everything
else belongs to Eliot."

Whoever Eliot is, he's accumulated an impressive mess. Old
tires pillar like stalagmites. Chrome bumpers grin without cars.
And whole pickets of hubcaps stretch in either direction.

Drew hiccups again.

I reach over, touching her arm.

"Two, six." She's counting. Something. "Eight—no. That
doesn't work."

She stops. Starts again. Stops.

I glance over at DeMott, hoping to warn him, but he's lowering
his window. The truck stops at a tower of crushed cars, with a

cave-like opening in the twisted metal.

"Eliot!" He calls out. "You here?"

The creature who steps out wears faded denim overalls and no shirt. Tattoos smother his pink skin. Those leaky blue tattoos that I've seen on convicts leg-chained in my dad's courtroom.

"I done paid the rent," he says to DeMott.

"Thanks." DeMott smiles. "Just wanted to look at that '57 Chevy."

"Too late."

"It's gone?"

"Going out today."

"But it's still here?" DeMott says.

Eliot's eyes peer out from swollen lids. Green eyes? I can't tell because he's also squinting at Drew. She sits beside me on the bench seat rocking and pointing out the window. I follow her finger point and see a yellow-shaded brass lamp on the ground, surrounded by more junk, its electrical cord trailing to nowhere.

"It's okay," I whisper to her. "It'll get plugged in."

Eliot says to DeMott. "You biddin' on that vehicle?"

He pronounces the word VEE-hickle.

"No. I just wanted to look at it."

"Can't."

"I can't look at it?" DeMott asks.

"I gots orders."

"How much will it cost?"

"Now you talkin." Eliot grins. A black gap separates his front teeth. "I tell you, that old Chevy's making me a purty penny."

"Classic car parts are hard to find." DeMott reaches for his wallet, takes out a twenty, hands it to Eliot.

Eliot holds the bill to the sky. Sunshine beams like a spotlight and Eliot squints up at Andrew Jackson, like he might just be a damn Yankee. Then he shoves the bill inside his overalls.

"I got a man from up north, he called," Eliot says. "Gave me good money for the whole she-bang."

"Congratulations."

"But don't be tellin' your old man." Eliot leans in. "Might could raise my rent."

"We're even." DeMott gestures toward us. "We never came here. Got it?"

Eliot's eyes are not green. They're brown, a hard brown, like dusty shale. He nudges his chin toward Drew. "What's wrong with her?"

Drew's wrapped her skinny arms around her knees, still rocking, staring out the windshield.

"Nothing," I say. Because a guy who collects random junk isn't likely to understand OCD. "Where's the Chevy?"

He points. Toward more junk. All I see are empty scaffolding planks stacked like some random stairway to heaven. Below them, dented washing machines slump dejectedly.

Eliot starts walking toward them. DeMott jumps out, jogging around the front of the truck to Drew's door. Once upon a time it bugged me that he opened doors for us. Then it dawned on me. He opens doors for the same reason my dad does. Not because girls are weaker, or to score points. He just really thinks girls are special.

"Drew." He guides her down from the truck, turning her shoulders to face him. "Are you okay?"

She points. That unplugged lamp.

"Could you plug in that lamp?" I ask.

DeMott runs over, picks up the lamp, and carries it into the hut-like structure of crushed cars.

I climb out and shrug into my backpack.

Eliot's turned left at a standing metal safe with its busted door hanging wide open. I take Drew's arm. She's making a sound I've never heard. One part little kid about to have a meltdown, one part the mutterings of a Mensa member. Which pretty much sums up my best friend.

"You know," I tell her, as we head toward the busted safe, "I've been thinking about that geometry in humming strings." Her arm feels like hollow bone. "It means there's order everywhere.

Even here. We just can't see it."

I walk around a dented refrigerator. Eliot's standing deeper into the metallic chaos.

"Order is everywhere, Drew."

She nods.

Eliot hollers, "Ain't she a beauty!"

The Cherrymobile sits on a flatbed truck behind him.

"This vee-hickle's strong enough to survive suicide!"

DeMott jogs up beside us. He waves at Eliot, trying to silence him.

"Detroit sure knew how to make cars," Eliot continues. "Not like that foreign junk we get these days."

"Thanks for your help," DeMott says. "I'll take it from here."

"If that girl'd been wearing a seatbelt, she'd be alive and kick-in'."

Personally I'd like to kick Eliot, but when I look over, DeMott doesn't seem particularly upset. He looks . . . wounded. And right there I realize another incredible thing about him. The whole world says he got every right to look down on people, but he doesn't.

"Appreciate your help," he says. "I'll let you know if we need anything else."

"Huh." Eliot's hands slide inside the bib. "Why y'all so interested in this vee-hicle?"

"The girl who owned it was their classmate," DeMott says.

Drew pulls away from my grip. She walks around the flatbed.

Eliot's shale eyes watch her. "So this's what, some kinda goodbye?"

"No." Drew keeps her gaze on the car. "It is nonsensical to say goodbye without first saying hello."

Eliot frowns. "So who you saying hello to?"

"Does the hood open?" she asks.

"Hey," he replies. "Does the Pope wear a dress?"

I look at DeMott. He shakes his head.

Eliot jumps up on the flatbed and walks the length to the damaged driver's side door. Where a window used to be, he reaches in and yanks something. The hood pops. "Born and bred in the U S of A."

"Thank you," DeMott says, his voice firm now. "We can take it from here."

"Don't take nothing, hear?" Eliot jumps off the flatbed. "Man from up north done bought the whole thing."

"You have my word."

Eliot squints like he did with that twenty dollar bill. My guess is that, unlike DeMott, Eliot's word isn't worth spit. He leaves, walking back around the busted safe.

Drew grabs the flatbed's wheels to hoist herself up. DeMott climbs up after her. Me? I want to run away. But Drew's head is swiveling back and forth like a bobble-head doll.

"Here, let me help you with that hood." DeMott carefully slides his hand under the crumpled metal. It takes several shoves, and the hinges squeal, begging us to leave them alone. When it's fully lifted, the hood blocks my view of them both. But Eliot's right, the rest of the car survived high-speed impact.

"Why do you want to see the engine?" he asks.

"Precisely."

Drew's on her own page.

I walk to the back end of the flatbed. The Cherrymobile's right rear fin looks like a shark's tail. I touch the white wheel tire below it and an image of Sloane floats across my mind. How she parked this car at St. Cat's. The Cherrymobile swallowed two parking spaces and made the nearby BMWs look like motorcycle sidecars.

"Say you wanted to kill yourself," Drew says. "Would you hit that tree head-on or sideways?"

I still can't see either of them. The crumpled hood's as wide as a queen mattress. But I can imagine the tortured look on DeMott's face.

"I . . . don't . . . know," he says.

"Headfirst," she says.

I take out my soil knife and pry the dull blade deep into the tire treads. Carefully, I lift out the soil. It's a weird orange hue, like that Pamunkey soil Teddy told me about. I stare at the grains, pretending this is just another geology project and Sloane is not gone-gone-gone.

I slide the soil into a Ziploc bag, swallow hard, and pinch the bag closed.

"So why didn't Sloane drive headfirst into that tree? She obviously turned the wheel. The car collided on the front left side."

I kneel on the ground, reach into my backpack, remove a Sharpie, and write today's date, time, and location on the plastic. Just like Teddy taught me.

She asks, "Can you explain this engine?"

DeMott's still quiet.

I circle around the flatbed and look up. Drew's no longer swiveling her head. Now she's putting things in order.

"Explain," she says. "Raleigh, look inside."

"What?"

"Look inside."

"Inside where?"

"The car."

"No. No. Way."

"Yes. Way. DeMott, explain the engine."

DeMott looks at me. His blue-blue eyes are pleading. But I can't help him. This trip was his idea. And no good deed goes unpunished.

I make my way around the flatbed. Something crunches under my shoes. Pieces of glass.

"Well." He clears his throat. "Have you ever seen those concrete barriers that separate two sides of the highway?"

"Be more specific."

"Rectangular blocks of concrete. They line up between the different lanes. So if a car going one way starts to drift, it hits the blocks instead of heading into oncoming traffic."

"Oh. Yes. I have seen them. Particularly the six miles of highway that connect Interstate 464 with Interstate 64. There are thirty seven of those blocks."

I wait.

He says, "An odd number."

"But if you add up 464 and 64—"

I look up at the sun, close my eyes, pray. *Help.*

"Good to know," DeMott says. Like my mother said last night, *Such beautiful manners.*

"But you haven't explained the engine." The pint-sized physicist has turned into a prosecuting attorney. "How are those barriers related to this engine?"

"Well. An engine this size works sort of like those concrete blocks."

"Protecting a driver from impact."

"Right. See how the engine cracked down the middle? But it's not completely destroyed. Even after a crash like that. Which is why somebody still wanted to buy the entire car."

"Is that the battery, there?"

I wait to hear his next response. But the tiny drill sergeant barks at me.

"Raleigh."

"What."

"Look inside."

I'm standing near the driver's side. "No."

"Do you want me to do it?"

"No. I've got it."

But I don't move.

"Because I will." Her voice rises.

I eyeball the torn-up metal, then carefully climb onto the flatbed. I take a seriously deep breath and look inside the car.

I could puke.

Blood smears the white leather seat.

"Raleigh?"

"I'm on it, Drew."

I manage to pry open the door. But sun's heated the seat leather, cooking the iron in the blood. It smells bitter, earthy. I gag and back away, gulping air.

"And the steering?" she asks DeMott. "Is that different too?"

"Yes. Back in the fifties, cars didn't have power steering. That meant you can't whip the wheel around with one finger. Turning takes real effort."

My gaze drifts to the steering wheel. Black molded plastic. Warmed blood glistens on the horn. My mind flashes with an image of Sloane's body hitting that unforgiving surface. At eighty-eight miles an hour.

She wanted to die.

"She could've lost control of the car."

"I suppose," he says. "But you could argue that either way."

Drew's silent.

"See?" I call out, trying to end this horror right now. "Sloane knew what she was doing."

DeMott chimes in. "And it's difficult to get this car airborne unless you're really trying."

"See?" I walk up the flatbed to where they stand at the hood. I am ready to guide Drew off the flatbed. *Show's over, folks.*

But she shakes her head "No. No. No." The wild hair waves. "Neither of you are factoring in the speed-weight ratio."

DeMott looks at me.

"Given enough speed," she continues, "and velocity, this car would become as light as a pebble."

Now I look at DeMott, waiting for him to block this idea.

But he says, "I guess that's true."

I groan.

Drew gives me a haughty look then says to him, "Tell me about the brakes."

I can't stand this.

I walk back down the length of the car. This is the most morbid thing in the world, and I'm sharing it with DeMott. How romantic.

"I checked the road," Drew says. "I didn't see any skid marks."

The next silence fills me with dread.

So much dread that I'm actually glad when an electronic bleat pulses from my backpack. I dig out my cell phone and check the number. Home.

"Hello."

"Come home now."

Helen.

But for once, I'm glad. This car makes me feel more depressed than at Sloane's memorial service. Too tangible, too real. And too disturbing when I realize this hunk of metal survived and Sloane didn't.

"What's going on?" I ask.

"I woke up," she says.

"Congratulations."

"And I want to go out."

After last night's party at Weyanoke, my mom was agitated. I woke in the middle of the night smelling smoke. Which always means she's burning things. Not food. Paper. She writes notes full of nonsense, what the voices say inside her head. Then burns them. I crept down the back stairs, listening. My dad was asking her why she took the batteries out of all the smoke detectors. She told him the detectors had secret cameras, filming us.

This morning at breakfast, my dad asked us not to leave her alone.

I left with DeMott. Helen had to stay.

"I'll be home soon," I tell her.

"Get me out of here. Now."

She hangs up.

"Raleigh," Drew calls out, "did you check inside the car?"

I stare at the driver's door. I left it open. Broken glass covers the floor mat under the gas pedal and brake. Like somebody dumped a bucket of crushed ice.

"Yes." I walk over, kneel down, and pinch a shard of glass.

Safety glass. Geologically, it's not pure silica. Manufacturers sandwich plastic film over the silica layers and bake it. So when the glass breaks, the pieces don't fly out and inflict more injuries. I glance up at the windshield. Cracks spider what didn't shatter.

"Raleigh, are you doing anything?"

"Yes." I pull out another Ziploc baggie and drop in glass. The edges aren't sharp because the manufacturers temper it—heating the silica then quickly cooling it.

But as I'm pinching the baggie closed, I see something else on the floor. Not glass. I pinch it. Gray and opaque, it has the rough porous surface of pumice. Igneous rock. But volcanic—where in Virginia is there volcanic rock? I hunt the carpeted floor for more grains and find some smaller ones. *Weird.* I drop them in another Ziploc bag, then stand and shove the door closed. The metal shrieks.

"You had better—"

"Drew, it's done." I step around the hood, dangling the baggies so she can see my work.

But DeMott's looking at something behind me. I turn to see Eliot. He's walked over to another stretch of chain link fence, fiddling with a padlock, as a dirty yellow car pulls up on the other side.

Eliot opens the gate. The car drives straight to the flatbed.

The guy who jumps out wears bib overalls with no shirt.

"Yo Cuz!" Eliot slaps his bare shoulder.

The guy slaps him back, then looks at the flatbed. "You got 'er up on there already?"

"I ain't dumb." Eliot sounds offended. "I never took it off. Man called that day, said he wanted the whole she-bang."

"You one smart dude."

Eliot beams.

CHAPTER THIRTEEN

W E DRIVE AWAY from the junkyard, me once again wedged between the two of them.

But now I'm struggling to even *like* my best friend.

Not just because she's counting every broken yellow line that runs down the middle of New Market Road.

Not just because I've had it with mental illness.

But because she is arguing with DeMott.

DeMott, who got up this morning and drove into Richmond. DeMott, who picked us up and drove all the way back out here. DeMott, who answered all her stupid questions about the Cherry-mobile.

"One fourteen," she says. "We must go there. One fifteen. One sixteen."

"I don't think that's a good idea," he says.

"—seventeen, I don't care. One eighteen, we *must* go. One nineteen."

At the curve in the road, the broken yellow turns into a solid double yellow line. Drew starts making another weird sound, like a plane about to take off.

"Drew," he says. "There's no way I'm going to Tinsley's house."

"Hmmmm, yes, hmmm, then leave me here. One twenty—"

The straightaway offers more broken yellow lines and her voice is rising. The pitch sounds frantic. Every other number, she interjects, "Must go!"

I know Drew. I know there's no stopping her. If she wants to contact Tinsley, she will ride her bike out here. On her own. And then what? Tinsley can manipulate her into anything.

I turn toward DeMott, staring at his profile. "We have to go."

"Pardon?"

"We have to go to Tinsley's."

He glances at me, then back at the road. "You're serious?"

"Very."

"One thirty-six," Drew says. "And you know where she lives, one thirty-seven."

"DeMott, you can stay in the truck," I tell him. "She just needs a minute."

He says nothing.

"Sorry," I add.

He says nothing, still.

TINSLEY LIVES IN the town of New Kent, which is still old.

But time in Virginia is almost geologic. We have the plantations on the James River that are like the Hadean era—formation of the earth. And then places like Tinsley's area, more Mesozoic. Still old, but by then dinosaurs were roaming.

We are coming up her driveway—long, but not nearly as long as DeMott's—and the plantation at the end looks odd to me. Wide porch. Check. Tall white columns. Check. But the siding. It's vinyl.

"Twelve." Drew says, "Doesn't that seem like a lot of lawn jockey statues?"

"One is too many," I tell her.

"Twelve's good, though. Months. Astrological signs. Tribes of Israel."

She keeps going with life's dozens, but I smile at DeMott. "Maybe we should put her on Jeopardy."

He turns off the engine.

She keeps going. ". . . and twelve days of Christmas . . ."

DeMott gets out and holds the passenger door open for Drew and for me. He also leads us to the front door. The concrete path is cracked.

"You don't have to come in," I tell him.

He rings the doorbell.

The woman who answers looks like Tinsley plus twenty-five years, right down to her perfectly-coiffed platinum hair. It's sort of disturbing. Like seeing Barbie heading for menopause.

"DeMott!" she exclaims. Her accent is deeper than Virginia. More like South Carolina. "What an unexpected pleasure."

"Good to see you, too, Mrs. Teager. Is Tinsley home?"

"Why, yes, for once my too-popular daughter's without prior engagements." She smiles at him. Then looks at us.

Mr. Good Manners introduces us. I think this woman's face is frozen. Maybe it's my imagination, but she stares at me extra-*extra* long.

"Twelve is a perfect number," Drew tells her. "Double perfect, in fact. Based on two sixes."

"Is that right?" Mrs. Teager's voice bevels down. "Thank you for letting me know."

This tone. People talk like this all the time with my mother. Basically, it means "Bless your heart, you bat-guano-crazy idiot."

And yet, like a true Southern Belle, Mrs. Teager's frosted-pink smile never so much as wavers.

"Will you please excuse me? I'll go find Tinsley."

We stay put in the small foyer, which, again, isn't even in Weyanoke's league. Mrs. Teager walks up the stairs that are nothing grand, not even opulent. They're not even as nice as our front staircase.

Drew counts the maple floorboards.

DeMott stares at his shoes.

And Satan's mistress appears.

"Hell-llo." Tinsley comes down the stairs wearing skin-tight skinny jeans, paired with a Christmas-red angora sweater. Probably all fashionable, but to me it looks like furry hemoglobin. "Don't tell me y'all were in the neighborhood and just decided to drop by?"

Drew blurts out, "Sloane did not kill herself!"

Tinsley halts mid-step.

Mrs. Teager, two steps above her, almost trips.

"I have no doubt whatsoever," Drew keeps going. "But could you ask your mom to keep walking? Up or down, I don't care, but she's on the fifth step and five is an odd number. She needs to get off that fifth step. Get off it. *Get off it.*"

Everyone looks at Mrs. Teager.

"Mother." Tinsley turns all the way around, holding the thin handrail. "You remember my telling you about Drew Levinson. Don't you? She's that *wonderful* girl in my class at St. Catherine's. The one who's so bright?"

Recognition slaps middle-aged Barbie. Her frosted mouth parts. And another expression quickly flashes in her icy hazel eyes. An expression I know oh-so-well.

"I'll leave you kids alone," she says, moving up the stairs. "Good to see you, DeMott."

"Yes, ma'am."

"Sloane's death is a matter of simple trigonometry," Drew blathers on, unaware of the vast undercurrent that just surged through the air space. "Speed times weight, added to momentum and—"

Mrs. Teager stops and looks back at us.

"—and just to make sure," Drew says, "I examined the Cherrymobile myself."

"You . . ." Tinsley pauses. "You did *what?*"

DeMott steps away from us.

"Checked out the car," Drew says. "My calculations are confirmed. Consider us on the case. Raleigh and I can prove Sloane did not kill herself."

Still on the stairs, Mrs. Teager does a slow head turn, like a turtle peering from its shell.

"Mother," Tinsley says, not even needing to look up at her.

"Would you mind?"

Mrs. Teager glides across the landing, out of view.

Drew sighs with relief. "Thanks," she says. "That last step, it was killing me."

CHAPTER FOURTEEN

W E DRIVE BACK to my house. But DeMott has zero chance of opening our door because when he stops on Monument Avenue, Drew flings open her door and races across the wide sidewalk. Her long brown hair waves from her head like there's a party in her brain. Right now, maybe there is.

He watches her navigate our front steps. Six steps to our formal entrance, so she doesn't need to double back.

"You need to reconsider your strategy for helping her," he says.

"You could've stayed in the car."

"Of all people, you had to go see *Tinsley?*"

He winces saying her name.

That should make me glad. But it doesn't.

"I'm sorry. I was only thinking about Drew. That wasn't fair to you. I'm sorry. Really really sorry."

His gaze focuses forward, down the block, where another Civil War hero marks the road. JEB Stuart rides a rearing horse, sword drawn in bronzed glory. Judging by DeMott's knotted jaw, the way his hands squeeze the steering wheel, he could be taking orders from the cavalry hero.

What if it comes down to this. I help Drew, and lose DeMott.

When nothing more is said, I lift my backpack off the floor and shrug it over my shoulder. The pack weighs a ton, but it's still lighter than my heart right now. I climb out and close the door. That metallic *clunk* sounds like some final goodbye.

I walk away.

"Raleigh."

He's lowered the window.

"Yeah?"

"I'll see you tomorrow."

My heart leaps. His eyes are the crystal-blue of tourmaline. "What's tomorrow?"

"Sunday."

Tomorrow is Sunday. So he'll see me at church. *That settles that.* "Okay, see you there."

"Do you have any plans after?"

I stop. "After church?"

He nods, smiles.

Warm relief spreads across my heart. "I have no plans after church."

"Now you do. Pick you up at noon."

BECAUSE IT FEELS like the world just rolled off my shoulders, I jog up our front steps and trot past the cornerstone marked 1902, skipping like a six-year-old down the brick path to the back patio. Drew is waiting there.

With Helen.

My sister smokes her cigarette like a hyperventilating dragon. Like said dragon, she opens her mouth and spews words like fire. "Do you have any idea how long you've been gone?"

"You're welcome. Where's Dad?"

"He had to go downtown. Something came up." She flicks her cigarette onto the slate, grinding it with the toe of her clog. "And FYI, she's lit up every fireplace."

Every bit of the warm fuzzy feeling from DeMott goes up in flames. My mom's in full purge mode now, moving from the stove to the fireplaces. Always a bad, bad sign.

"Fine, I'm here now. What time are you coming home?"

But Drew lifts a stiff arm, pointing at the crushed cigarette butt.

"Someone is going to pick that up, correct?"

Helen stares at her. I bend down and pick up the disgusting frayed bits of tobacco and smashed fiberglass filter.

"Thanks." Drew opens the back door and walks inside.

Helen looks at me with a smirk.

"Raleigh, someday you're going to wake up and realize you've wasted your life taking care of crazy people."

THE HEAT-THICKENED KITCHEN feels like a tropical jungle.

I check the stove, making sure the gas got shut off, then lead Drew up the back stairs. Years ago, around the time my mom started saying the CIA had placed listening devices in the water faucets, Helen and I colonized the third floor of this house. The old servants' quarters.

It's even hotter up here.

I bang on my bedroom window, forcing the old wooden frame to give six inches of fresh air. Then I dump my backpack inside my closet and stick a piece of Scotch tape between the bottom of the closet door and the wood floor. A simple security device in case anyone—e.g. my mom—comes snooping. If the tape's torn, I know to prepare a good explanation for these baggies of rocks and glass in my backpack.

Drew sits cross-legged on the floor, rearranging my staurolite samples. Way back when life was almost normal, my dad and I used to jump in the car after heavy rains and go rock hunting in southwest Virginia. The minerals in the ground reacted with the rain, littering the ground with white crosses of staurolite. The locals called them "fairy stones." Legend says the rain is actually angels crying over the death of Jesus, and their tears turn into to white crosses.

Drew's lining up the crosses by size.

"You okay?" I ask.

She doesn't look up. "Can I spend the night?"

Saturday night. Jayne'll tie on a good drunk. Which she probably did last night, too.

"Sure. You can spend the night."

"Thanks."

"No problem." I stare down at my rearranged rock collection and push away Helen's words about taking care of crazy people.

"Hungry?" I ask her.

IN THE TROPICAL kitchen which now smells like wood smoke, we strip down to T-shirts and dig through the cupboards for cookie cutters. Trees. Santas. Snowflakes. I even find sprinkles, only two years past their expiration date. But, hey, when is sugar ever too old to eat?

"Drew," I force good cheer into my voice, "we are officially going to get into the Christmas spirit."

"I'm Jewish.

"So was Jesus."

"Your point?"

What is my point? I can't think of one, partly because those certain poor shepherds are still coming down the hall.

"Your mother has played that particular part of the song three times in a row." Drew sounds anxious.

"Keep counting," I tell her. "I'll bet there's a bunch of prime numbers."

I pull out my grandmother's *Housekeeping in Old Virginia*, left behind when Frances Harmon moved out. It was six months after her son married my mom, adopted me and Helen, and moved us into this huge house. Flipping through the pages, I find all kinds of weird medicinal cures, stuff like herbal poultices. Then the shortbread recipe which—*Hallelujah!*—calls for pounds of butter.

But the other reason I'm using it is because the recipes call for "pinches" and "dabs" and "dollops." I hand the book to Drew and tell her convert those instructions into precise measurements. Tedious work. Perfect for calming the storm inside her head. For a little while.

But only a little while.

I'm whisking the eggs when she says, "That is now the *eleventh* time your mom's played that song. Eleven is a good place to stop."

"Prime?" I whisk the eggs way too hard.

"Yes. The decimal system's smallest two-digit prime number."

I mix in the creamed butter.

"And eleven raised to the nth power," she continues, "is the nth level of Pascal's Triangle."

Add the flour, punch my fists into the dough. Pounding and pounding.

Drew opens the little bottle of expired sprinkles. *Oh, God.* She's counting them. I drive my knuckles into the dough. The recipe does not call for beating it into a pulp, and I don't care.

The *First Noel* is turning sixteen when the kitchen door swings open. My dad stands there for a moment, taking in the scene. Cold air washes into the room and makes me want to run outside. And never come back.

"Hi, Drew."

"Mr. Harmon, did you know the Chinese were aware of Pascal's Triangle five hundred years before Pascal himself?"

"I did not know that." He closes the door, removes his coat.

"The Chinese recognized the pattern in the eleventh century. Raleigh, what did I tell you about the number eleven?"

"It's really special." I give my dad a significant look.

He throws it right back at me. And then some. "Raleigh, can I talk to you—in my office?"

I practically sprint down the hall, chased by the number eleven from one end of the house and *noel-noel-noel* from the other. I leap into my dad's office, like it's one of those safe rooms that protect people from assault in their own houses. I drop into the only chair not covered by legal briefs. "Thank you," I tell him. "It's a nightmare."

He walks over to his desk. "Is it?"

His cheeks are red, almost inflamed. He walks a lot during

difficult cases. I shouldn't feel a pang of jealousy. But I haven't been able to run for days. "I'm losing my mind."

"What are you and Drew up to?" he asks.

"Right now we're making Judeo-Christmas cookies. And later, since Drew's spending the night, I'll be imbibing some seriously high doses of Benadryl. You've been warned."

"Drew won't be spending the night."

I sit up. He knows all about Jayne's bad habits. Which is why I never can spend the night over there. And why he always lets Drew spend the night here. "Because of Mom?"

"Call your sister, tell her to come back. She can stay here while I drive Drew home. I'd like you to ride with us."

"Dad, what's going—"

"Raleigh." His voice. The tone is sharper than I've ever heard. "This is not a request. This is an order."

CHAPTER FIFTEEN

THE SOUNDTRACK FOR our ride to Drew's house comes courtesy of the AM dial's Golden Oldies station.

Neil Diamond croons about chestnuts roasting on an open fire, while Drew gives my dad the precise directions to her house. He knows how to get there. But when she's agitated, exactness is her comfort.

And my dad knows she's upset because he's indulging her with math questions.

"How 'bout those Pythagoreans," he says.

"Yes. The Pythagoreans." Drew's talking fast. Somewhere in her tortured mind, she knows if my dad's taking her home instead of letting her spend the night, something's very wrong. "The Pythagoreans maintained a number theory. But it was more pseudoscience than mathematics."

"How so?"

"They believed even numbers were feminine. Odd numbers were masculine."

"That doesn't sound the least bit scientific."

"Each individual number also represented an abstract concept. Please take a right at the corner, right at the corner."

He takes a right at the corner. "What kind of abstract concepts?"

"Numeral one represented reason. Two stood for opinion. Three, harmony. Four, justice. Left at the light."

He turns left at the light. "I already see a problem with the number four. I'm a judge—a number four—but I'm masculine, which would require an odd number."

"Correct. Turn into my driveway."

My dad turns into her driveway and stops at the door.

I hop out before he can stop me. "I'll be right back."

I follow Drew's floating hair through the dark. The cold air forms an invisible ice on my tongue, jolting my brain like a defibrillator pad. Drew counts her trips up and down the backdoor steps, then digs the key from under the tortoise. All those years it bugged me that she and Jayne didn't lock this door. Because my formative years were spent in a criminal courtroom. Now, I wish we could go back to those days. All that simple trust is gone.

In the sunroom, Sir Isaac Newton—the most stuck-up cat in Virginia—hisses at me. Drew pets his head as we pass through into the kitchen. The kitchen is perfectly clean kitchen because nobody in this house cooks.

We discover Jayne in the den.

Passed out on the couch.

The wine glass sits on the coffee table.

On the TV, Emeril yells, "Bam!"

Jayne doesn't even flinch.

"Want some help getting her upstairs?" I ask.

Drew shakes her head, vehemently, as if trying to throw away a bad memory.

"You alright?" I ask.

"We can talk tomorrow," she says.

"Or call me tonight. If you need to."

I turn to leave.

"Raleigh?"

I look back. She's so small, she could be eleven years old. "Yeah?"

"Thanks."

"For what?"

"For today."

"Oh, sure." I nod. "Thanks should go to DeMott."

Hint, hint.

Her dark eyes fill with gratitude. "It means so much to me that you agree about what happened to Sloane."

Oh, man.

I look away. Jayne's sprawl has all those weird and uncomfortable angles of the drunk and the dead. When I glance back at Drew, I smile.

"Hey, you'll figure this out," I tell her. "I'm counting on you."

"Counting," she says. "Funny."

But she doesn't smile back.

CHAPTER SIXTEEN

WHEN I OPEN the car door, my dad's singing with the radio.
"Repeat the sounding joy—"

I climb in and slouch down.

"—re-pe-EEET! re-pe-eee-EEET!"

Between my mom and Drew, any repeating word right now makes my teeth itch. But he's repeating the word "repeat." In a Christmas carol. After living through all those "noels."

I glare at him.

He flings out an arm, hitting the last notes with re-soun-ding joy. His operatic moves usually make me laugh. But I've just witnessed Jayne's drunken carcass and left Drew in there. He's not getting off the hook that easily.

"Why can't she spend the night?" I ask.

He eases the car onto Westhampton Road.

"Dad?"

"Not tonight, Raleigh."

A hallowed silence fills the car. The next song warbles from the dashboard. At the stoplight on Libbie Avenue, we hear about that little town of Bethlehem. I stare at the shops on Grove Avenue. Christmas here looks so different from my house. Here, a white-light winter wonderland sparkles from the shops. People whisk down the sidewalk swinging festive bags and dash into restaurants I can only dream about. My life seems to suck even more. I am going home to another winter casserole . . . how very still we see thee lie.

"What's Mom making for dinner?"

"I'm sure it's something good."

I repress a groan.

"But before we go home," he says, "we have one more stop."

I look over. His tone. Serious again.

"If this is about presents," I tell him, "don't worry. I got something for Helen. Something nice." Tiny granite rocks that can be frozen for ice cubes. For cocktails at Yale.

"I'm glad you remembered her."

"And I made something for you and Mom." That's his rule: homemade gifts. "So I don't need to go shopping right now."

"Good." He keeps driving. "Because I'm not in the mood to shop."

My heart sinks. "Where are we going?"

He looks over, studies my face. "You're doing a good job being Drew's friend."

"That's exactly what it feels like—a job." But I'm still not letting him off the hook. "And why can't she spend the night?"

"I'm sorry that being her friend feels like a job. That might be what's ruining things."

"What?"

"Raleigh . . ."

I grit my teeth. *"Pardon?"*

He turns onto Broad Street and drives right past Allen Street, which would take us to our house. Each passing street light feels like the second hand of a clock, ticking past. I swivel toward my window.

"Did I ever tell you what C. S. Lewis said?" he asks.

I groan loud enough to drown out the stupid holly-jolly Christmas on the radio. My dad's got this horrible habit of dropping quotes on me, always opening with: *Did I ever tell you what so-and-so-famous thinker once said?* When he knows he's never told me.

"I don't care wha—"

"Lewis said friendship was unnecessary."

"What?"

"Pardon."

"What," I say, just to bug him.

He stops at the light on 14th Street. On the opposite corner, some people have gathered outside a pub, all bunched together under a street light like a flock of moths.

"Lewis said friendship wasn't essential to survival. Not like food, water, or air."

"So?"

The light turns green.

"Friendship has no survival value. But friendship is what gives survival its value." He looks over. "See the distinction?"

We are driving across the Mayo Bridge, heading north, away from downtown. I sit up. "We're going to your office?"

He nods.

"But it's Saturday. *Night.*"

"I'd like you to talk to somebody."

"Who?"

The next silence smothers me. My heart thuds. He drives up Hull Street, deep into northside Richmond. Night gets darker and darker.

"Dad?"

He turns into the courthouse and puts the old Mercedes in the space marked RESERVED FOR JUDGE D. HARMON.

"Dad?" I squeak.

He pulls out the key and exits the car.

THE LOBBY'S GRAY marble floor echoes every step, no matter how softly I walk. A burly guard sits behind a reception desk near the elevators. His voice echoes, too.

"Evenin', Judge. They ain't here yet."

They?

"Thanks, Bobby. Send them up as soon as they arrive."

I follow my dad into the elevator. He pushes 5. The stainless steel doors slide shut.

"So, that's great. The guard knows who's coming, but I don't?"

He gazes up at the numbers flashing above the doors. When they open, he steps out. I hesitate, but what am I going to do, run away?

I follow him down the hall. Usually this place crackles with energy, a panic soup simmering with justice and deadlines and guilt and remorse. But now the entire building feels hollow and cavernous, the clerk's desk so empty it looks like nobody's ever coming back.

"It's rude not to tell me." He's never done this to me before. It makes me feel panicky.

Unlocking his office door, he flicks on the fluorescent lights and steps into his chambers.

I don't follow. His inner office is my safe haven. The way other kids have forts or clubhouses. But tonight's going to change that. I can feel it.

I drag my feet to the doorway.

Red-leather books line the walls behind his desk. All those laws of Virginia. They've always comforted me, too, the unwavering boundary that insists people are crazy but we still have rules. Firm rules. But suddenly all that red leather looks just as threatening as Sandbag's pen marking up my English papers.

I appeal to the judge, reminding him he's a proper Virginia gentleman. "The polite thing would be to tell me what's going on."

"Raleigh." My dad takes off his coat, hangs it on a tree near his desk. "Have a seat."

Out of spite, I stand by the far window and gaze down at Hull Street. The road looks cold and empty until two police cruisers slice down the block, lights flashing. Saturday night, trouble starts early. Still facing the window, I shift my gaze, using the black glass as a reflection to see my dad. He's reading some papers at his desk. So calm it creeps me out.

"You know—"

The phone rings. He pushes a button, speaks into the intercom.

"Bobby?"

"Yeah, Judge, they's heading up now."

"Thank you."

I glance at the door. His black judicial robe hangs nearby on a hook. When I was a little girl, that wide-winged robe made me think his job was being an owl. Wise and kind. Now it looks like a black ghost.

The elevator *bings*. My dad gets up, walks to the outer office, standing at the hallway door.

"Josiah," he says, in a serious tone. Then his voice softens. "Susannah, thank you for coming. I'm sorry to disturb you like this."

I brace myself.

But nothing could prepare me for who walks into his office.

Mrs. Stillman.

I almost swallow my tongue.

And right behind her is the white-haired man.

CHAPTER SEVENTEEN

"*T*HIS IS MY daughter, Raleigh."

Mrs. Stillman's dressed in all black. Her eyelids are puffy, but her gaze is like crystalline spears.

The white-haired man extends his hand to me, offering a firm shake. "Josiah McNeill," he says.

His gray eyes aren't exactly friendly, but they're two hundred degrees warmer than Mrs. Stillman's.

"Mr. McNeill is the Stillman family attorney," my dad says.

Attorney?

Mr. McNeill gently seats Mrs. Stillman in one of the four chairs that face my dad's desk. Two for defense. Two for prosecution.

Mr. McNeill also holds a chair for me. Virginia gentleman. I take a seat on defense. He sits in the chair between me and Mrs. Stillman. Like a mediator.

My dread increases.

"Josiah," My dad sits at his desk, "thank you for coming on such short notice."

Mr. McNeill crosses his legs. Long legs and he places a pair of leather gloves on one knee. "Raleigh, do you know why you're here?" he asks.

I glare at my dad. "I have *no* idea why I'm here."

McNeill nods. His white hair glitters under the lights. "As I told your father, it's my firm belief that you intend no harm to the Stillman family. However, this afternoon we were made aware of your visit to see Sloane's car."

My heart bangs against my ribs.

Mrs. Stillman's voice stabs the tense air.

"Why in the world would you *do* such a thing?" She grips a small black purse. It shakes. "It is completely morbid!"

A cold sensation runs down my arms. It has a name. *Tinsley.* She ratted on us. I knew it. This whole stupid thing with the car and Drew was another set-up. The serpent strikes again. And I fell for it.

"Raleigh." Mr. McNeill looks over at me with pity. "This family has been shattered by tragedy."

I look away. Then I look back. His gaze. It's not scorn. Or even judgment. In fact, there's even kindness. Like a grandfather who discovers your baseball accidentally shattered the neighbor's window, and offers to pay for it.

"Raleigh, I understand you knew Sloane. Personally?"

"Yes, sir."

"Then you undoubtedly know how the Stillmans guard their privacy. They've never sought the limelight. Even when their accomplishments merited public attention."

Shame creeps up my throat, fills my face with heat.

"Unfortunately we live in a world that no longer considers privacy a human right." He sighs. "Someone already divulged the contents of Sloane's suicide note."

"And her antidepressants!" Mrs. Stillman glares at me. Like I leaked those details.

I steal a glance at my dad, pleading for the defense. But the judge is entirely focused on Mrs. Stillman.

"There is, however," the attorney continues, "one detail that has managed to remain private. Until now."

I wait. But he says nothing.

Instead he starts rearranging the fingers of his gloves. Mrs. Stillman unsnaps her black clutch and removes a white handkerchief. She presses it to her mouth. Then gives a tiny nod.

"Mrs. Stillman bravely decided to share this one detail here, within the confines of confidentiality." He glances at my dad, then me, making sure that last word sinks in. "She's doing this out of respect for your father, Raleigh. She believes that you will understand the seriousness of what's happened. And you will respect family's needs. And you will respect Sloane."

My dad's eyes flick toward me.

"Yes, sir." I can't even swallow. "I'm listening."

The lawyer looks over at Mrs. Stillman, as if checking. She sniffles into the handkerchief and gives another tiny nod.

When the lawyer looks at me, his long face seems even sadder. He draws a deep breath. "Sloane was pregnant."

My mouth falls open. I look at my dad. His face reveals nothing. But I stare into his eyes, and it hits me. He knew this fact. That's why I'm here. To hear this terrible detail, directly from these people. So my shame can be nailed deep into my heart.

Mrs. Stillman presses the handkerchief to her mouth so hard it's like she's staunching a scream. The lawyer adjusts his gloves again, this time arranging them so that each finger touches the other, like praying hands.

Everyone is waiting for me to say something. But the words in my head are so . . . not . . . good enough.

"I'm . . . very . . . sorry."

Her sob breaks.

The lawyer looks like he's about to cry, too.

"Thank you, Raleigh," he says. "We learned about it from the coroner."

I shift my gaze to the red-leather books. They offer no sympathy, no pity.

My dad asks, gently, "Any idea who the father is?"

"None."

Mrs. Stillman is crying now. The lawyer reaches over and places a hand on her back. Her cries slow down at his touch.

"I'm sorry." My voice chokes. "I never intended to cause you more pain. Sloane was a friend and we just got . . . curious . . . "

"I believe you," Mr. McNeill says. "And your friend, Drew? Is that her name?"

"Yes, sir."

"We've heard about her own suffering. Our hearts go out to her family. Truly. And we recognize that you're attempting to help her. But, Raleigh, by indulging in your friend's obsession you're inflicting tremendous pain on Mrs. Stillman. A grieving mother. She should not be forced to indulge the wild fantasies of a troubled young woman."

Mrs. Stillman looks over at me. A knife slices into my chest. I've seen plenty of sorrow. In my dad. In Drew. In my own mirrored reflection when my mom says I'm not her "real" daughter.

But nothing—*nothing* compares to Mrs. Stillman's eyes. The knife sinks deeper.

"Drew doesn't mean any harm, she thinks she's helping—"

"Helping?" Mrs. Stillman's voice drips with disgust. "How is this morbid curiosity supposed to help anything? Disrupting Sloane's funeral the way she did? Poking around the wreckage of her car? You want me to believe she's trying to *help*?!"

"Susannah." Mr. McNeill leans forward. "They're just girls."

"So was my daughter."

Nobody says a word.

Mrs. Stillman folds the handkerchief with shaking hands and places it back inside her purse. The brass clasp makes a crisp metallic "click."

The lawyer stands, helps her from the chair.

My dad and I stand, too. It's polite.

But Mrs. Stillman has the best breeding. She extends a still-shaking hand over the desk and thanks my dad for his time. She offers me a wordless nod that would seem fine to anyone who hadn't heard this whole conversation. And then she walks out the door, her back straight, as if none of these awful things had been spoken, as if David Harmon's daughter didn't just rip a bandage off her heart, making her bleed all over again.

CHAPTER EIGHTEEN

THE DRIVE HOME is a silent night, all the way.

And when we walk in the door, something unholy waits. Another casserole.

My mom stands by the dining room table, narrow-eyed with suspicion. "Where did you go?"

My dad kisses her cheek. "We took Drew home."

"Why did it take so long?" Her hands clutch a dishtowel the same way Mrs. Stillman gripped that monogrammed handkerchief. Fear.

No. Terror.

"I swung by my office," he says. "Raleigh was patient enough to come with me."

She glances at me, like I'm going to reveal something more. But right now, I am numb. So numb I might not even taste this so-called food.

My dad opens his arms, takes her in, hugging her. "I'm sorry, sweetie. I should've called you."

While he tells her how wonderful she is, I drop into my chair at the table. My sister's chair beside me is empty. There's no place setting for her, either. And no Christmas carols are playing from the dining room.

My dad looks over, noticing the settings. "Helen's not eating with us?"

My mom looks away. "She left."

"When?"

"When you took so long driving Drew home."

I unfold my napkin. Really, I can't handle this right now. My mind is still teetering on the fragile edge of Mrs. Stillman's breakdown.

"I should've called," he tells her. "I had a problem to take care of. But everything's fine now. Problem solved."

He guides her to the table, raving about the delicious food she's prepared. The two of them are totally wrapped up in each other. Like I don't even exist.

And for once, I'm grateful.

FIVE HOURS AND sixteen minutes later, I tiptoe down the servant stairs into the dark kitchen. My growling stomach wants me to rummage through the cupboards—even expired sprinkles—but I tell it to wait.

Prying open the French door, I step outside and glance up at my parents' bedroom window. On Saturday nights, they go to bed early to be ready for church the next morning. But it's past midnight and a light still shines up there.

My dad. Waiting up for Helen.

Or my mom. Waiting for the voices in her head to stop talking.

I creep across the slate and creak open the back gate. Then sprint down the alley.

The cold black air scrapes down my throat, rips open my lungs, and fuels my legs. I run hard, heading west through the empty streets, through a darkness that threatens to make me stop. It takes a full mile for my breathing to catch up with my stride. But nothing in my life has ever matched running. It's like some kind of self-generating miracle. I can start out tight and scared and moving too fast. And then a hush comes. A quiet that falls like a trance. My breath, my feet, this cold air. Even the dark falls away. Fear leaves. And I can feel the city, it's hushed anticipation, like Richmond is a little kid holding its breath because Santa is landing on the roof.

The night feels perfect.

Two point four miles later, my fingers so cold the bones ache, I manage to dig the key from under Drew's stone tortoise. Fortunately, Sir Isaac Newton isn't in the sunroom. And Jayne's no longer passed out in the den, although the cooking channel's still on the TV and the wine glass still stands on the table, like it won the first round and waits for tomorrow's Round Two.

Upstairs, light shines from under Drew's closed bedroom door.

I tap quietly. "Open up," I whisper. "It's me."

She yells, "You don't need to be quiet!"

I open the door. She's sitting at her desk, typing on the computer.

"Alcohol dulls the sensory perceptions," she says. "Jayne can't hear a thing."

I close the door. After the cold outside, the room feels too warm. I wipe sweat from my forehead.

"Conversely," Drew continues, still typing, "alcohol exaggerates everything else. So if you stick around long enough you, too, can observe the unnaturally loud volume of her inebriated stupidity."

I sit on her bed. On the wall above it, Richard P. Feynman grins from a life-size poster. I wait for Drew to finish. She's typing one-handed. The other hand is tapping the keys of an algebraic computer.

I yank off my sweatshirt. The wait is making me sweat even more. "Aren't you at all curious why I'm here?"

"To every man is given the key to the gates of heaven." Feynman. She is quoting Feynman, and it is past midnight. "The same key opens the gates of hell. And so it is with science."

"And parents."

Her fingers stop typing. She looks over at me. "Explain."

"Mrs. Stillman called my dad."

She goes back to typing.

"Drew." I stare at her profile. That long thin face framed by torrents of wild long hair. "This is serious. He drove me to his office after we dropped you off. Mrs. Stillman showed up. With the family attorney."

She continues typing.

"Hello? They're upset that we're looking into Sloane's death."

She punches the totaling key. Squints at the calculator. "Something's really wrong."

"Are you listening to me?"

"Closely."

She swivels the chair toward me. Her dark eyes are so intense I suddenly feel light-headed. Like maybe there's no oxygen in here.

She says, "Let's build a hypothetical parallel universe."

"What."

"Let's say Sir Isaac Newton committed suicide."

"Is this the universe I'm hoping for?"

"Raleigh, you are referring to my cat. You may not care for his company, but I love him."

My eyes widen. This girl. This one—she is *Drew*. Not that obsessive-compulsive freak. My Drew. Yes, she's still counting, but if she's using a calculator, then it's real numbers. Things with some meaning, that add up to other meanings. Here, in the safety of her bedroom, the big bad world can't get her. Drew is back. I lift my sweatshirt and rub it over my face, wiping away the burn in my eyes.

"Sorry," I tell her.

"Apology accepted. Now, let's say after Newton dies, someone comes to me and says he didn't commit suicide. In fact, his death might have been an accident. Or, worse, he was murdered."

"I would be your first suspect."

"Naturally. But let's move on to the key question. Would I ask whoever's telling me this information to shut up, to go away, to stop causing trouble?"

"Only because your best friend could go to jail for killing him."

"Not even then."

"Really?"

"First, my cat is awesome. Second, finding the truth is the only way to live." She lifts her narrow face, gazing up at her planetary mobile that hangs from the ceiling. Jupiter and its rings float on waves of the invisible air moving around us. "My paramount concern would be to find out what really happened to Newton. Do you agree?"

"Yes."

"Good." She lowers her face, and levels me with an intense expression. "You are built the same way as me, Raleigh."

We both know what she means. She's here, in her room, obsessively pursuing Sloane's death. But I did the same thing in October. When Drew went missing. When nobody would listen to what I was saying. We stare at each other for a long, long moment. And it's like an invisible something becomes so real I could touch it. For just one split-second, it's like I can feel the force that holds the universe together, that keeps all the real planets from flinging off into black holes, that makes sure they orbit perfectly around the sun. The same force that brought us together as friends. It's like I could touch it, in the air between us.

"Are you going to ask me why I'm here?"

"Actually, my question is, why did you waste valuable friction running to my house to arrive at 12:17 a.m.?"

"I need to tell you something."

She swivels back the computer. "Don't bother."

"*What.*"

"Raleigh, I know you don't believe my theory."

Yes. This is the real Drew.

"I changed my mind."

She looks over at me, her eyebrows shoot way up. Dark, thick, Mediterranean eyebrows. Like Richard P. Feynman's. "Then say it."

"Sloane Stillman did not commit suicide."

She stares back at me. Then swivels to the computer. Typing.

"Drew?"

"You really didn't believe me. Not even a little. So you were humoring me, like some charity case. You didn't believe me."

"Believe is a strong word."

She whips around. "Of course *believe* a strong word. I'm not interested in milquetoast babble. The stupid chitchat that passes for opinion. The dumbass dialogue of people who have no beliefs."

I hold up my hand, signaling her to stop. "Are you going to let me explain what changed my mind?"

"I'm still amazed that people say there are no stupid questions."

I tell her about the drive from her house tonight, how my dad wouldn't even say who was meeting us at his office. As I talk, Drew picks up her Rubik's cube. listening. Her cube isn't the colorful plastic model. It's the prototype, with solid wood squares that are all the same color, just different shapes. The colored plastic cube proved too easy.

"Tinsley." She looks up. "She could've called Mary Vale who told her mom—"

"Or, Mrs. Teager, who called Mrs. Stillman," I add. "And the attorney knows my dad, so he got involved." Plus, both men are dealing with shattered women, some brotherhood of brokenness.

She twists the cube, lining up the shapes. "Their lawyer told you to back off?"

"He was actually pretty nice, considering. But . . ." I wait until she looks up. "Sloane was pregnant."

Drew's hand freezes. "How is that possible?"

"I know it's challenging being a fourteen-year-old sophomore so let me explain. There's this stuff called sperm. It can fertilize an egg when people—"

She throws the cube at me. I duck. When it smacks the wall, Richard P. Feynman gets a cleft chin.

The physicist keeps grinning. But I hold still, listening.

Drew grabs the cube off the floor. "Jayne can't hear anything. I told you. And I was asking, Who's Sloane's boyfriend?"

"I don't know. I've been racking my brain." I even thought back to my wretched memory of the Homecoming dance in October, when everything whirled down the drain with Drew. But I can't recall seeing Sloane at that dance. Or any dance. She wasn't that type of senior. In fact, Sloane probably stayed away from Homecoming to work on some science project.

"But I remember the spring science fair?" I open my hands, Drew tosses me the cube. "You won."

"Again," she says.

We both smile.

Last spring, Drew built something called an audio oscillator. It could measure the sound waves of a fastball connecting with a baseball bat. Everyone knows that distinctive *"crack!"* But Drew then calculated the time it took for fastballs to arrive in left, right, and center fields. Then, she averaged the number of fly balls caught by spectators with where they sat. And finally, she proved that by sitting in right field, a person could gain valuable seconds between hearing that *"crack"* and the arrival of the ball.

Her study made CNN news.

Back then, baseball was Drew's main obsession. That was then. Now all her baseball collections stuff are gone. Even though I hate baseball, I hate even more the evil that caused her to give up something she loved.

"Do you remember Sloane's experiment?" I twist the cube. "It had to do with sheep."

"The experiment where she used lactose to switch on the gene for beta-galactosidase production in E.coli?"

I stare at her. "The experiment involved *sheep.*"

"Yes, I heard you. But Sloane had two experiments with sheep. The second one focused on genetics, how meiosis can produce variations in offspring."

"All I remember is sheep."

"Raleigh." Her eyebrows are up again. She takes the wooden cube from my hand. "Stop ignoring everything that doesn't involve minerals, rocks, or tectonics."

"You are incorrect, professor. I remembered the sheep."

She forces a smile. "Let's fast-forward. Get to your hypothesis."

I've been thinking about it the whole night. Through dinner.

Laying in bed, trying to sleep. On my run over here. "When Sloane was giving her presentation about the sheep—"

"The information you ignored."

"Not entirely. She was going on and on about blood samples."

Drew looks up, surprised.

"Yes." I lift my hand. "I heard her say something about one of the sheep. How after she took its blood, it got sick. And I remember how her voice changed. She sounded upset. Which wasn't like Sloane. She looked at the sick sheep's blood and realized it was pregnant. And after she took its blood, the sheep had a miscarriage."

"*That's* what you remember? Raleigh, that stuff had *nothing* to do with her experiment."

"Fine. But her voice, when she said that baby sheep died—"

"Technically, a lamb."

"Drew, listen to me. If you weren't so focused on experiments and results, you would remember this, too."

"But it wasn't her point."

"Okay, it was a tangent. But Sloane said all her biology textbooks described that dead baby sheep—lamb, whatever—as a fetus. But she saw it. After the mother sheep miscarried. And Sloane said that 'fetus' was incorrect. I remember her exact words."

"Because of her voice."

"*Yes.* She said, 'It had had a beating heart. And that means it was a living creature.' "

"Congratulations, Raleigh. You paid attention to something that had nothing to do with geology."

"Then you're the one who needs listen. Think about it, Drew. *Think.*"

For several minutes, the only sound comes from her hands, snapping the Rubik's cube. But then I hear the humming of her computer. Two computers, actually. One that sits on her desk. And the other inside her beautiful head, where synapses fire at super-human speeds. I watch her fingers, twisting wooden cube. All the rows, in perfect order.

She looks up at me. Her brown eyes glow.

"You're saying Sloane Stillman could not kill a baby inside of her."

My eyes water. "Do you remember, how she started complaining about the cafeteria food? She wanted vegan food. She even refused to eat anything with eggs."

Drew sets the Cube beside her computer. "Start with a theorem."

"Did Sloane Stillman kill herself?"

Drew types the words, then says, "My theorem is, No, she did not. And physical evidence from the crash scene backs up my theorem."

I stand. My legs are stiff from sitting after a hard run. I rest my hands on the back of her chair and lean forward, read over her shoulder.

She types, Who is the father?

"Here's another question," I tell her. "Where was Sloane going that night?"

Drew types that question. Then another. Why was she driving so fast?

"Anything else?" she asks.

"Yes." I reach around her and type out the question that's bugged me all night.

If Sloane didn't write that suicide note, who did?

CHAPTER NINETEEN

S UNDAY MORNING, I sit in our family pew at St. John's and
listen to the antique pipe organ baptizing the air with the joy of
man's desiring. Bach's tune clears away some of the despair that
hung here like a suffocating shroud just three days ago, during
Sloane's funeral.

But Reverend Burkhardt is preaching with the same fervor.
"Have you ever tried to guess what's inside a Christmas present
just by how it's wrapped?"

My gaze drifts to the front pew where DeMott sits with his
family. His parents are on either end, their three kids between
them. Another front pew holds the Teagers.

"A man once put a blue Tiffany's box under the family
Christmas tree. Every time his wife walked past that present, she
imagined expensive jewelry."

I stare at the back of Tinsley's head. Last night, on my run
home from Drew's house, I decided it wasn't Tinsley who ratted us
out. It was her mother who would've called Mrs. Stillman. They're
cousins, somehow. And Mrs. Teager would want to protect Mrs.
Stillman.

But Tinsley? All she cares about is her own reputation. She
wants us to restore Sloane's reputation. So Tinsley can bask in it.
But I also figure nobody told Tinsley about Sloane's pregnancy.
An out-of-wedlock baby? With an unknown father. That would
ruin the fabled bloodline. Tinsley would let Sloane rot for that
trespass.

"On Christmas morning, the wife tore open that Tiffany's box. Guess what was inside? A pair of socks. The husband thought he'd played a really funny joke." Reverend Burkhardt lifts his head, gazing out at the congregation. "Men. Do not repeat his mistake."

Chuckles rumble through the congregation. I glance over at my dad. He's holding my mom's left hand. But her right hand grips a pen. She's writing on the church bulletin.

I tilt my head. She's written one word, vertically.

N
O
E
L

She then writes something after each letter. An acrostic.

No
One
Else
Leaves

"Jesus comes to us like that," Reverend Burkhardt says. "Everyone expected that blue Tiffany box. They were waiting for the King of Kings. The king wearing royal robes and commanding powerful armies and defeating the enemy on the battlefield."

My mother writes NOEL again. But each letter gets a different word.

Not
Only
Evil
Lies

"But what do the Wise Men find? A baby born among filthy farm animals. With parents who can't scrape together two coins. And yet, the Wise Men *knew* this baby was the King of Kings."

He leans forward, peering out at us.

"How many of you are holding onto expectations like that for Christmas? You expect a Tiffany box with jewelry. But God will send what he chooses to send. Will you accept it?"

Reverend Burkhardt is still talking but my palms prickle with sweat. And my head starts to pound.

Her next acrostic reads:

Notable
Objections
Eager
Liar

She's writing about me.
The eager liar.
The girl she thinks isn't her daughter.
The girl named Ray.
And then, that name hits me.
I get it.
No-el.
She's saying, No 'L.'
Because my name with no 'L' would be, Raeigh.
Ray.

I want to grab her pen and chuck it across the church. I want to stand up and scream, "I am not Ray!"

But I can't. Not here.

Not anywhere.

The world has no room for what I feel.

So I face forward and pretend to listen, and blink back that familiar burn in my eyes.

CHAPTER TWENTY

JUST PAST NOON, DeMott arrives at my house, but I'm already outside, already changed from church clothes into jeans and my Chuck Taylor sneakers, already jumping into his truck so fast he doesn't have a chance to open my door.

I toss my backpack in first.

He looks at it and says, "Most girls carry purses."

"It'll only take a minute."

"Really." His blue eyes are intense. "*What* is only going to take a minute?"

"You don't even have to come inside." I beg him with my eyes. "I promise."

He shifts the truck into gear and gazes into the rearview mirror. Like he'd rather go back and start over. "Where am I not going inside?"

TEN MINUTES LATER, we're in the driveway of the small brick house in the West End of town, with its shutters slanted and gutters clogged and wooden wheelchair ramp still smothered by autumn leaves.

"One minute," he says.

"Maybe two. Or five."

"Or ten." He sighs. "Or twenty."

And yet, Mr. Manners still follows me up the ramp to the front door.

I have to pound on the door several times before Teddy opens it.

His red hair stands up, like every strand is screaming, "Fire!"

"Don't got time for whatever this here's about," he barks. "I'm leaving for West Virginnie in one hour."

DeMott backs off, apologizing.

But I turn and say, "Come back in an hour."

Of course, all his fine Virginia breeding insists he should say something. And for several excruciating seconds, I watch his gorgeous face go to war between a frown and a polite smile. Most people would probably walk away.

But DeMott?

He says, "I hope you have a nice Christmas, Mr. Chastain."

"Stuff it. Christmas stinks."

Teddy slams the door.

DeMott's mouth hangs open.

"Sorry." I touch his arm. "I'll see you in an hour."

I open the door, step inside, and slam it behind me before Teddy can do anymore damage.

"That was really mean," I snap.

"Where's the soil?" he growls.

I reach into my backpack, glaring at him, and pull out the Ziploc baggies with soil from Sloane's car. And the bag with the broken glass. "All yours, Mr. Scrooge."

He snatches the baggies from my hands, drops them in his lap, and pivots the chair, hard, so the wheels squeal really loud. "I hate Christmas."

"Gee, really?"

Teddy gets like this every Christmas. I've finally decided that something rotten must've happened to him during the holidays. Maybe even what snapped his spinal cord. In which case, it would really suck to hear people talking about "the most wonderful time of the year" when you can't even walk anymore.

His house, naturally, has no Christmas decorations, but there wouldn't be room for them anyway. Every horizontal surface—

shelf, chair, table, floors—is cluttered with rock specimens or geology journals or structural maps of places like the Appalachian mountain chain. But in the back room, he keeps it cleared enough to function as a geology lab. The microscope is already turned on. I feel a small warm feeling for the curmudgeon. He turned it on, after I called this morning.

I take a seat at the long table. He slides in beside me.

"What's this?" He holds up one of the baggies.

"Safety glass. From Sloane's car."

"Who cares?"

"Fine. Take the other one."

I grab the small plastic tub of Vaseline near the microscope and smear a super-thin layer of petroleum jelly on a glass slide. I reach into the baggie and pick out some gray stones. I drop them on the slide, then place it under the scope.

"Huh." Teddy's ignored the other baggie. He's pinched out one of those tiny gray stones. "Ain't glass."

I'm not letting him divert me. I adjust the focus knobs.

He says, "That boy's still hanging around."

"Not after your stunt. You're a real charmer, Teddy."

"*I'm* the problem?" He chuckles. "Check out your predicament."

I lift my head from the scope. "What?"

"Ain't no way purebreds should be bred with hounds."

"Did you just call me a dog?"

"Quit trying to cheer me up." He nods at the scope. "Git back to the soil."

I drop my eyes to the lens. The polarized beams of light cross over the compact gray stones. Each grain looks almost cubic. But these are not crystals. The surfaces are air-pocked. Porous as pumice. I don't look up from the eyepiece. "Where would pumice come from in Virginia?"

"Get outta the way."

I sit back. He wheels up to the scope, peering into the lens. His damaged hands work the focus knobs.

"Yerp." He reaches down, moving the slide, shifting it between the lights. "Got it."

"Great." I wait. And wait. "Care to share?"

"Why should I?" he asks.

"Because you just insulted DeMott."

"He can take it."

"Maybe I can't."

"Nah. You can take more'n him. Any day."

"The grains, please?"

He lifts his arm, checking his watch.

"Come on," I beg him.

"Gimme a good first guess."

"I just did. Pumice. It's porous. Volcanic."

"What else?"

"No layering." Layers come with time. "No developed crystallization." Crystals come with time and enough space, so minerals can develop to their full atomic structure. Volcanics usually offer neither time nor space. Hot liquified rock explodes, leaving behind air holes in the soup, or the stuff oozes into confined spaces that mold it into a solid mass. The way white veins of quartz snake through most granites without looking like individual crystals.

Either way, volcanics rarely produce layers or crystals.

"That's why I think these stones are volcanic."

"So," he says. "What's the problem?"

"One, we don't have active volcanics in Virginia. And two, all these grains look alike. Almost unnatural."

"You like him?" he asks.

"Why?"

"Because I'm like a Richter scale. I'm giving you the heads-up on some small tremors so you can get the hell out of Pompeii."

I stare into his eyes, that green glowing bright as Christmas lights. Only right now it's fueled by some kind of bitterness, or anger. This messy house crowded with rocks and books suddenly seems very, very empty.

And whatever Teddy sees in my own eyes, it makes him look

away.

"Ah, hell, just ignore me. Every Christmas I'm like a bull trying to crap barbed wire."

"There's an image I would like to remove from my brain."

"That boy's a right nice dude. He ain't got one mean bone in his body. Problem is, he ain't the dude for you."

"Where does this volcanic soil come from?"

"Changing the subject."

"You brought up the barbed wire."

"Diatomaceous earth."

"Dia—what?"

He spells out *diatomaceous*. "It's a rare soil, 'specially 'round these parts."

"So how did it get into Sloane's car, with the busted safety glass?"

He grins. "I'm givin you a nice fat puzzle for Christmas."

I stare at him. "That's the sum total of your help?"

"Yerp."

"Sloane was pregnant."

The joker is gone. His eyes hold mine as I describe all that's happened since Drew and I invaded his lab on Friday afternoon. He listens without a single interjection.

"You're sayin Drewsky might be right?"

I nod.

"Man alive." He shakes his head, runs a hand over his wild red hair. "You need to get a book on diatomaceous earth. It's in the science library."

"Here's a news bulletin, Teddy. School's closed."

He shifts his weight and reaches back into his pocket, pulling out a key ring. He gives it a shake, jingling the keys like bells.

I smile at him. "Maybe you're not Scrooge after all."

CHAPTER TWENTY-ONE

A FTER TEDDY UNLOCKS St. Cat's main entrance and drives off in his van—belching black smoke down the road—I wander my school's dark and silent halls. Chills run up my arms. Not from fear. But because some stuff makes me doubt God exists. Things like suffering and death. My mom's mental illness. Tinsley's popularity.

But other things do just the opposite. They make me believe in something holy. Oceans do this to me. Mountains. Rivers. Perfectly formed crystals.

And books.

I pry open the science library door with all the reverence of a penitent sneaking into church. Sunlight pours through the high windows, framing a sky that's the blue of stained glass. It lights up the long room so much I don't even need to turn on the lights. As my feet float over the jewel-green carpeting, I have to keep myself from bowing at the shelves of books that stretch from floor to ceiling.

The tightest corner of the L-shaped room holds the geology books. For several moments, the book spines whisper to me, trying to lure me into the secrets they guard. Dinosaurs buried in radioactive mud. Earthquakes fracturing miles of bedrock. Floods that threw black sand on sugar-white beaches. All the ancient devastations are here, waiting for a geologist to care enough to tell the story again, with words.

I force myself to search only for the book Teddy said was here.

My hands hover over the spines. I see titles about volcanics. I hook my index finger into one of the books, sliding it out, just as somebody coughs.

The book hits the floor with a *bang*.

"Who's there?"

An adult's voice.

Oh, crap.

I reach down, grab the book, and run for the darkest corner.

"Who's there!"

A man's voice.

"I know you're in here."

Coming closer.

What if it's Ellis?

"Come out—now! Or I'll call the police."

I creep out of the dark corner.

The good news—it's not Ellis.

The bad news—he's still a teacher.

Mr. Turner teaches Latin, Life Sciences, and Spanish.

"Raleigh?" He squints, like he can't make sense of it. "How— what—why are you in here?"

My hands shake. I lift the book. "I was, uh . . ."

"You—what? The doors are locked."

My mouth isn't working. Part of the problem is Mr. Turner's face. His dark eyes are bloodshot. And his black goatee glistens. Another church-ish feeling sweeps over me. Like walking into the sanctuary and finding someone praying. Mr. Turner looks like he's been crying.

"Speak up!" He draws a hand over his goatee, wiping away the moisture.

I raise the book again. "Tedd—Mr. Chastain—he sent me. To find a book."

"For an assignment?"

"Uh, yes. Yes, sir. An assignment."

"Then be quick about it." He wipes his eyes. "*Acta non verba.*"

Latin. *Deeds not words.*

"Yes, sir."

He offers a firm nod, then walks to the other side of the library.

I don't move. But my gaze follows him to the back wall, to the Plexiglass display case. The clear plastic door is open. And next to the case, a cardboard box sits on a table. Mr. Turner sniffles and reaches into the case. He takes something out. Places it in the box. Then another sniffle. Maybe he's got a cold. That time of year. Lots of people have colds in December.

Right? Maybe . . . But . . .

He holds two objects in his hands. Small things. White.

Plastic.

Sheep.

I stare at the display case. Sloane's sheep experiment. Drew won the science fair, but Sloane got the display. Because Ellis decided Drew got enough publicity with national TV coverage.

I take a half-step toward him. "Mr. Turner?"

"Yes?" He faces the case, his back to me.

"I'm sorry, sir. I didn't mean to interrupt."

He raises an arm, waving me off. I stare at his back. His hair is kind of long, and the dark curls touch the collar of his corduroy jacket. Michael Turner was hired two years ago, to replace Ernest Stivers, an exoskeleton of Pre-Cambrian age who droned through his lessons day after day. Biology was the most dreaded class at St. Catherine's—which is saying something, since Sandbag teaches English. But Mr. Turner? Not only is he cute in that casual-preppy way, but he's a really good teacher. His classes are so popular, the school's added summer biology camps. Drew even got sidetracked from physics to biology for a while.

But my heart is beating too fast. Who helped Mr. Turner run those summer camps?

His star Biology student.

Sloane Stillman.

I shift toward the geology shelves, hunting for my prey. Teddy said the diatomaceous earth book wouldn't be shelved with the volcanics. Diatomaceous earth is sedimentary, so the book would be shelved among the silts and sands, seashells and limestone. Those volumes sit on the top shelves. I grab the rolling ladder and climb up, setting myself on the perch.

But my attention keeps going back to Mr. Turner. It's like he's forgotten I'm here, totally absorbed by packing up Sloane's science fair display. And still sniffling.

I finally find the book. The opening pages describe diatoms. Single-celled algae whose walls are made of silica. Silica is what makes sand. Diatoms appear with lots of fossil deposits. And algae.

Algae. Fossils. Biology.

I look over at Mr. Turner.

Why not?

"Excuse me, Mr. Turner?"

"Hmm." He still doesn't look over here.

"Would you happen to know anything about diatoms?"

He glances over his shoulder. His gaze climbs up the ladder to where I'm perched. "Diatoms? Yes. Why do you ask?"

"Tedd—" I correct myself again. "Mr. Chastain's assignment has to do with diatoms." I lift the book, pointing to the cover that says *DIATOMS*. Like that proves I'm not lying.

"Very well," he says. "What would you like to know?"

His voice. It sounds faraway, like he's in another world. *Thinking about Sloane?*

"Raleigh, what would you like to know?"

"Uh, like, where would I find diatoms? I mean, nearby."

He reaches into the display case and picks up a Petri dish. From the ladder, I can see inside the box. Everything has been placed in there with careful order. Even the plastic sheep stand together in a flock. He puts the Petri dish in the box. There's a red plastic sheet inside the dish, simulating blood.

My heart thuds into my chest. "Any ideas where I might find it?"

"Diatoms?" His voice sounds dreamlike.

"Yes." I climb down the ladder and walk over to him.

"I led a . . ." He swallows, clears his throat. "I led a field trip to a quarry last summer. His voice gets even weirder. "It was part of the school's biology camp. The girls took samples of diatomaceous earth."

Was Sloane helping you at that camp?

Instead, I ask, "Where's the quarry?"

"Near the town of Ashland."

"And it has diatoms?" I watch him carefully. But all he offers is more Latin.

"*Ad abundantiam.*"

In abundance.

"Great."

"I'm sure Mr. Chastain can give you more information about it."

Except Teddy never gives me answers. Only breadcrumbs. "Well, uh, sir . . . Mr. Chastain left for West Virginia."

"Then he'll fill you in after the holiday break."

"That might be a problem."

He looks over at me. He's got one of those nice goatees, dark and full, not scraggly. "What would that problem be?"

"Mr. Chastain wants me to finish this project now, over break. Before Christmas."

He stares at me another long moment. "Is that so?"

"Yes," I lie. "Absolutely that is so."

CHAPTER TWENTY-TWO

A ND THERE HE IS, waiting.
    DeMott.

Parked at the curb outside the school's entrance. His head rests against the truck cab's back window. Eyes closed, like he's napping.

I walk toward the truck and hear those crucial words from Friday night. Spoken into the starry darkness under a centuries-old tree.

He said, *I can wait a very long time.*

How long, I asked.

Forever.

Barely three days later, I'm already testing his promise. For several long moments, I stand by the passenger door watching him. The winter sun burns the windshield, bathing him with golden light. He looks more handsome than ever. But beyond that. A handsomeness that's both kind and calm. My eyes want to linger.

I open the door. "Hey, there."

He pushes himself upright. "Hey."

I climb in. "You should lock your doors."

"I'll take my chances. Especially since a beautiful girl just climbed in."

Heat rises through my chest, threatens to sear my throat. "Were you waiting long?"

"Teddy said you might be awhile." He smiles, a little wearily. "Get what you came for?"

I lift the book, illegally borrowed from the science library.

He reads the cover. It's not a long title. But he stares at the book for a long time. "Do you always do this?"

"Do what?"

"Turn free time into work."

The heat that was rising up my throat plummets. A solid thud in my gut. I reach around my right shoulder, grabbing my seatbelt, avoiding his question.

But in the side window, my reflection stares back at me.

My hair is loose, carefree. But my face? It stops me. Right there, mid-seatbelt. My face looks blank. Even though emotions are rioting inside because the guy I really *really* like just said something that really *really* hurt. Something completely, undeniably true. DeMott wanted a Sunday date. And here I am, working through a desperate quest for answers. I stare into my eyes. Large and amber and hiding confessions. Yes, I need to know what happened to Sloane. That's part of it. But maybe even more, I want to vindicate Drew. Show the world she's not that just some kook who interrupts funerals and asks to play the turkey in *A Christmas Carol.*

I click my seatbelt. "I've never been a big fan of unscheduled time."

He says nothing. And I don't look over at him. I stare out the windshield, watching the breeze scatter dead brown leaves over the empty sidewalk.

"Raleigh."

His voice. I can't look at him. I glance out my side window again. Then close my eyes. I don't even want to look at myself.

The truck's engine turns over.

"Okay," he says. "What's next on today's agenda?"

I want to blurt it all out. Everything about Sloane's pregnancy and Mr. Turner crying in the library and how Drew's not totally crazy. Taking a deep breath, I turn and look into his blue eyes. They are pools of acceptance.

"I'm sorry." I swallow, and it hurts. "I need to do this. Today.

If you can drive me, that would be great. But if you can't, I understand."

It seems impossible a guy this handsome could get even better looking.

But he smiles. And says, "I'm here to help you."

INTERSTATE 90 IS definitely the fastest way to go. But Mr. I-Can-Wait-Forever takes the oldest highway in America, Route 1.

The two lanes meander into Hanover County. When we reach the small town of Ashland, he asks, "Which way from here?"

I'm reading the map Mr. Turner drew from memory. How to get to this particular quarry that has diatomaceous earth. Mr. Turner told me he took the biology campers there so they could see what diatoms really look like, in the soil. Simple answer. But this memory map drawn by the weeping biology teacher who may or may not be the father of his late star student's baby is a really bad sketch. I turn it sideways.

"I think we're supposed to head toward the South Anna River."

But when we do that, we end up driving around Ashland for twenty minutes. Cows, fields, horses, goats. Old farm farmhouses with red barns.

But no quarry.

DeMott pulls to the side of the road. My mood sinks, like his tires sinking into the road's gravel shoulder.

"Let me see that map."

I hand it to him.

"You sure it's not *south* of the river?" he asks.

"No."

He turns the paper twice. Holds it up to the windshield, trying to get it to match the road. I look out the window.

"Raleigh."

In the field across from us, a white goat chews dead winter grass.

"Don't shut me out."

"I just gave you the map."

"Not that," he says. "A wall went up."

"When?"

"Back at St. Cat's. When I asked about free time."

"I don't know what you're talking about." I grab the map. "Let me see that."

But he lifts it over his head. I lunge for it. He moves the paper to his other hand. I click out of my seat belt and wave both hands like a basketball guard. I manage to get one corner of the paper. But he doesn't let go.

"You're going to rip it," he says.

"Then let go!"

He only pulls back. And I yank. The paper's tearing, I can hear it, but neither of us is letting go. I yank.

"Great." I hold the torn corner, ragged in my hand. "Happy?"

He offers me the map. But as I'm taking it, his hand slips behind me. He pulls me into him, kissing my mouth.

The kiss rolls through me. I am weightless. Falling backward. But DeMott's hand is there, too, catching my fall, holding me steady.

The next kiss is . . . perfect.

But he pulls back.

I open my eyes.

His head's turned, looking out the driver's side window.

I sit up.

The officer wears mirrored aviator shades.

"Where did he come from?" I ask.

The officer makes a motion with one hand, signaling DeMott to lower the window.

I scoot back into my seat, straightening my clothes.

"Officer," DeMott says. "Everything okay?"

From all the years spent in my dad's courtroom, I'm not surprised by the pause that follows. Cops know how to use silence like sword. I glance at the embroidered patch on his brown parka. Hanover County Sheriff's Department. A deputy.

"You two experiencing some engine trouble?" he asks.

"No, sir." DeMott keeps both hands on the steering wheel.

"Then can you tell me why you parked on the side of the road?"

DeMott nods toward the torn paper, laying on the floor. "We got lost. Our map isn't very good."

"Sure it's the map's fault?"

My face feels hot. DeMott looks over at me. His face is red too. I lean forward. The aviator shades shift toward me.

"We're looking for diatomaceous earth," I say.

The aviator shades shift back to DeMott. "License, registration, insurance?"

The cop carries the paperwork back to his cruiser, parked behind us, the swirling lights on. I glance out my window. The goat's right by the fence, full of curiosity.

"You don't have some kind of criminal record, do you?" De-Mott asks me.

"Not yet."

The cop comes back, returns the license and papers to DeMott. His attitude's changed. Maybe he searched the name Fielding. "What is it, exactly, you two are looking for?"

I lift the library book. "A quarry."

The officer holds out his hand.

I give him the book. "There's supposed to be a quarry mine around here."

"You mean the pit?" he asks.

Quarry, pit. Both holes in the ground. Geologically, that's like the difference between saying, "tomato," and "toe-mah-toe."

"How do we get to the pit?" I ask.

"Follow me," he says.

CHAPTER TWENTY-THREE

Q UARRIES ARE FABULOUSLY filthy places. Bulldozers. Rough-cut rock.

And clouds of dust.

DeMott coughs, following the deputy's cruiser down a gravel road northeast of Ashland.

He coughs again. "You notice I'm not asking *why* we're here."

"Yes."

Through the dust clouds, I see a Quonset hut. The deputy's cruiser stops, we park behind him. A blanket of beige dust settles on DeMott's hood.

"But I'd like to know," he adds. "What *are* we doing here?"

"Looking for answers.

"And that's not one of them," he says.

The deputy waves, and drives away. A guy steps out of the Quonset hut. He's our age, with blonde curly hair. He waves at the departing deputy.

"I probably don't want to know," DeMott says.

"Probably right."

I climb out of the truck.

DeMott gets out, too, coughing, waving a hand in front of his face. I can feel the fine-grained dust on my tongue. Gritty. And a little slippery. Sand, combined with clay.

The guy walks toward us. His face is round, childlike, the long blonde curls all over the place. I introduce myself. His hazels eyes are clear, but one seems to drift.

I'm about to introduce DeMott, when the guy turns and says, "DeMott Fielding, right?"

There's an awkward silence. DeMott almost kind of panicked, like we're in Mr. Manners' nightmare—he doesn't recognize this guy.

But, as usual, he recovers. "How are you?"

"Charlie." The guy points at his chest. "I'm Charlie Judisch. I went out for baseball. Last Spring. St. Christopher's. Remember?"

"Oh, right." DeMott looks even more embarrassed. He extends his hand. "Good to see you. You work here?"

"Own it. Well, actually, my parents, *they* own it." He gives a bashful smile. "I work here. Weekends, after school. Not a problem since I got cut from baseball." He laughs, with no trace bitterness. "But what're *you* doing here?"

DeMott looks at me. I raise the book. Charles's eyes scan the title. Well, one eye scans. The other eye drifts. When he glances up at me, his gaze seems to go over my left shoulder.

"Very cool," he says. "You need some diatomaceous earth?"

"I need information about it."

"Oh. I thought maybe you were some of the art people." He takes in our blank stares. "For sculpting. Our clay molds into any shape."

I nod, like this is important. "I heard about some biology camps out here, too. From St. Catherine's School?"

"Yeah. They came to study the diatoms." He looks at DeMott, as if sensing his confusion. "Diatoms are basically marine algae. Each cell's enclosed in this really amazing double-shell of silica."

"Bivalves." I add. "One shell fits over the other."

"Like a lid on a box!" Charlie grins.

"The St. Catherine's biology teacher said you have some good examples."

"Yes! Our bivalves are ancient. Way, way back in fossil time. That's why the biology teacher and his assistant—"

I sort of hear the rest of his exuberant explanation. But my mind combs over that one word. *Assistant*. Sloane? I wait for

Charlie to finish.

"Was his assistant a tall girl?" I ask. "Short brown hair?"

Charlie's face droops. All that exuberance drained in an instant. "The girl who died last week."

"Sloane Stillman."

"You *knew* her?"

DeMott turns, facing me with a pointed expression. "Raleigh goes to St. Catherine's."

Uh-oh.

"Wow, gee," Charlie says. "Then you know what happened to her."

I nod, although the reason I'm here is because I *don't* know what happened to Sloane—or why there was diatomaceous earth on the floor of her car.

I shift my stance to avoid making eye contact with DeMott. "Any chance I could see your quarry?"

"Absolutely!" Charlie says.

"I'll wait in the truck," DeMott says.

He offers me a flat expression and walks back to the truck, which is now dusty as a ranch vehicle. Every step he takes moves him not just physically farther away but emotionally, too. If it wasn't for his perfect manners, I'd be worried he'd drive away without me.

"Well come on!" Charlie starts walking around the Quonset hut. "You gotta see this!"

On the other side, the dust thickens the air even more. On the ground, a hard-packed soil spreads out like a plateau. And at the far edge, some twelve-wheel dump trucks wait under metallic claws of diggers, each bucket depositing a gray-brown soil into the truck's open containers, filling the air with more dust. Circling it all, a water truck sprays the soil, some futile attempt to keep the fine-grained sediment from going airborne. All the truck windows are rolled up, drivers inside.

I have to raise my voice over the diesel machinery. "What's the soil used for?"

"Fat Cat!"

"What?"

"You've never heard of Fat Cat?"

I shake my head.

"Premium kitty litter—the best!"

We don't own a cat. And I don't exactly pay attention to evil Newton. But Charlie's off on another enthusiastic explanation.

"Our soil's the key ingredient. Diatomaceous earth can absorb its own weight in cat pee!"

"Really."

"Yeah!"

This guy. After all the snooty girls at St. Cat's and the upper crust at Weyanoke, I almost forgot people like him existed. But then I realize, he reminds me of Drew. The old Drew. The girl who used to get so excited about scientific phenomena she was totally oblivious to everything else.

And I want old Drew back.

I reach into my jacket and pull out the baggie with the gray stones. "Does it look like this stuff?"

Charlie opens the baggie, reaches inside and takes out one of the tiny stones. He squeezes it. "I think it's clean," he says.

"Clean?"

"Unused." As far as I can tell.

He touches his tongue to the tip of it. "Yes!" He almost bounces up and down. "This is Fat Cat. Know how I can tell?"

"No idea." I'm still kind of shocked.

"I can taste the bentonite!"

"Clay?"

"Whoa." He looks at me in amazement. "You know about bentonite?"

Credit goes to Teddy, who has taught me about clays in everything from so-called beauty masks that absorb zit-oils, to clays used in medicines like Maalox to absorb gas.

"So this diatomaceous earth absorbs cat pee?"

He nods and explains how this diatomaceous earth alters the

ions in cat pee. "That takes out a big 'stink factor' in cat boxes," he says.

"People probably pay good money for that."

"You bet!" He laughs. "Still, there is a saturation point. I mean, too much pee and it'll come in contact with cat poop. Cat pee plus cat poop equals bad bacteria."

I bite my tongue to keep from laughing.

"Kinda gross," he says.

"Well . . ."

"That's why I think we should start a different line of products." He digs into his back pocket and whips out a business card, handing it to me.

I read the business name. *Play with Clay.*

"This stuff is perfect for sculpting. I got this idea. My dad's letting me run with it. I already sold some to an art school up north."

"Congratulations." I slip the card into my pocket, then kneel down and pinch the soil at our feet. The texture is silken, so fine-grained. "Can you tell me anything about the biology teacher's assistant?"

He stares at me. That wandering eye. It's endearing, like a lost puppy.

"She was really different," he says.

"How so?"

"Not like the other girls at St. Catherine's." He gives a start. "Oh, gee, I'm sorry."

"Actually, I agree with you."

"And you're not like them either. They're all so stuck-up. But Sloane wasn't like that. At all."

I nod. Because that's how I saw her. But she was taking antidepressants. And she was pregnant. And she might've been having an affair with one of her teachers. I brush the soil off my hands. A dump truck rumbles past. Charlie waves at the driver.

"Sloane was here with the biology teacher, right?"

"Yeah. Mr. Turner. I think that's his name."

"They got along okay?"

"Well, yeah."

"They were close?"

"I think so."

"How close?"

He is still for a moment. "Not the usual teacher-student thing. More like friends."

"Good friends?"

"Is there another kind of friend?"

I smile. In Charlie's world, there are only good friends. No manipulations. No deceptions. No lying. I stare into his sweet round face and feel like a mean little terrier that dug up someone else's bone.

"You know what's the worst part?" He watches another dump truck driving away. "I keep wondering what I could've done to help her."

You know what I wonder? How a guy like this survives among the ruthless jocks at St. Christopher's. But I know how. He stays invisible. Just like Drew. Like me. Keep your head down, get through the day. And it works. DeMott isn't a ruthless jock, but even he failed to see Charlie.

"Her death is not your fault," I tell him.

"Thanks for saying that." He looks over at me. That wandering eye drifts away. "But I'm always gonna wonder. Probably for the rest of my life. Maybe she needed some help. You know what I mean?"

"Yes," I tell him. "I know exactly what you mean."

CHAPTER TWENTY-FOUR

W E DRIVE AWAY from the quarry, leaving the dust behind us. The sunshine seems brighter than ever. But my head still feels cloudy.

And my heart?

I glance over at DeMott. My heart rattles, like somebody climbed inside and is pounding on the walls for answers. Along the back country roads, I search for the right words.

But I know the right words. Three words. *I am sorry.*

"Hungry?" he asks.

"Starving."

Within ten minutes we're seated at a barbecue joint named for those three little pigs. The air is heaven—roasted meat, barbecue sauce, and good ol' American grease.

DeMott orders ribs.

I order "the family meal."

I wash my hands and dusty face in the restroom, and come out to find the food has already arrived at the table: two pulled-pork sandwiches, side of onion rings, side of hush puppies, side of mashed potatoes, side of coleslaw—my one concession to vegetables—and one large Coke, no crushed ice.

"You're going to eat all that?" DeMott's eyes widen.

"Yep." I lift the sandwich bun and place two onion rings on top of the pulled pork, then add coleslaw and a squirt of barbecue sauce. I say silent grace, and pray the boy across the table doesn't think I'm the fourth pig in the fairy tale because I don't know when I'll see food like this again.

I bite down.

An involuntary hum vibrates up my throat. Southern food that wasn't cooked by my mother.

"I take it that you like your food," he says.

Another blush wants to creep into my face, but I swat it down. No way. I am not going to feel guilty for enjoying food. But, I do wipe my mouth with a napkin and finish chewing before speaking.

"How well did you know Sloane?" I ask.

A baby back rib was on its way to his mouth. But it stops mid-air. "Why do you ask?"

"Just curious."

"That's not the impression I got at the quarry."

I sail right over that. "Did you know Sloane was on antidepressants?"

"Everything looks different in hindsight."

"Everything?"

"Sloane wasn't the person we thought she was."

"You mean, that she was depressed?"

"Raleigh, I'm really not comfortable talking about this." His blue eyes refuse to meet my gaze. "Can we discuss something else?"

I take another big ol' bite and leave the silence hanging there. At the table next to us, a family of four sits down. All the kids have identical straight black hair and brown eyes. DeMott smiles at the parents.

"Mama." The littlest kid points at our table. "Lookit all that food!"

I polish off the first sandwich.

"You must've know Sloane pretty well." I start building the second sandwich with more onion rings and coleslaw. "Being neighbors and all."

He chews, a long long time. "You're not going to let this go, are you?"

I shake my head and take a monster bite.

"Alright, let's talk about Sloane," he says. "I was her escort last spring."

I stop mid-chew. "Escort? What is that, some service you provide?"

"Very funny. The debutante ball was at Weyanoke. I was Sloane's escort. Or date."

I grab my Coke to clear my mouth. The drink's ice cold. But that's not what sends the chill down my back. "You two dated?"

"No. Escort's a formality. You'll see."

"I'll see . . . what?"

"When you turn sixteen. You'll be a debutante."

"No way. No. No. *No.*"

"Raleigh, you'll get an invitation. The Harmons are a first-family."

"Then how come my sister wasn't—" I stop. If Helen was invited, I don't need to hear her colorful response. I pick up my sandwich for the distraction. "Let's get back to this escort thing."

"The debutante committee chooses them."

My jaw drops. "There's a committee?"

"You'll see."

I bite down, stuffing my mouth. I'll eat broccoli for the rest of my life before I'll go to a debutante ball.

"There's no romance with the dates," he adds, as if to reassure me. "We're just there to take care of the debutantes."

"Oh. Okay. So what was Sloane like that night?"

"Cold." He doesn't even have to think about it. "Cold as ice."

Odd. Who could be cold to DeMott?

"Cold to everyone, or just you?"

He shrugs. "She clearly didn't want to be there."

"I don't blame her."

He doesn't answer.

I take another big bite, watching him. And trying to ignore my taste buds. They're dancing with the salt-sweet tang of barbecue, the coleslaw full of my beloved mayonnaise, and that particular breaded crunch of onion rings. A taste so glorious it gives me courage to press him even further.

"Maybe Sloane was afraid her boyfriend would get jealous of you."

DeMott's blue gaze locks on mine. He lowers a baby back rib, slowly.

"I don't like talking about this," he says. "But there's something you should know." He glances at the family next to us, then leans forward, his voice almost a whisper. "Sloane was a lesbian."

"Lesbian!"

His head snaps back. He glances at the family. They stare at us.

"Sorry." I lower my voice. "Who told you she was gay?"

He picks up his ribs, takes a bite.

"DeMott?"

His eyes are glacial. "Let's not talk about it."

"But we are. So now you need to finish the topic. Who told you she was gay?"

He leans forward again. "This is not the sort of thing people broadcast in public."

I grab my Coke, gulping it down to cool the heat rising in my face. The carbonation explodes in my throat. I count to twenty. "I didn't mean to . . . I just . . . I don't believe it."

"Believe it. Sloane had no interest in guys."

Four good bites remain on my second sandwich. But I my hunger is gone. Sloane obviously had *some* interest in guys if she was pregnant. Maybe her romance with Mr. Turner made the escort-boys seem beneath her.

DeMott is wiping his fingers clean. I count to ten.

"Can we drop by Drew's house?" I ask.

"What for?"

"Just need to check on her."

He sighs. "Raleigh, at some point are you going to spend time with me—just me?"

The pain on his face. It stings my soul. Our hangout time was spent with Teddy, the quarry, questions about Sloane. I know how he feels. My mom disregards my feelings every day. My stomach clenches.

"I need to apologize." I take a deep breath. "The best part of this whole day was ripping that map."

He smiles. "Thank you."

"But." I stare down at my almost-empty plate. "But I have to help Drew. This whole thing with Sloane, it's needs to be resolved. I'm sorry."

My hands twist the napkin in my lap. The noise grows louder around us—kids and radio music and waitresses bustling past. But there's also a black hole of silence.

I look up.

Maybe Teddy's right. Maybe this relationship will never work.

"Yes," he says.

I blink. *Yes, this relationship will never work?*

"Yes . . . ," I hesitate. "Yes, what?"

"Yes, I'll drive you to Drew's."

"Oh." *That* yes.

He tilts his head. "Was there something else you were wondering about?"

"No." I shake my head. "Nothing."

And everything.

CHAPTER TWENTY-FIVE

I T'S SUNDAY AFTERNOON, but Jayne's car isn't in the driveway. Maybe she left to buy more wine.

I dig the key out from under the stone turtle, and step inside the sun room with DeMott behind me.

Newton offers his customary hiss.

"His name's Sir Isaac Newton," I explain. "Drew named him. She's also the only person who loves him."

DeMott follows me into the kitchen. "You don't care for cats?"

"Just not that cat."

Upstairs in her bedroom, Drew's wedged the purple Princess phone between her shoulder and ear so both hands can fly over her keyboard. "Bernie, news flash. I'm not old enough to drive."

I motion for DeMott to step inside, then close the door.

Drew keeps speaking into the phone. "But if mass times velocity gives me momentum, the larger the car, the harder it is to stop. Correct?"

I can feel DeMott's glance. But I pretend to be fascinated by the books on her shelves. Books about integrals, derivatives, summations. *Ugh.*

"Momentum." *Type-type-type.* "Yeah, force. And change in velocity. But how do I define it? Force of impact times time of impact?"

I open one of the books and scan the pages. But no words are visible because there's a gigantic plank in my own eye. I scorn DeMott's manners, but, really, is my behavior toward Drew any different? I pretend to be okay with her OCD. I pretend to care about vectors and Feynman quotes. I pretend I'm not pretending. How is that any different from DeMott's too-polite manners?

"It's a matter of degrees," Drew says, as if answering my question.

Finally, she hangs up.

She swivels the chair toward us, so fast centrifugal force sends her hair flying. "How's this for luck?"

"There's no such thing as luck."

"Raleigh, the jury's still out on that matter. And Bernie's a classic car collector."

I turn to DeMott. "Bernie is the physics librarian at MIT."

"MIT," he says.

"Massachusetts Institute of Technology." I put the book back, exactly where I found it. "So you're telling me Bernie knows about old Chevys."

"Correct!"

She says it with the same enthusiasm as Charlie Judisch. *Maybe I should set them up.* But as I'm hatching the plan, she picks up a spray bottle. It's marked C_2H_5OH. She spritzes the Princess phone and fumes of alcohol fill the air. I can feel DeMott's gaze again. I'm sure he's wondering, *If she's the only person touching the phone, why is she spraying it for germs?*

"Bernie," she says, wiping off the alcohol with a sterile cloth, "agrees that no person with a triple-digit IQ would attempt suicide by aiming that particular Chevy at a tree. Statistically speaking, Sloane was more likely to survive the crash than die."

She turns to the computer screen, scrolling through a document. "He said, and I quote, 'Those Chevys were built like armored tanks.' "

"Did you tell him she was taking antidepressants?" I ask.

"Why not drive off a cliff? Why not close the garage door and start the engine?"

"Drew—"

"But there's more. I talked to Mary Vale."

For a long, long moment, I can't speak. "Mary Vale—Stillman?"

"Raleigh, please. We both know there is no other Mary Vale. She agreed to allow me to examine Sloane's bedroom."

"Excuse me." DeMott waves his hand, as if brushing away the alcohol fumes. "Mrs. Stillman already told you two to stop—"

"How do you know that?" Drew asks.

He looks at me.

But it's a good question.

"DeMott, how do you know about Mrs. Stillman talking to me?"

"She . . . expressed her displeasure to my mom."

"Displeasure." *Wow*. I stare at him. *Displeasure*. Most definitely the polite word for southern fury.

Drew narrows her eyes. "Were you the one who ratted us out about the junkyard?"

"Pardon?"

I jump in. "Drew's just wondering who—"

"He needs to drive us to Mary Vale's," she says. "Take him downstairs so I can change into clean clothes."

In a flash, he is out of her room, heading down the stairs. I race after him.

"DeMott." He's a step below me. I reach out, put my hand on his shoulder. "Stop. Please."

He stops. I can feel the tension through his sweatshirt.

"I won't pull you into another embarrassing trip."

He turns. His eyes search mine. I look away.

"But if I don't drive you," he says, "you two will still go out there. Am I right?"

I pull my hand away. Still can't look up. "Yes."

"How, riding your bikes?"

"Probably."

"Then I have to take you."

He walks down the stairs without another word.

CHAPTER TWENTY-SIX

OUTSIDE THE FABLED Still Waters plantation, DeMott parks in the half-moon driveway. His expression looks chiseled from quartz.

Drew hops out of the truck, oblivious to the tightrope of tension.

"I'll call you when we're done," I tell him.

"I don't carry a cell phone," he says.

"We'll find another way home, you aren't responsible for—"

"No." He looks away, glancing in the rearview mirror. Like somebody might actually be coming down the long empty driveway framed by boxwood bushes. "I'll be back in thirty minutes."

I climb out. And watch his truck head back to New Market Road. He turns right, toward Weyanoke. I suck down a deep breath of cold air.

"Fifty-two . . ." Drew is saying.

I turn to see that she's counted every step from the truck to the grand porch. The Stillman's classic white plantation house comes complete with a double-sized black front door garlanded in pine and red velvet. Perfect Christmas decorations. Only as I get closer, I can see how the decorations are sagging, limp, like the whole place is mourning Sloane.

I try to grab's Drew's skinny wrist, but I'm too late. She pushes her finger into the doorbell. *Bong-BONG-bonngggg . . .* The doorbell keeps going, sounding like the Ghost of Christmas Past.

The door whips open. Mary Vale hisses, "Shhhhhhhh!"

From inside the house, a man's voice calls out. "Miz Mary Vale?"

"Yes, Otto. It's for me."

The man appears behind her, an older black man wearing a dark suit. And suspicion.

"They're just some friends from school," she says.

"Y'all be quiet. Your mama needs her rest."

Mary Vale throws Drew a pointed look.

"What?" Drew says.

Mary Vale looks at me.

"She doesn't know," I explain.

"What," Drew says. "What don't I know?"

After seeing Mrs. Stillman three times this week, and my own mom when she's zombie-fied on medication, I think it's clear.

"Mrs. Stillman's napping."

"Oh." Drew lowers her voice. "I will be very quiet."

Mary Vale wastes no time, leading us briskly across the foyer. I wish she'd slow down because the floor has an amazing inlaid wood pattern, like a giant compass. But Mary Vale's already heading down a big hall with carpeting so plush our footsteps suddenly fall silent. She glances over her shoulder, making sure we're following, and each time she does, her face strikes me all over again. Sloane was pretty, but Mary Vale's one of those Victorian paintings, the kind with some epitome of female loveliness stranded in an oarless rowboat, floating away on the lily-strewn waterway so poignant you just know disaster's heading her way, like that rowboat's about to plunge over a waterfall.

"Hold it." Drew stops. Points.

There's a large sculpture filling an alcove. At first, I think it's a toy. Balls connected to each other by sticks.

"Can I touch it?" Drew says.

"Shhh." Mary Vale keeps walking.

"Please?" Drew begs.

"*No.* Be quiet."

Drew looks at me, brown eyes wide with reverence. "Methyl-pyroxine-phenylcetylene-oxide!"

"Shhhh!" hisses Mary Vale.

I grab Drew, pulling her forward. "Later."

Mary Vale stands waiting at a door, one hand on the shiny brass lever. "You have to swear not to tell anyone about this."

"What about Tinsley?" Drew asks.

"My cousin *told me* to let you two in here." She sounds bitter. "But you can't tell anybody else."

She pushes the lever. But she doesn't open the door. She just stands there, and in that split-second hesitation, the Victorian painting comes to life again. Only now the damsel in the boat has realized that the waterfall's up ahead, that her lovely life includes a grisly death. And somehow, the knowledge of tragedy only makes Mary Vale look even more beautiful.

Drew rushes past her.

Sloane's bedroom.

Drew goes straight to the computer on a desk.

I want to leave. *Now.*

But Mary Vale ushers me in, closing the door, leaning her back against it.

The sorrow. It hangs in the air and pushes my heart all the way down into my stomach. I glance at Sloane's unmade bed and feel sick. The covers are thrown back like she just got up. And something worse. A smell.

Not just that.

A bad smell.

I glance around. The room doesn't have one speck of dust. *How can a room this clean smell this bad?*

"Password protected," Drew mutters, fingers on the keyboard. She looks at me. "How did you find my password?"

"Educated guessing."

No wonder I don't like it in here. This room feels too much like Drew's bedroom in October, when I was hunting for answers. When I didn't know if Drew was alive or dead. "Try something with biology," I suggest. "Or maybe sheep."

"No." Mary Vale's voice quivers. "*Biology is life*. No spaces. That's her password."

Drew types it. "We're in!"

"Please." Mary Vale hangs her head.

I rush over and whisper in her ear. "Drew—quiet!"

She nods, but is totally focused on the computer.

I glance over at Mary Vale. Her face looks like a porcelain teacup that's about to fracture into a thousand pieces.

And I can't handle this stench. I walk over to the bed. The sheets are clean, not to mention finely-spun cotton with about ten thousand threads per inch. The bedside bookshelf holds stacks of tomes. Biological cell reproduction. Genetics. Organic chemistry. There's also a framed photo of her dad, the famous chemist Skip Stillman. Another photo shows Mary Vale making a funny face. But not one photo of Mrs. Stillman.

I glance back. Mary Vale hovers behind Drew as she skims through the computer's folders and files.

I take one book from Sloane's shelf: *Fuel for Centuries* by Stephen "Skip" Stillman.

Mr. Stillman discovered Methyl-pyroxine-phenylcetylene-oxide, a compound added to unleaded gasoline to increase fuel efficiency. Every time someone gasses up their car, the Stillmans collect .05 cents on every gallon. The family was wealthy even before Mr. Stillman's discovery. Now they collect checks just for breathing. Why not erect a molecular model sculpture.

"She planned to take over operations."

I turn. Mary Vale's large eyes are the same blue as spring's first sunny day. She nods at the book in my hands.

"Sloane," she says. "She planned to run Methyl Corporation. She wanted them to branch into biogenetics."

Methyl Corporation manufactures the gasoline additive, among other chemical compounds. The company employs thousands of Richmonders.

"She would've been great at that."

But the expression on Mary Vale's face makes me look away. *Can this knife sink any deeper into my heart?* I replace the book. A familiar sadness creeps over me. The feeling I had in October, standing in Drew's room when she was nowhere to be found. But with Drew, there was still a chance she was alive.

Sloane?

She's stone cold dead, forever.

"Mary Vale?" There's a knock at the door. "Mary Vale, are you in there?"

It sounds like Mrs. Stillman.

Drew continues typing, as if nothing's happening. I place my hand on her wrist.

"Hey—"

And clamp my other hand over her mouth.

Immediately I regret it.

Her eyes. That deep brown color fills with a feral expression. The look I prayed I'd never see again. Her hand claws at my fingers, desperate. But I can't let go.

The door level rattles. "Darling?"

Locked. *Thank God.*

"One moment, Mother!"

Mary Vale rushes across the room and flings open a different door. I see clothing, shoes, luggage. A walk-in closet. With my hand still covering Drew's mouth, I drag her across the room, all ninety-eight pounds of her wired tight as a steel spring. Mary Vale closes the door behind us.

Drew is gasping, sucking air through my fingers.

"Hold on," I whisper. "It won't be long."

"Darling!" Mrs. Stillman's voice is right next to us—she's in the bedroom. "Why? Why . . . would . . . you come in here?"

"I just wanted to. You know."

"No . . . I don't know." But then her voice snaps. "Her computer? You turned on her computer?"

I really want to hear Mary Vale's response, but I'm literally gagging. That smell. It's coming from here—in the closet. A stink so powerful it's like a finger poking the back of my throat. I bury my nose in Drew's hair, whispering, "You smell that?"

She nods, mutters something into my hand.

"Just go away!" Mary Vale cries. "Leave me alone!"

My eyes water.

"I cannot cope," Mrs. Stillman says. "You cannot be—"

Drew says something, her hot breath tickling my palm.

Mary Vale's yelling. "Mother, take another pill!"

I press my mouth to Drew's ear again. "Promise you'll whisper?"

She nods. I lift my hand one inch.

"Ammonium," she whispers.

I shake my head. *What?*

She points.

There's a sliding glass door behind us. And my first thought is, *Who has a sliding glass door in their closet?* Oh. Right. *People who collect five cents on every gallon of gas.*

But Drew points again. On the floor there's a plastic box with gray lumps inside it.

"Get out!" Mary Vale screeches. "Get out of here!"

I glance around the closet. It's bigger than my whole bedroom. Clothes hang on two walls. A third wall displays shoes. The fourth wall is the glass door. All the clothes and shoes aren't a puzzle—Sloane always dressed really nice—but I'm trying to recall if she smelled this bad at school.

"Mary Vale, darling, you don't look well."

"Check the mirror, Mother. You don't look so hot yourself."

Moments later, a door slams.

"Ammonium nitrate," Drew whispers. "That's what we're smelling. Cat box."

I close my eyes. *Kitty litter.* It must've gotten into the bottom of Sloane's shoes. Then inside the Cherrymobile.

"Feline urine contains compounds other than ammonium nitrate," Drew begins.

I hold up my hand. First of all, I've heard enough. And second, she and Charlie Judisch are made for each other. But third, and most disappointing, is that all that work on the gray "volcanic" stones and diatomaceous earth only proves one thing. The Stillmans buy premium kitty litter.

What a revelation.

Mary Vale opens the closet door. "She's gone."

But now an orange cat is in Sloane's bedroom. The cat looks up at us.

Drew walks right back past it and sits at Sloane's desk.

The cat saunters into the closet and climbs into the tray. His sharp green eyes remind me of someone.

The cat must be cousins with Tinsley, too.

He lifts his head, haughty, like his poop doesn't stink. Which, of course, confirms he's related to Tinsley.

Drew's opened a document on the computer. She pages through it, muttering as she reads. Mary Vale and I stand behind her chair.

"Counselor," Drew points at the screen. "Who was her counselor?"

Mary Vale leans down. "What are you reading?"

"The time stamp says this document was the last one she opened. The night she died."

Nobody says anything.

The cat swishes grains around the plastic box.

"Do you want me to clean up?" I ask Mary Vale. "Apparently kitty litter works better if you remove the feces."

"Her journal?" Mary Vale says. "You're reading my sister's *journal?*"

"Of course," Drew says. "People write journals. People read them. And right here she keeps referring to her counselor. Who says Sloane needs help."

I lean down. "Help, for what?"

Drew scrolls through the document. "Doesn't say, specifically."

The cat steps out of the closet. Mary Vale snatches him up,

clutching him the way a little girl might cling to a teddy bear.

"My sister didn't have a counselor." She strokes the cat. "She would've told me." Her hand stops on the cat's back. "But . . ."

"What?"

"She also never told me about the antidepressants."

I wait, wondering if she knows about the pregnancy. If nobody's inflicted that pain on Mary Vale, no way am I doing it. "Any idea who the therapist is?"

She shakes her head.

"Did she have any close relationships? Teachers, for instance."

"I don't think so."

"She and Mr. Turner sure seemed close."

Mary Vale frowns. Her skin barely wrinkles. "The biology teacher?"

I tell her about how I saw him this morning in the science library. I don't tell her that he was taking down Sloane's science fair exhibit. "He seemed really upset. About your sister."

Mary Vale gazes down at the cat purring in her arms. "Mr. Turner was her mentor. He helped get her into Harvard early. She was, I guess you'd say, like, a protégé."

"And nothing more?"

"More, how?"

"I don't know. Romantic?"

That early spring blue in her eyes disappears into winter. And suddenly I see the family resemblance to Tinsley.

"You can leave now," she says.

I don't move. And Drew keeps typing.

Mary Vale walks over to the closet and crosses to the glass door. She pushes it open. The cold winter air sweeps inside, brushing over my face.

Drew keeps typing. "So was she sleeping with Mr. Turner?"

"Drew." I touch her arm.

"Huh?"

"We need to go."

"Uh huh."

"Now."

I start for the closet. Drew glances up, then clicks the mouse, muttering about something. As I pass Mary Vale, I see tears in her eyes. Large tears, tragic. Just like those Victorian paintings.

"Sometimes we don't know everything," I tell her. "Even about family."

She's a beautiful crier. No wincing. No blotchy skin. Her tears simply roll.

But there's another knock on the door. "Miz Mary Vale?"

She sniffs. "What, Otto."

"Where're those girls?"

She points at the open glass door. "They're gone."

I reach for Drew, holding a finger to my lips. She types one last rapid fire entry, pushes Enter, and follows me through the closet. To get across the stinking cat box, I have to stretch my stride, one foot outside, one inside.

I look across the lawn.

And there he is.

DeMott.

In the driveway.

Waiting.

CHAPTER TWENTY-SEVEN

O VER THE FIELDS we go, counting all the way.
　　Counting every broken yellow line on New Market Road. Counting every road sign into Richmond. Every Christmas flag flapping on Grove Avenue.

DeMott doesn't say one word; Drew won't shut up.

Sitting between them on the bench seat is like wearing headphones stuck on mono.

"We are definitely uncovering truth," Drew babbles. "But the first principle is you must not fool yourself—and you are the easiest person to fool."

Richard P. Feynman strikes again.

We turn down Westhampton Road, then into her driveway.

"I won't call you tonight," she keeps talking right up to the moment the truck stops. "But tomorrow, we'll talk. We will know something, Raleigh. We will. We will. We will. We will."

Four. She can stop on four. *Please, God. Stop her on four.*

"Okay," I say.

She leaps out, makes her clumsy run for the back door, and goes through the whole up-and-down the stairs routine.

As soon as the back door closes, DeMott drives away.

More silence.

My heart. One minute it's slamming into my ribcage. The next it's stopping dead, filled with anger.

"You don't understand," I say, as we head down Monument Avenue. Dusk is settling over the city. The dark gray clouds match my mood. "You just don't understand."

"Neither do you," he says.

When he stops in front of my house, I grab my backpack and open my door before he has a chance to.

"Merry Christmas," he says.

"Yeah, you too." I slam the door.

IN SOME ALTERNATE universe, bells on bobtails ring.

But inside my house, everything is falling apart.

"*Finally*," Helen says. "Now I can leave."

I haven't even closed the kitchen door. And those angels are singing to certain poor shepherds.

Helen grabs her coat. "Enjoy the circus." She rushes out the door.

I left this house with high hopes and my backpack. Now, hope is gone and the only physical object added to my pack is that thin book on diatomaceous earth.

I trudge upstairs. My pack feels like it weighs a hundred pounds. I drop it on my bedroom floor and climb in bed, pulling the pillows over my head, in case any of those angels come singing.

IN MY DREAM, I'm back in Sloane's bedroom. Someone's knocking on the door.

But when my eyes open, I'm in my bedroom.

Someone is knocking on my bedroom door.

"Raleigh?"

I sit up. The bedside clock says 6:52. I look out the window. Darkness. I can't tell if it's a.m. or p.m.

"Come in."

My dad's wearing a white dress shirt, red tie askew, sleeves rolled up to his elbows. Work day. And nighttime. *Did I really sleep through an entire day?*

He steps in, closes my door. "Sorry, I had a commitment."

"Oh."

Not like *commitment*, meaning *previous engagement*. My dad's one of the state's hand-picked judges who rules on emergency commitment hearings. When somebody goes so nuts they get sent to the state hospital—against their will. It's obvious why the state picked my dad. But these commitments always pop up without warning. And every single one wears him down.

"Sorry," I tell him. "Bad?"

"They're always bad." He sighs. "The holidays make them worse. Speaking of which, tomorrow I need you girls to make a real effort tomorrow."

"What's tomorrow?"

"Raleigh." He looks wounded. "Christmas Eve."

"Oh. Right." So it must still be Sunday. Tomorrow's Monday. "Christmas Eve. Got it."

He stands there a moment, like he wants to say something more.

"Helen went out," I add. "But I'm home for the whole night. If you need me to do anything . . ."

"Come downstairs." He smiles, but it's tired. "Hang out with your boring parents?"

"Sure." I throw back my covers. My sweatshirt is wrinkled. We both know what that means. She'll be suspicious, like a wrinkled sweatshirt means I'm up to something. Which, I guess, I am. "Don't worry, I'll change."

He nods. "Maybe we can play a board game?"

It's painful to watch your parents deal with certain things. But the most painful for me is this: my dad trying to patch things together here at home. Like hopeful and futile combined. But especially bad after he's just heard about somebody's loved one getting sent to the state hospital. *There but for the grace of God, go us.*

"Yeah, a board game sounds great." I *hate* board games. "But let's not play Scrabble."

"What's wrong with Scrabble?"

"Hard to play with no Ls."

It takes him a moment. Then he smiles.

But his eyes are moist.

SWEATSHIRT CHANGED BUT head still fuzzy from the late nap, I walk down the back stairs and head straight for the fridge. Board games with my parents. This calls for serious reinforcements. I dig through the shelves, searching, searching, searching, for one can of Coke.

When the phone rings, I don't make any move for it. One, I hate talking on the phone. Two, Drew said she'd call tomorrow. And three, it's probably one of Helen's weirdo boyfriends, realizing she's back in town.

My dad walks into the room. "Raleigh . . ."

"I'm already playing a board game. You can't expect me to answer the phone, too."

He picks up the phone. "Hello?"

On the bottom shelf in the far back, shoved past two pans of leftover casseroles—one can of Coca Cola. *Hallelujah!*

"She's not here," my dad says.

Yep. Call for Helen.

I pop the can and guzzle like a girl lost in the Sahara.

"I'll check." My dad lowers the phone, covers the receiver with his palm. "Have you seen Drew?"

Drew?

"She was at her house."

He lifts the receiver, repeats what I just said, but then turns back to me. "Mrs. Levinson says Drew's not there."

I hold out my hand for the phone. Seriously. Jayne must be so bombed. "Hi, it's Raleigh."

"Where did she go?" Jayne's voice is tight.

"I dropped her off at your house." Third time I've said this, but it's not making dent. Alcohol. "Around five o'clock."

"I saw her, I talked to her. She was here." Jayne takes a breath. "But she's *gone*."

Something flickers through my stomach. "You mean, she left?"

"Her bike is gone!"

I glance at my Dad. Just what he needs. More drama.

"I'm on my way," I tell her.

CHAPTER TWENTY-EIGHT

MY DAD DOESN'T want me going by myself. Which leaves only one option.

Helen.

And the Hippiemobile.

I jog in the icy air until I find her old VW. It's parked at the curb outside of Buddy's, the dive bar in the Fan district. Helen's home away from home. I call her from the curb. When she steps outside, she's swaying.

"You can't drive," she says.

"Neither can you."

"I've only had four beers."

I push her into the passenger seat, then I climb behind the wheel. Her VW bug is forty years old. I grind the gear shift into first. Turn the key. Release the clutch. The car lurches forward, threatens to stall, but rattles down to The Boulevard.

I hand Helen my cell phone. "Hit redial, on Speaker."

The phone goes right to Drew's voice mail. "Thanks to the scientific breakthrough of wireless communications, you have reached the recording component of Drew Levinson's cell phone. Please take advantage of technological progress and leave me a message that will interest me enough to call you back."

At the beep, Helen holds the phone to my mouth.

"Drew." I lick my lips. I have no spit. "Call me. Immediately."

I manage to drive us down Grove Street to St. Catherine's. Helen stays in the car, I walk around the building. Every window is black but a December moonlight presses through the clouds. The world looks as murky as muddy water. I check both bike racks. They're empty.

Questions ping around my head. *Would Drew come here?* I cup my eyes to the windows. The classrooms are empty. My mind, however, is full of bad memories.

I back away.

In the car, Helen's smoking. And tugging her parka around her body.

"Real cars," I tell her, "have heat."

"This has heat." She points her lit cigarette at the dashboard vent. Air leaks out like an old man's dying breath. "And don't take this out on me. She's your friend."

I drive the Hippiemobile to River Road and coast down the hill past the Country Club of Virginia, where exclusiveness is made even more noticeable by the delicate yellow lights dotting the pristine white building. At Huguenot Bridge, I turn left and park in the gravel lot, yanking on the emergency brake and leaving the gear in Neutral so the so-called heater can stay on. Helen stays in the car.

I walk down to the water. Black water. "Drew!"

The answer comes back. A steady rush of water.

I jog over to the trail that leads into the woods. The weird moonlight makes the bare trees look like petrified cobwebs.

"Drew! Are you here?"

My heart pounds so hard it hurts. I do not want to walk into the woods. Alone. *Maybe Helen* . . . I look over my shoulder.

And jump. "What are you doing?"

Helen bundles the parka around her. "If she wants to be alone, why bother?"

"Don't sneak up on me." I head back for the car. "And if Drew wanted to be alone, she would've stayed in her room."

"Did you check?"

"What?"

"Her room."

Fair question.

Maybe Jayne's so drunk she didn't see Drew come back from her bike ride.

The Hippiemobile rattles up River Road. And since the streets are empty, and I don't know how to work a clutch on a hill, I roll right through the red light.

"That's more like it," Helen sighs with smoke.

Jayne's car is parked in the driveway. Helen follows me into the sunroom.

"What a gorgeous cat," she says.

Perched on the loveseat he's shredded, Newton gives me a withering expression. Helen sits down beside him. "I wish we had a cat."

Jayne steps into the room from the kitchen. "Did you find her?" *Duh.*

But I keep my mouth shut. I'm hoping Jayne will stay with Helen and Newton. But this is definitely not my night.

Jayne follows me through the kitchen, and into the den, where for once the TV's not playing the cooking channel. It's the local news. She trails me up the stairs to Drew's room.

The bed is so tightly made the Marines should be jealous. Feynman grins from his poster.

"What're you looking for?" Jayne's got this voice. It usually sounds really confident. Which is why she's a high mucky-muck in public relations with Reynolds. The woman can't reheat a can of beans but she can make other women go wild about plastic turkey bags.

But now there's a weird quiver in her voice. Something I've never heard, even in the worst of times.

"Did you guys have a fight?" I ask.

"No!"

But she looks away.

"What did Drew say?"

"She was going for a bike ride."

"At night?"

"I . . ." She twists a cell phone in her hand. "I wasn't paying attention. There. I said it. Are you happy?"

No.

"Anything else I should know?"

She shakes her head. Her hair's usually coiffed. But all kinds of weird strands are sticking up, like electrified.

I scan the bedroom. Drew's stuck Post-It notes on her digital clock. And her computer monitor. The handwriting is precise. Each one reads, No Power. Another OCD thing—Drew's afraid of an electrical fire. So she unplugs things. Three cords snake across the carpet. I lean to the side and find a third Post-It, stuck to the printer. Only there's also a fourth Post-It on the printer's bottom tray. The precise handwriting reads *Copy for Raleigh.*

"She should answer her cell phone," Jayne whines. "She knows how worried I am."

I take the paper from the printer, and glance over at Jayne. There's a red wine spot soaked into her jeans.

"Did you call the police?" I ask.

She looks away again.

"You're waiting—*again?*"

"No . . ."

I take her phone, push three buttons. 9-1-1.

Then hand it back to her. "Tell them everything."

CHAPTER TWENTY-NINE

J AYNE STAMMERS INTO her phone. Half of me wants to grab it and explain the whole thing.

But my wicked half wants her to suffer.

I shuffle through the pages Drew left for me. First page shows an April date. This year. I read a couple paragraphs. Drew's marked every use of "counselor" in purple highlighter.

It's a journal.

Sloane's journal.

How did Drew—oh, I know. Mary Vale screamed at Mrs. Stillman, Drew went back to the computer. Probably emailed herself a copy of the journal.

I feel kind of sick.

Pulling out my cell phone, I walk downstairs, leaving Jayne behind, and call information. The automated voice connects me to the number. When I walk into the den, Helen's gone. I listen to the ringing phone and walk back to the den.

In the phone, I hear the deep voice of Otto. The butler. "Still-man residence."

"Is Mary Vale there?"

The pause goes on long enough that I have to ask, "Hello?"

"One moment, please."

I stare at the television. Commercials.

When Mary Vale picks up the phone, her voice hisses. "Stop calling my house."

"It's Raleigh."

"How many times do I have to tell you?"

"But I haven't call—" *Wait.* "Did Drew call you?"

"Six times!"

"Why?"

"Oh, *please.*"

"Mary Vale, seriously, I don't know." The television shows a commercial for some hard-to-find Christmas toy. A doll, some kind. "Mary Vale, I need to know. What was Drew calling you about?"

There's a long pause.

The doll cradled by a little girl. But the doll starts crying. The girl starts wiping its tears. *Who buys these things?*

"Mary Vale, are you there?"

"The counselor." Her voice is so soft, I almost miss the words.

"You mean, Sloane's counselor?"

"How many times are you going to make me say this? I didn't know my sister was seeing counselor. Okay? My family doesn't even believe in therapy."

"You told Drew this?'

"Yes! But she still kept calling. I finally told her *she* needs the counseling. I told her that woman at school is free."

"Did Drew say anything else?"

"She said our phone number adds up to a prime number."

"Oh."

"Thirty-one."

"Okay."

"Like I care."

"Mary Vale, if she calls you again, will you call me—please— right away?" I recite my cell phone number.

"Is that a prime number too?" she asks.

Her tone is so snotty, I cut off the call without saying good-bye.

HELEN APPEARS TO have a bottomless pack of cigarettes.

She's puffing away as I get into the car.

"Want one?" she asks, mistaking my fixed gaze for something else. "Calms the nerves."

I roll down my window. "Nicotine is a stimulant."

"So's sugar and caffeine, but I don't see you giving up your precious Coke."

I push in the clutch, shove the gear into First. We lurch down Westhampton Road. I roll through yellow lights, hang turns instead of stopping for red. And steal glances at my sister. "Did you ever go to the school counselor?"

"All the time."

I blink. "You're kidding."

"Hello—Mom?"

"You talked to the school counselor about Mom."

"Of course." She lets out a stream of smoke.

"What's wrong with that?"

"It's family. It's private."

"Yeah, well." She puffs. "Get through it your way, Raleigh. I'll get through it mine."

I take a left on Cary Street. The headlights carve two white columns down the empty road.

"And for your information," Helen says, "that counselor called *me* into her office first. Seventh grade. She wanted to discuss what she called 'the situation at home.'"

I don't say anything. Because I got that same request. Written on a school permission slip. "And?"

"And she let me smoke in her office."

"Wow, great therapy."

"Raleigh, you might want to consider seeing her."

"Uh-huh." I'm forced to rattle to a stop beside Windsor Farms. I can't even count how many girls from St. Cat's live there. But Drew wouldn't bike in there.

Helen stubs out her cigarette in the tiny ashtray, which is already jammed with butts. "What's it like," she asks, "without me around the house?"

"Fine."

"That bad?" Her tone. She seems to hear it too because she turns away, gazing out her side window. Maybe the beer's wearing off. "Sorry."

The light flashes green. I ease my foot off the clutch. The car pops forward, coughs, dies. "Crap."

Helen sighs. "You need to be patient."

I stomp on the clutch, turn the key, glance in the rearview mirror. Nobody's behind us. But in the opposite lane, a car's heading toward us. Probably a cop. Then I might believe in luck. Bad luck.

"Hurry," Helen says.

"I'm trying."

She shakes a fresh smoke from the endless pack. "Just let the clutch out, slowly."

"I'm trying!"

The car is right in front of us. I'm trying to time my feet on the pedals, when Helen says, "What's that?"

I only see her hand, flashing in the oncoming headlights. Pointing with the unlit cigarette. The headlights strike something on the ground. Metallic. An ornament. Christmas decoration. But it's half-buried in the ground.

The headlights swoop away.

I lean forward. Thin spokes radiate in a half-circle. Wheel.

Bike wheel.

I stomp on the gas and clutch and swerve into the first driveway. The car dies. I bolt out the door, racing down the road. Another car heads toward us. The lights brush over the side of the road. The bike's in the ditch.

I run for it. But my legs aren't working.

The purple Schwinn.

And a girl, lying in the ditch.

Drew.

CHAPTER THIRTY

THE LAST PLACE on earth I want to be.

Again.

"They must design hospitals so you're glad to leave." Helen paces the waiting room floor at Stuart Circle Hospital, outside the emergency room. "Why else spend money to make something so damn ugly?"

She looks at me, as if expecting an answer. But I've got my own unanswerable questions. And the longer they bounce around my head, the more I realize what they really are—bargains.

Save Drew, and I'll stop lying.

Helen sighs. "I need a smoke. You want anything?"

Yes. But I want it so badly that all I can do is shake my head *No*, keep my eyes fixed on this stupid vinyl chair where thousands of people have sat and sobbed and made these exact same bargains with God. And did those bargains work out?

Just the thought of that makes me drop my face into my hands. I close my eyes. They burn like I've been staring into fire. I can't get that image out of my mind, Drew lying in that ditch, blood trickling down the side of her head. I take a deep breath, tasting the oily scent on my palms. Fear and panic. Drew's right back in the hospital. Drew. The girl who wouldn't hurt a fly.

Aren't you supposed to protect her?

"Hey." Helen. I feel her body plunk down in the seat beside me. But I don't take my hands away from my face. "I called Dad, told him what's going on. He asked if you could spare me."

"What?"

"Can I go home, or do you need me here?"

"Go. I'm fine."

When there's no movement, I lower my hands. She smells like an ashtray.

"He told Mom you're spending the night with Drew."

Which is true. I'm spending the night with Drew—in the hospital because of a hit-and-run. The man never lies.

"Sure you're okay?" Helen stands up.

"Fine."

But she doesn't leave. I glance up. It's like looking at my long-lost sister from deep childhood. The nice one. The one who let me sleep in her bed whenever my insomnia kicked in. Who told me stories about our birth dad and life in North Carolina, when we were poor and rode city busses everywhere.

"Thanks," I tell her.

"Call me if you need anything."

I watch her black clogs scuff cross the shiny white floor. Her ashy scent fades, replaced by something worse. Disinfected air. I drop my face in my hands again. Every swallow hurts.

Why can't life pick on somebody else?

I hold my breath. My mind flashes with images. That bleeding head. The ambulance. I take a breath. Then another. *Do not cry.* The disinfectant smell fades. I start praying. *Help Drew. Help Jayne. Help me.* I take a deep breath. There's a new scent. Not cigarettes. Not hospital. It smells like . . . clean laundry.

I lower my hands.

DeMott Fielding sits next to me.

"How long have you been here?" I ask.

"I don't wear a watch." He takes my hand, his fingers feel warm. "But not long."

Two medics pushing an empty gurney through swinging double doors. The speaker crackles, paging Dr. Deaver.

"How did you know?" I ask.

"Your sister called." He almost smiles. "She said, 'Get your butt over there'."

Helen. I blink back the sting.

"But she didn't give me any details," he adds.

I wait until my voice is steady. Then I describe this night, start- ing with the phone call from Jayne and how we found Drew. "The back wheel of her bike's mangled. Somebody must've hit her from behind. Then just drove off. How do people live with themselves? Her head—" I start to tell him how her head was bleeding. But my throat chokes shut.

"Her helmet?"

I shake my head.

"Don't tell me." He looks horrified. "She wasn't wearing a helmet?"

I say nothing.

"That seems . . ." He chooses his words. "That seems unlike Drew."

My thought exactly. The girl who panics about germs on her phone. Why didn't she wear a helmet?

He closes his fingers over my hand.

When Jayne steps out of the swinging double doors, she looks like somebody who just walked through a wind tunnel.

"They're keeping her in a coma." Her voice sounds empty. "Safer. For the brain. They moved her upstairs." Jayne smooths a hand over her hair. "I'm going home, clean up. Will you . . .?"

But I'm already walking to the elevators.

". . . stay with her?"

THEY'VE PUT HER in a shared room. A closed curtain separates the beds. Drew's on the far side.

DeMott walks to the window, sits on the ledge.

I stand beside her bed. Plastic tubes run to her nose and mouth, connected to machines. Lights dance on the monitors. The machines beep.

"You think I don't pay attention," I tell her.

Her head's shaved, wrapped with gauze. A deep purple bruise washes down the side of her face. Blood pools in her jaw. Her thin body. It barely changes the outline of the white sheet and blanket.

"But I pay attention. I hear everything you say. Like how Richard P. Feynman said he didn't understand physics."

I wipe my nose.

"He said nobody does. So you better wake up, Drew. Somebody's got to explain this stuff."

My throat aches.

"And I pay attention when you recite Newton's three laws of motion. I know you don't believe me. But one. An object remains at rest unless acted upon by an external . . ."

Force.

I can't say the word. Right now physics is too real. Drew. And the force that acted upon her. That put her back in the hospital. Hooked up to machines. Lost to some internal landscape so far, far away that her expression looks blank. Like she's no longer a genius.

I take her hand. The fingers are limp.

"Richard P. Feynman also said religion is a culture of faith. Science is a culture of doubt. So. There. We have to balance each other."

The machine beeps.

Steady, regular. Inhuman.

"I didn't want to tell you this part. But Feynman said physics wasn't the most important thing."

Beep.

"He did. I was saving this, until you were ready to hear it."

Beep.

"Feyman said the most important thing is *love.*"

Beep.

Beep.

Beep.

I recite everything she's ever told me. All that theoretical knowledge I still don't understand. Foucalt's pendulum and

Fibonacci's sequence. That weird String Theory.

When Jayne finally comes into the room, my throat is dry. Her brown eyes are shiny. Like polished stones.

DeMott stands.

I forgot he was here.

Jayne sways. "Thank you, Raleigh." She adds four Rs to my name. "You can go now."

I pick up the pen and paper next to the room's phone, and write down my cell number. Hand it to Jayne. The alcohol on her breath smells worse than the hospital's disinfectant.

"Call me," I said. "The second she wakes up."

CHAPTER THIRTY-ONE

NEED AIR, fresh air.

DeMott follows me outside.

Standing on the sidewalk outside the hospital, I pull in the cold winter air and stare at the statue across from us on Monument Avenue. Cavalry hero JEB Stuart glances over his shoulder, wielding a sword.

"How about we take a drive?" DeMott asks.

His truck navigates through the Fan's narrow streets. Christmas lights gleam from the row houses, brighter than ever, like there's some sudden surge of electricity this close to the high holy day.

When he crosses into Oregon Hill, I feel an odd calm. The simple satisfaction that someone sits next to me, who doesn't feel the need to speak or fill the painful silence with empty words. I take another deep breath and catch that good scent of him. Clean and clear.

"Can I show you something?" he asks.

Ten minutes later, he stops at a grand iron gate. Two words arch over the entrance: Hollywood Cemetery.

The parking area is empty. Who visits a graveyard in the middle of the night?

DeMott, that's who.

He gets out of the truck, walks around the front, and opens my door.

I want to stay in the truck. Drive until dawn cracks open the night sky. Find Drew awake and everyone celebrating Christmas

Eve—especially my genius Jewish friend.

But he opens his arms. "Come here."

I get out. He closes his arms around me. His breath is silver in the night air.

"Closer," he says.

My hands are stuffed into the pockets of my jacket, even as my whole body sinks into his. I breathe in, drinking in his comfort, and lean my face into his shoulder.

He whispers. "I knew it."

"Knew what?"

"We fit."

I want to nod but I'm afraid to even breathe, afraid to break this spell. He smells of clean laundry and winter and night and Boy. A feeling explodes inside my chest.

He shifts his arm, draping it over my shoulder. "Let's walk."

I count our steps, the beats of my heart, and wonder if this is why Drew counts. To steady herself. To create order when everything feels like chaos.

We cross through the cemetery under that murky moonlight. The gravestones look gray, faded. DeMott turns his head, kisses my forehead. The softest kiss of my entire life.

I tilt my head, looking up at him. "Thank you."

"You're welcome. It's a strange Christmas," he says. "But it's still Christmas."

We walk toward a knoll. At the top, DeMott steps back and takes my hand.

"What do you see, Raleigh?"

Down below, the James River runs like a channel of tarnished silver between charcoal hills.

But DeMott's looking the other way. At the cemetery.

I turn. Rows of marble headstones and white crypts. Gray granite markers that in this light look blue as slate. An iron trellis arches over the plot of President Madison.

"I see dead people."

He doesn't even crack a smile.

"DeMott, what am I supposed to see?"

"Look." He points at the ground.

I step away, letting go of his hand. This strange light, everything looks ghostly.

"See it?" he asks.

The soil curves upward. Fresh soil. About six feet long, three feet wide. The brass name plate gleams in the moonlight.

STILLMAN.

I turn away."

"Raleigh, look at it."

"No."

"Look."

"*Why?*"

"Because. We're all going to die."

"Wow, DeMott. Way to kill a moment."

"Listen to me." He grabs my hand, pulling me toward Sloane's grave. "Don't you see? It can all end tomorrow. Or even tonight."

"This just gets better and better."

He wraps his arms around me again. But I don't lean into him.

"When they buried her, I stood right here. Her mother's face was nothing but agony. And Mary Vale? She cried so hard she collapsed. That family's been shattered. Destroyed. And you and Drew, you're making it worse."

"You're wrong."

"No, Raleigh. You are."

I push away, heading back down the knoll.

"Raleigh." His voice slips through the night, comes up behind me. "You can stop all this now."

"Oh." I turn on him. "Since Drew's in a coma? Let's just pretend nothing weird happened to Sloane?"

He says nothing.

I start walking.

"Life is too short," he says. "Don't make it harder than it has to be."

The frosted grass crunches under my feet.

"Raleigh?"

I keep going. A rushing sound fills my ears, like the river was right here beside me.

He grabs my arm.

I yank it away. "You don't know."

"I don't need to know. I was here. If you'd seen them put her in the ground—"

"Sloane didn't kill herself."

His eyes look gray, like ash. "You don't know that."

"Yeah, I do." I want to tell him—spill all the sad and confusing details. Tell him how Drew's physics now make sense. How Sloane was probably having an affair with a teacher and got pregnant. How she wouldn't kill her own baby.

But none of that would change his mind.

DeMott wants Sloane to rest in peace.

And that's the problem.

Until we know the truth, she'll never rest in peace.

CHAPTER THIRTY-TWO

H E PULLS UP to the curb outside the hospital, but makes no move to get out and open my door.

I step out. Lights glare over the hospital entrance.

"You should go home," he says. "Get some sleep."

"Will do." *Not happening.* Walking into my house right now would rocket my mother's paranoia into orbit. "Thanks for coming all the way down here."

I close the door.

But I don't move. And he doesn't drive away. We just stare at each other.

He lowers the window. "If you can get away for a little while tonight, we're having a party."

"Another one?"

He sort of smiles. "Close friends only. We do this every Christmas Eve."

Christmas Eve. I glance at my watch. 12:09 a.m. Tomorrow is Christmas.

"You can bring your whole family," he says.

"I don't know if . . ."

"It's casual," he adds. "Nothing fancy."

"I'll think about it."

I turn away.

"Either way," he calls out, "will you let me know how Drew's doing?"

When I look back, his eyes hook me. That blue, it's gemstone quality. I tell myself Teddy's right, this relationship will never work. He should leave, never come back. But he's waiting for me to say something. Anything. And all I want to say is, *Can I get back in the truck?* Hit reverse, go back in time to where your arm was around me, and we fit, before either one of us said things we both regret? Instead of me walking back into this stinking hospital to see half-dead Drew and her drunken mother and my own sorry state?

I say none of it.

He frowns. "Okay. See you around."

The window goes up.

I lift my hand weakly, but I don't know if he sees it.

IN THE WAITING area, Jayne's talking to a cop. And chewing gum—hard—probably to cover the alcohol fumes. I move across the shiny vinyl, trying to get close enough to eavesdrop. Jayne doesn't always tell the whole truth and nothing but the truth.

I'm trying to stay invisible, but the cop turns toward me.

Officer Lande.

I haven't seen her since October, and her face surprises me all over again. She's got these sharp cheekbones carved above a hard jaw, her chin almost pointed. She sees me alright, but her cat-tilted eyes shift right back to Jayne, all without ever moving her head. Cops. They know how to do this stuff.

"—worried sick about it." Jayne is talking fast-fast-fast. "I asked, I did. I asked. She wouldn't tell me, I asked who, she said it was about school, something about school, she had to go now. Couldn't wait."

"And you don't know who she was going to see?" asks Officer Lande.

"I do not."

"But I do."

They both look at me.

"The school counselor." I tell them—well, I tell Officer Lande, because I'm not really talking to Jayne—about Sloane's journal. How Drew was reading it and highlighted the word *counselor* over and over. But then I have to back up and explain because Jayne has no idea what's going on at St. Cat's. Typical. But then, being Jayne, she butts in. Like she knows.

"She had all this paper," she tells Officer Lande. "A whole stack of paper."

"Who?" Officer Lande asks.

"My daughter! Are you listening? She put the papers in a big envelope. I followed her outside. I just. I just. I just—"

"Alright, Ms. Levinson. Drew had some papers?"

"She put the envelope in her bike basket." Jayne looks pointedly at me. "Then she put a *rock* on top."

Like somehow the rock makes everything my fault.

"Anything else?" asks Officer Lande.

"I offered to drive her. I did. But she wouldn't let me. Because—because—"

Because you're drunk.

"It's alright, Ms. Levinson, continue."

"We've been working on things. Really." Jayne's eyes shine like brown glass. "And she has a light on her bike. Two lights. Front and back."

Officer Lande writes that part in her little notebook. Then turns to me. "Do you know the school counselor?"

"Her name's Collingworth." I know because she sent me that *come talk to me* note Helen got, too. "Bettina Collingworth."

Officer Lande reaches up and taps the small radio clipped to the shoulder. She asks the dispatcher to put her through to Holmgren. That would be Detective Holmgren. When his deep voice cracks through the radio, Officer Lande tells him to look up Bettina Collingworth. "Currently employed as a school counselor at St. Catherine's School."

"St. Cathinerine's?" Holmgren replies.

"And I'm standing here with Raleigh Harmon." She glances over at gum-chewing Jayne. "And Drew Levinson's mother."

Radio silence.

Then Holmgren says he'll get back to her.

Officer Lande asks Jayne some more questions, about how Drew's been lately, if she's getting along with her parents. I'm about to interrupt because if Jayne's out here, and I'm out there, then nobody's with Drew. But just as I'm about to say that, Drew's dad comes out of the double doors.

In the rest of Richmond, winter is here. But Rusty Levinson wears flip-flops and cargo shorts. His T-shirt is spattered with paint and clay.

He halts when he sees Officer Lande.

"Mr. Levinson," Officer Lande says. "I'm very sorry."

Rusty tugs on his dark hair. His fingertips leave behind white flakes of plaster. "Let me guess." His lips tighten around each word. "You cops can't find the monster who did this to my daughter."

"We're doing our best. Drew's bike has been taken into evidence and forensics is looking at it." Officer Lande's words sail over Rusty's head. She turns to me. "Anything you want to share?"

I shake my head.

And Rusty's already diverting attention by launching missiles at Jayne. Jayne's a total drunk but Rusty's a total dope-head. And even I know misdemeanor possession for pot could land him in jail for thirty days. So he shines the spotlight on his ex-wife. "Why would you let her ride her bike in the dark?" he asks.

"Don't you dare start—"

"And no helmet? You're supposed to be her *mother*."

"And you're supposed to be her father. Stop telling her to break the rules!"

"This is different, Jayne. We're talking life and death."

"She's *fourteen*, which you would know if you ever remembered her birthday!"

"Have another drink, Jayne."

Jayne blinks. Tears spring into her eyes.

I look at Officer Lande. Her feet are spread wide, doing that detached cop thing where they seem like they don't care but actually they're preparing for someone to take the first swing. So I've got to ask now or forever hold my hypothesis.

I step closer. Her eyes shift toward me.

"Did you guys take the envelope?" I ask.

"What envelope?"

"Drew put an envelope in her bike basket." I look at Jayne, confirming. "Right?"

She nods.

Officer Lande taps the radio again. Holmgren comes on. No-body's shown him any inventory on evidence, he says. "But I've got an address for Collingworth."

Officer Lande writes down the address, her pale eyes flicking to the big clock on the hospital wall.

"*Now*," I tell her. "I don't care what time it is, we're going. Now."

"We?" she says.

CHAPTER THIRTY-THREE

RIDING SHOTGUN IN a police cruiser is definitely better than riding in the back seat. Which is where I usually ride in Officer Lande's cruiser. But the back seat's laminated in hard black plastic, smells nasty, and feels haunted.

"You know this counselor personally?" Officer Lande asks, as we drive over the Powhite Parkway on Cary Street.

"Sorta."

"Sorta, how?"

"Sorta like she wanted me to come see her but I didn't."

"You didn't go."

With Officer Lande, there's no use bluffing. Check out her face—those angles tell you she's not the warm fuzzy type. "Factually speaking, I once walked past her office."

"So you knew her address when I asked Holmgren for it?" She looks over. Her face almost softens. Almost.

"I thought he should look her up."

She thinks about that. "Did the counselor want to talk to you about what happened to Drew?"

I shake my head.

"Your mom?"

I nod.

"So why didn't you talk to her?"

I wait to answer. First, because the police cruiser is pulling into the counselor's driveway off Cary Street. And second, because all those years sitting in my dad's courtroom have taught me how certain statements can have a prejudicial effect on a jury.

So all I say is, "You'll see."

Officer Lande taps her shoulder radio to give the dispatcher her location. We get out and walk toward the blah-beige Craftsman. It's only a half mile from where Drew got hit. I head around the side of the house, where the counselor keeps a private entrance for clients.

"Watch your step," I say.

Tree roots push against the concrete walkway, cracking the surface. When I was checking out this place, all those fractures and fissures and fault lines seemed like really disturbing metaphors for what would happen inside the counselor's office. *No thanks.*

It is 1:17 a.m. on Christmas Eve when Officer Lande knocks on the door. The leaded glass at the top of the door is black as the night. Officer Lande knocks again. Then a voice on the other side asks, "What is it?"

What.

Not *Who.*

"Richmond police, ma'am. I need to ask you a few questions."

A light flashes inside. The counselor's head pops up. She has a shiny moon of a face. She cracks the door, staring over the chain, looking at Officer Lande. Then me.

"Bettina Collingworth?" Officer Lande asks.

"Yes." She squints at me. "Do I know you?"

Which is exactly why I never came to see her. I look at Officer Lande.

"Ma'am, could we speak inside?"

She lets us into the foyer. A skateboard sits next to a pair of black Nike high tops. The day I walked past here, a boy with eyes rimmed in black liner, his hair cut into ragged tufts, went in without knocking.

The counselor gestures toward some chairs in a small sitting area, just past the foyer. The chairs are in a triangle formation, facing each other like group counseling. I look around at the paintings of artistic confusion. Officer Lande flips open her notebook and gets right to the point.

"Did you see a girl named Drew Levinson this evening?"

"Drew Levinson." The counselor clutches the collar of her pajamas. "That's what this is about?"

Officer Lande says nothing.

"We spoke by telephone."

"Drew Levinson called you?"

"She asked to speak to me in person. And I made myself available. But she never showed." Bettina glances at me. "I figured she changed her mind."

Like me spurning her attempts to *reach out.*

"Ma'am, did Drew tell you what she wanted to talk to you about?"

"That's confidential."

Officer Lande clears her throat then informs Bettina that Drew's been in a hit-and-run accident. How she's in a coma at Stuart Circle Hospital. "We need to find out who struck her and at what time."

The counselor's hand climbs to her mouth. Not that I need another reason never to come here but I get one: her eyes show zero emotion. Maybe that works for Helen, but it looks to me like a trap.

"Anything you can offer will help," says Officer Lande.

Bettina nods. But still says nothing.

"Have you personally interacted with Drew before tonight?"

"I've reached out to her, for quite some time," she says. "That's why I rearranged my night when she called. To accommodate her needs. I dropped everything. I had a Christmas party to go to."

Okay, another reason: like she's doing us poor psychological slobs a big favor.

"So you were reaching out to Drew for some time. Because of what happened to her recently?"

"Yes. I read about the tragedy in the paper, of course. But the school asked me, as well. Drew, it appears to me, is suffering from post-traumatic stress disorder. Anyone would, after what she went through. But the PTSD is compounded," she looks at me, "because Drew's in denial."

Final reason: denial. These people call everything denial. And what are you going to do, deny it?

"Tell me about her phone call to you."

Collingworth sits back, gives the pajamas another tug. "She told me it was an emergency."

"She used that word, 'emergency'?"

"No, actually. She said, 'urgent.' She was quite passionate. So I called off my prior engagement and waited. But she never showed up."

"Did you try to find out why she didn't come?"

Collingworth takes a moment. "My reputation with these young people rests on their knowing I will not inform their parents."

"Ever?"

"Officer, that's my right."

"Unless they're in danger to themselves or others." Officer Lande lets the silence stretch out. "And Drew *is* in danger now."

The silence stretches. On and on.

And on. Nothing like a show-down between a cop and a coun-selor. Both keep silence in their tool boxes.

Collingsworth finally concedes. "You're sure it was hit-and-run?"

"Why do you ask?"

"Because Drew Levinson is a suicide risk."

"What!" I jump up. "You're nuts!"

"We don't use that word," she says, calmly.

Officer Lande gently pulls me down into my chair. She tells the counselor, "Please go on."

"I could hear it in Drew's voice. She was experiencing a severe manic episode. With traumatic disorders, mania often precedes a suicide attempt. Particularly in teenagers."

I hate this woman. "You don't know what you're talking

181

about."

But Officer Lande actually writes down this crap. Without looking up from her notebook she asks, "If she's a suicide risk, don't you think you should've called someone when she didn't show up?"

I want to smile.

Collingworth's round eyes focus on the notebook. "I should add, Drew asked me some questions about another girl. A classmate who recently committed suicide. Drew wanted details. Clearly, a cry for help. And clearly, I didn't take that cry seriously enough."

I stand up again. "Can I use the bathroom?"

Collingsworth evaluates me, like she's trying to measure my bladder. "It's down the hall, on the right."

Socket night lights make the rooms glow. I pass a dining room full of that Stickley furniture that says *sit up and behave*. Four chairs. At the end of the hall I can see a kitchen. On my right is the bathroom. But there's a room next to it with an open door. I glance over my shoulder. They're still talking.

I slide down the hall.

The room holds more of that Stickley furniture but also a couch. *Lie down and tell me all your problems in one hour.* I step over to the desk where a nightlight shines up from the wall. The desk top is covered with glass. Photographs are under the glass. I bend down. I see that kid with the ragged hair. And one of Collingworth herself wearing a black graduation cap-and-gown and sunglasses. Also a group photo with some women her age. And then.

Hold it.

I lean in so close my nose almost touches the glass. It's him.

Michael Turner.

Behind him, a sandy beach stretches out. He holds a lobster by its tail.

I move back into the hallway, step into the bathroom, and flush the toilet.

When I return to them, Collingworth is giving Officer Lande her background, something about her style of therapy. But Officer Lande looks up at me. Her face seems different.

"Raleigh," she asks, "did you know why Drew was interested in Sloane Stillman?"

"Yes." I look at Collingworth. "Drew found Sloane's journal. She wrote about her counselor. A lot. Before she died."

Collingworth's round eyes harden into stones.

Officer Lande asks her, "Were there any signs? Any indications that Sloane was a suicide risk?"

The silence returns. "St. Catherine's asked me to contact Sloane."

"When?"

"The beginning of the school year."

"Why?"

"Sloane's grades were falling. She'd been a straight-A student since elementary school. But she began getting Cs and Ds. She refused to discuss it with her teachers."

Like hearing about the antidepressants. I'm stunned Sloane ever sank below an A. But I'm tempted to ask, *What grade did Mr. Turner give her?*

But that question feels dangerous right now.

"When a student changes suddenly, it's standard procedure for the school to contact me. Of course, any number of factors contribute to poor grades." She pauses. "In Sloane's case, she explained that she was granted early admission to Harvard. As long as she maintained a C average, Harvard would hold her spot."

"So you spoke with her?"

"Yes."

"And you suspected nothing, no suicidal tendencies?"

The stones return to her eyes. "Sloane Stillman appeared calm, intelligent. Rational. Her reason for the falling grades made perfect sense. She had achieved her goal. Why work harder than necessary?"

"And then she . . ." Officer Lande holds the pause, "she just kills herself?"

Collingworth sits back in her chair and clasps her hands. "If there are no further questions, officer, I think that's all the time I have for you."

CHAPTER THIRTY-FOUR

DRIVING AWAY FROM the counselor's house, Officer Lande radios the dispatcher.

"Heading downtown." She cuts the radio and looks over at me. "I'll take you back to the hospital."

"Actually, can you drop me off at Drew's house?" I bite the inside of my lip. "Her cat. He needs food."

"Sure," she says. "Run in and feed him, I'll wait."

I stare out the window. Her cruiser's passing the little shops of Carytown. the street twinkling like a Christmas village. Every inch of Richmond, poised for the big day. When I glance over at Officer Lande, she seems lost in thought.

"I don't want to go back to the hospital right now," I tell her. "And I can't go home because my dad told my mom I was spending the night with Drew."

"At the hospital?"

"Not that part."

In one smooth motion, with her palm flattened to the steering wheel, she takes one of those cop U-turns. The car doesn't even seem to slow down but all of a sudden we're heading west.

"The truth suits you, Raleigh. Don't give up on it."

Her dashboard glows with electronics. Her gray eyes look like smoky pearls.

"Your mom okay?" she asks, turning into Drew's dark driveway.

"My mom's crazy." The truth. "Like, literally. Like, beyond

that counselor's help."

She puts the cruiser in Park. "But you're not in any danger?"

A number of replies come to mind. *What kind of danger?* The CIA bugged our water faucets. Our mail is full of poisons planted by the FBI. I am somebody named Ray.

Officer Lande's pearl-gray eyes demand the truth. But I don't have time.

"I think you need to run a background check on somebody."

She nods. "The counselor."

"Yeah. But there's a teacher at our school, Michael Turner. I'm pretty sure he was having an affair with Sloane Stillman."

Her head pulls back. "You're *pretty sure*? Or you know this?"

"Sloane was pregnant." I let that sink in. "I know Virginia law says statutory rape only applies to age fifteen and under. But, it's wrong. If he's the father."

The cop-silence fogs up the windshield.

So I tell her the whole long tale of Drew's weird idea about Sloane not committing suicide. How it morphed into something plausible after Mrs. Stillman showed up at my dad's office. And how Mr. Turner was crying in the science library. "And now this counselor, she has a picture of Mr. Turner in her office."

"Hold it." She lifts both hands. "Her office—at school?"

"You heard her yourself. She gave me permission to enter the premises."

"Raleigh—"

"I did not violate her rights for search and seizure."

"What did you—"

"She gave us permission to enter the premises. That means, by law, anything within sight is reasonable grounds for evidence."

"Raleigh." She sighs. "Please tell me this photo was in her bathroom."

"But I didn't know where her bathroom was. Remember?"

She gazes out the windshield, her face sculpted from stone. When she taps the radio, she asks for Holmgren. She asks him for a background check on Michael Turner. "He's a teacher at St.

Catherine's School."

"Not that school again." Holmgren sounds angry. "It's Christmas Eve. Any background check can wait until after the holiday."

I touch her arm. "Remind him that NCIC is open every day of the year. Christmas Eve, too."

Officer Lande taps the radio again. "Holmy." Her eyes almost crinkle with her smile. "Raleigh wanted to remind you that the NCIC is always open. Including holidays."

The National Crime Information Center. It's a computerized database of criminal justice records. Everything from stolen property and fugitives to past arrest records.

I touch her arm again but she holds the radio to my mouth. "And it's open twenty-four hours a day," I say.

"Holmy," she says into the radio. "You got that?"

There's a crackling silence.

When Holmgren comes on again, he sounds even more angry. "The name 'Michael Turner' doesn't exactly narrow things down."

Hundreds, maybe thousands of guys named Michael Turners could be in that database. So I give Holmgren an approximate age, height, and weight for Mr. Turner, along with how long he's been a teacher at St. Cat's.

Officer Lande tells him she needs the info ASAP, then cuts the radio.

When she looks out at Drew's house, she frowns. "Sure you're alright in there?"

"I'm fine."

She waits as I dig the key out from under the stone tortoise, unlock the door, and step inside. She flashes her headlights, acknowledging my wave, and drives away. Part of me wants to run after her cruiser, ask if I can stay with her all night. Until this nightmare is over.

But that's not helping Drew.

In the pitch-black sunroom, there's no hiss from Sir Isaac Newton. So I walk into the kitchen. Jayne's left a light on and Newton lays on the floor beside his food bowl. Lifting his Siamese head, he gives me this pitiful look. Then, to emphasize his point, he gets up and dips his face into the empty bowl, licking the plastic with his rough tongue. A sound like sandpaper. But I don't move.

Something feels wrong here. The heat breezes through the floor vents. The cuckoo clock clicks out the seconds. And by the sink, a wine bottle stands, red droplets smearing the label like blood. Still another bottle lays inside the stainless steel sink. I glance up at the cuckoo clock. Almost 2:00 a.m.

I walk over to the phone, hit redial.

"Stuart Circle Hospital," a woman's voice answers.

At least Jayne called while she was here.

"I wanted to check on a patient. Drew Levinson. Can you tell me if she's awake?"

"We can't give out—"

"I'm family. I just need to know if she's awake."

The woman puts me on hold. Newton minces over. When the woman comes back on the line, all she'll say is that Drew is not awake.

I hang up and look down. Newton is winding his taupe body around my ankles, back and forth, making the sign of infinity.

Drew's favorite symbol.

"I agree, Newton. This night feels endless."

I grab a can of Fancy Feast from the cupboard, pop the aluminum top, and scoop the food into the bowl. Newton scarfs it down.

When my cell phone rings, I check the number. No Identification Available. Maybe Drew woke up.

"Hello?"

"Hi, Raleigh." Officer Lande. "Everything okay?"

"Just feeding the cat."

"Good. I wanted to let you know. Detective Holmgren got a hit. There's a Michael Turner who was relieved of duty at a private girl's school in Louisiana. Same Michael Turner is now living in Richmond."

" 'Relieved of duty.' For what?"

"Doesn't say. But there is a paternity suit, outstanding. Never settled."

Newton licks his whiskers and stares into my eyes like he can hypnotize me into opening another can of Fancy Feast. "But wouldn't St. Cat's have done a background check on him?"

"People get around those things. You know that. And the paternity suit charges might've gone into the system after he was hired. So unless your school renews its background checks every year, they might never know."

And why do another background check on Michael Turner? He's a fantastic teacher. His star student got into Harvard, early admission.

"Tell Detective Holmgren thanks."

"Will do. But he said to tell you not to bug him. He's already checking on any outstanding child support." She pauses. "Sure you're alright?"

"I'm fine."

"Call me if you need anything, Raleigh."

"Thanks."

I put the phone in my pocket and look at the cat.

"Ready?"

Newton follows me upstairs.

CHAPTER THIRTY-FIVE

S ITTING ON DREW'S bed beneath the grinning Feynman, I read through the copy of Sloane's journal.

And feel queasy.

Maybe DeMott's right. Because reading Sloane's thoughts feels like I've exhumed her body from Hollywood Cemetery.

No. Worse than that.

I'm digging up her soul.

She wrote tons of stuff about her biology experiments. Three pages describe that sheep from the science fair, all about the miscarriage. The biological details turn my stomach. The summer entries talk about how glad she is to work all day with Turner. How much she learns from him. How "special" he is. But the affair itself isn't detailed here. Maybe Sloane was worried people would find out.

Drew's purple highlighter marks all entries about "my counselor."

But again, no details. No name for the counselor.

But the entries change in the fall. Darker. Even grim. On October 31, Sloane writes bitterly about costumes and masks and why people enjoy this "profane holiday for the dead."

Drew's purple highlighter shows up again, on the entry for November 15.

Against all that is healthy and normal, we are going to the
Bahamas for Christmas. Mother refuses to listen to my

argument. Beach vacations are an expensive method for a temporary frontal lobotomy. We do nothing at the beach but sit in the sun, burn our skin cells, risk later melanoma, before showering and shuffling to some boring high-priced dinner where mother will sip umbrella drinks so she can sleep for twelve hours. And the next day and the next and the next: we only repeat the entire ignoble routine. Kill me now.

But Mother is a medicated robot. She seems determined to feel nothing.

"A nice change of scenery," she says, in that voice that tells me she's taken a double dose of the prescription.

Poor Mother. Stuck in a tragedy of her own devising.

And a boring one at that.

At least Peery Fielding is lively.

Peery Fielding.

DeMott's mother.

Did Drew highlight this section because of the connection to DeMott? I don't see the importance. Unless it's for the statement "kill me now."

I read through more pages. Drew highlighted some short passages about the Cherrymobile. A mechanic said the engine was not running right. Sloane seems really bothered about it.

I even talked to the counselor about it. Knows everything about old cars. Says I'm far too attached to this 'sentimental object.' That it is not healthy. Typical response.

Collingworth. She would say something like that. Just to say something.

The next section Drew highlighted comes just before Thanksgiving.

> Harvard letter arrived. I got in. Blissful. That's how I felt. Mary Vale said, "Dad would be really proud."
>
> Then we cried.
>
> But today I realized something I've only read about in French literature. A _frisson_. I felt it during the Thanksgiving party at Weyanoke. Mother and Peery were talking, quite animated on Peery's part. But suddenly neither one was speaking to the other. Definite _frisson_ at the Thanksgiving table.
>
> On the ride home, I asked Mother what happened. She wouldn't tell me. Confirming said _frisson_.
>
> But I'm fairly certain she must have mentioned the counselor, and Peery reacted. Peery disapproves. And mother, having imbibed three glasses of Cristal champagne, combined with the prescription meds, probably said something to the effect of, "It's none of your business."
>
> If true, then the secret is out.
>
> Counselor is now public knowledge.

I look up, staring into Feynman's face without really seeing him.

Bettina Collingworth.

She made it sound like she barely saw Sloane.

So either she's lying, or Sloane had a different counselor.

I flip back through the pages, searching. But Sloane mostly wrote about Harvard, how she worried she wouldn't get in, and about leaving Mary Vale. Sloane was a really good older sister, unlike someone else I know.

When Newton leaps onto the bed, he walks past me and settles into a tight feline circle. Then digs his claws into the purple comforter.

"Right."

I read again the sections Drew highlighted, where Sloane mentions Mary Vale. Referred to as MV.

> December 1
>
> Feeling so protective of MV. Mother's abdicated her maternal role, Dad's never coming back. So I'm MV's real parent. But I don't want to ruin life for her.
>
> I am considering deferring my admission to Harvard. Would they let me take off a year? Two? I could enroll in some classes at VCU, continue my studies.

VCU.

Virginia Commonwealth University, here in Richmond.

> Then I could stay home until MV graduates from St. Cat's. With tutoring and diligence, we could get her grades up, so she could go to Harvard with me. Or bring MV with me to Harvard next year, find her a private school in Massachusetts. There's enough money in the trust fund. I wouldn't have to leave her here alone.

The next day, she writes:

> I told MV my idea about moving to Massachusetts. She laughed.
>
> "I am never leaving Richmond," she said.
>
> I wanted to scream at her. "Get out while you can! Before you get destroyed!"
>
> But that would only scare her. And that's my job. I am scared so MV doesn't have to be. I'm the chemical buffer element in this experiment in dark deception.
>
> Speaking of, counselor's planning to see me again.

Very soon I know.

Kill me now.

I yell at the page, "Who is your counselor?!"

Newton opens one eye.

I rifle through the pages. Teachers. Students. Even famous biologists are mentioned. Her mother, Mary Vale, Michael Turner. The mechanic who works on the Cherrymobile.

But Sloane never names the counselor.

Why not?

What is the big deal about Bettina Collingworth?

I get it, Sloane was ashamed about the counseling. She's disgusted by her mother's drug dependency.

So was it about taking the antidepressants? Is that what bothered her? I can understand. She doesn't want to be like her mother. That's my fear, too.

I read over the final entries.

November 27

I convinced Mary Vale to join the drama club. She says she's too shy. But I am insisting. Long rehearsals, keep her busy, away from this house.

Then Drew highlighted this section:

December 15

MV "thrilled" about the news.

How do I tell her the rest of it?

The rest of what—the pregnancy?

But that doesn't make sense. Mary Vale wouldn't be "thrilled" about that news.

The last entry:

Mother taking MV to New York. The Plaza, of course. The whole Eloise experience. Happy for MV, even though she's much too old for this kind of thing. So am I. But I would go. I am afraid here, left behind.

And then she died.

I look over at Newton, sound asleep. I stand, shaking sleep from my legs.

What did Drew see in those sections with the counselor? Collingworth isn't named. But Drew called her.

And something made her jump on her bike, at night, in such a hurry she forgot her helmet.

Collingworth said Drew used the word "urgent."

And what if Drew wakes up and can't remember why she highlighted these sections?

I stare out her window. The sky is leaking that pre-dawn gray-blue, the color that always sends a wave of fatigue over me after a sleepless night. My perverse Pavlovian response to insomnia. Darkness makes me anxious and dawn makes me sleepy. Sometimes it feels like my brain tells my body, You made it through the night, now you can sleep—when everyone else is getting up.

I lean my forehead against the window. My mind drifts back to Sloane's bedroom. Her computer. That stench from the cat box. Kitty litter and clay. And then my thoughts jump to Drew's dad. Sculptor. And Charlie Judisch wants to start a business selling diatomaceous earth to artists.

My eyes open. I reach into my pocket and find the business card in my back pocket. *Play with Clay.* The clay, he said, could form into any shape. Any shape at all.

I glance out the window. Dawn's here. I can see through the trees to Westhampton Road, where it stretches to Cary Street. Where a car hit Drew. The picture comes back with nauseating detail. Her bike. The road. That soft gravel shoulder she disappeared from.

The clay can be shaped into anything. Anything at all.

I walk over to the purple Princess phone. Drew's digital clock reads 6:12 a.m. She probably synchronized it with Greenwich mean time.

I dial the number on the card. A sleepy voice says, "uhl-lo?"

"Charlie?"

"Uhmm. Who's this?"

"Raleigh."

No response.

"Raleigh Harmon. I met you yesterday. At your quarry. I wanted to know about diatomaceous earth?"

"Hey, hi!" His voice is suddenly bright as sunshine. "Hey. Wow. But, like, it's—kinda early?"

"I just found your card."

"Oh." Pause. "Okay? But you couldn't wait until reasonable daylight hours."

"Right. It has to do with your clay."

"Our clay!" Puppy boy runs back. "What about our clay?"

"You said it could be shaped into anything. Right?"

"Anything!"

"Are you old enough to drive?"

There's a moment's silence.

"Depends on who you ask."

Good answer. "I just was wondering if you could bring me some of that sculpting clay."

"Like . . . now?"

"Yes," I tell him. "I also need some water and a clean kitty litter box."

"*Now?*" he repeats.

"Right now."

CHAPTER THIRTY-SIX

D REW ONCE EXPLAINED to me how neutron bombs work. How the explosion kills people but leaves all the buildings standing. It has to do with the thermonuclear reactions that send out murderous amounts of radiation in only a minimal explosive blast.

Physics is deadly.

And as I run down Westhampton Road at dawn on Christmas Eve, after a night of not sleeping, the world looks like one of those neutron bombs went off.

No people, anywhere. Houses and parked cars and bare winter trees encased in frost are here. And above me, ominous gray clouds hanging like funeral veils.

I keep running. My legs protest every step. And my jeans aren't exactly track gear. But when my mind finally shuts off, my breath and feet fall into the pace of my swinging arms. Effortless, weightless. Peace.

I'm rounding the corner to Grove Avenue when a high pitched whine shatters the still morning air.

It sounds like a real neutron bomb falling out of the sky.

But it's car coming down the road.

No. A Jeep. Camouflage green. With a gold star on the hood. And half a windshield that barely covers the driver's face.

Charlie Judisch.

He stops in front of me and lifts the goggles he's wearing. They match his leather aviator's cap and white silk scarf. The

World War I flying ace.

"Hop in," he says.

Literally, because this Jeep has no doors. Or front license plate. Which is a Class 2 misdemeanor. "Is this thing legal?"

"Depends on who you ask." He grins and puts the goggles back on. "You'll want to wear these." He reaches down to the floor, and offers me a hat and goggles like his. "When I say this is a cool ride, I mean it."

I hop in. The passenger seat feels hard as a wooden church pew. I yank on the cap, goggles, and turn to him. "Okay?"

"Okay!" His grin spreads. The puppy who gets into mischief.

He roars the jeep down the road. I give him directions.

"Roger that!" he says.

The roads are so empty, the houses so dark, that the jeep's engine noise seems even louder. But it gets weirder when Charlie starts singing. "Over hill, over dell—" at the top of his lungs—"we will hit the dusty trail—" raising one arm, waving at the gated estates on Cary Street "—up and down, in and out! Countermarch and right about!"

The Jeep chews up the road like General Patton on the battle-field. It's all too weird. Too much like a dream that ends with me waking up—and wondering how my subconscious ever came up with *that*.

But it's real. Happening. Now.

And as he sings, something rises inside me. Maybe it's the diesel fumes seeping through the floorboard. Or the hard seat pounding my hips. But as he waves at another brick-walled estate, I lean forward, face in my hands. Am I laughing, or crying?

"Hey," he says. "Where are we going?"

I look over the half windshield. We are right where Drew got hit. "Pull into that driveway."

"Roger, driveway!"

It's the same driveway the ambulance used last night. Beside it, a small vinyl-sided rambler, curtains drawn. I reach over, turn off the jeep's engine. "I don't want to wake anyone."

Charlie whispers, "Is this where you live?"

I shake my head, point over my shoulder. "The road. That's why we're here."

He lifts his goggles, squints at the road.

"That's why I need the clay," I explain. "I'm going to make an impression."

"Raleigh." He grins. "You *already* made an impression."

That wandering eye. That sweet attitude. Charlie Judisch makes life seem totally playful.

And totally unlike my life.

"Can I see the clay?"

"Yes!" He hops out. "And I've got the kitty litter box. Can't wait to see what this means."

I follow him around the back of the jeep, and carefully explain that a friend of mine was hit by a car last night.

"Drunk driver?" he asks.

That was my first thought. But Drew's got a super bright light on the front and the back of her bike. So even if somebody was driving drunk, human nature would cause them to veer away from the blinking light. If anything a drunk would cross over into the next lane.

Somebody meant to hit her.

Charlie reaches up, taking off the cap, loosening the white scarf. His blond curls bob around his face. "Wasn't she wearing a helmet?"

I gesture to the cap. "I don't think you're in a position to judge."

"Point taken. But—"

"But since she wasn't wearing a helmet, that tells me she was really hurrying. Desperate to get somewhere."

"Where?"

The counselor's house.

The counselor, who denies Drew showed up. The counselor who denies being Sloane's counselor. The counselor who knows more than she's saying and wants to keep her cushy job and has a cute photo of Mr. Turner on her desk. The counselor Sloane refused to name.

"Supplies?" I ask.

He pulls back a tarp. "Clay, kitty litter box, water."

I reach into my pocket and pull out a pair of rubber gloves taken from under Jayne's kitchen sink. She'll never miss them. After I put them on, I scoop out the dry silty soil and set it inside the empty kitty litter box. The stuff is fine as talcum powder.

"Water, please," I say.

"How much water?" Charlie asks.

"We're making fudge."

He dribbles in water. I mix it with the fine soil, turning my face to the side to avoid the dust. "How long does this stuff take to dry?"

"In this cold, not long. Why?"

"You'll see."

When the mix is basically gray fudge dough, he carries the plastic box down the driveway and follows me down the road. One car passes. The elderly couple inside stare at us. Why not. Two kids walking down the side of the road on Christmas Eve morning.

"It's okay if you don't want tell me," Charlie says. "But it'd be kinda nice to know if our clay has some other use."

"I just don't know if this is going to work." I keep walking along the road. The shoulder's made up of black sand, silt, and tiny gravel. The tire tracks are dug into the soil. And two thin lines. Bike tires. They're followed by tire tracks. Until the bike tracks slant right, and disappear. Into the ditch. My stomach knots so tightly it hurts to keep walking. But I don't stop until I find the perfect set of treads. No bike tracks here.

So Drew was still riding on the road.

I turn and look at Charlie. "I want to make an impression of these tire tracks."

The tire tracks run about twenty yards before the bike tracks appear. Long enough that Drew must've felt headlights on her back. Noticed the light beam burning around her. Did she slow down? Or maybe her OCD was running so high she didn't even notice the car following her. Too busy counting? Thinking about her appointment with the counselor.

I kneel down. The car's right front wheel crosses onto the shoulder first, sinking into the soil. About five yards later, the back right wheel follows. Still feeling sick, I motion for Charlie to set down the kitty box. I reach inside with both hands, pulling out the wet clay, massaging it between my gloved hands before laying it carefully over the tire tracks, patting gently until I've covered a two-foot area.

"*That's* the impression you want to make."

I nod.

"You think I could sell this clay to police departments?" he asks.

"Maybe, if this idea works." I stand up, feeling nauseated. This wet clay reminds me of that stuff the orthodontist used to make a plaster cast of my teeth.

Charlie gets the idea. "So, when you take this off, it should have a reverse image of the tire tracks, in three-dimensions."

"Right."

"But how do you know these exact tires belong to the car that hit her?"

Good question.

"I don't, completely." I wipe the back of my wrist over my face, pushing away stray hair from my eyes. "But the ambulance parked in that driveway. And the police wouldn't park on the road. We'd see more tracks." I point my clay-gloved hand up the road. "And I pulled over up there."

He looks back and forth, curls bouncing. "But maybe somebody just drove on the shoulder."

"Only this road is so wide." Officer Lande pulled a U-turn on it without touching the shoulder. "So unless their car breaks down, nobody needs to use the shoulder. And I know that didn't happen."

"How?"

"When a car breaks down, the car stops on the shoulder. The

wheels sink in really deep. Instead, this car sped up."

He does another double-take. "How can you tell that?"

I walk back, showing him where the tires first touched the soft sand-and-gravel shoulder. "You can see how the car slows down, how the tires sink deeper. But over there, the tracks almost disappear. The car sped up."

"I still don't know how you know that."

Drew. That's how. After everything that happened in October, I started running longer distances. Ten miles wasn't even enough. But the added mileage hurt my feet. But Drew, who hates exercise, told me to just run faster. It made no sense. But she explained the physics. Higher velocity, she said, would mean my feet made less contact with the ground. I sped up. The pain disappeared. At least, the pain in my feet did.

When I explain it all to Charlie, he gives me one of those funny grins.

"She sounds really smart!"

The front door to the small house opens. The man who steps out has gray hair and a face pinched with annoyance. I don't blame him. Last night some kid wound up in his ditch. Ambulance, cops, flashing lights. Now Christmas Eve and . . .

"I'll go talk to him." Charlie crosses over to the front yard, waving. "Merry Christmas!"

The man picks up the rolled newspaper on the ground. He scowls at Charlie.

"I said, Merry Christmas!"

Puppy boy.

I kneel down to the clay, tapping the surface. That Charlie. I wonder if the world can ever wear him down.

"What do you want?" the man's tone says it's the last thing he wants to know.

"We are gathering evidence."

"You with the police?"

"That girl is their support staff."

I look up. Charlie is pointing at me. Beaming with pride.

Wha . . . ?

"Support staff?" The man mulls over the ambiguity. "So you're with the police, or not?"

"I'm definitely not totally against them."

I lift the edge of the clay. Tiny bits of gravel and sand stick to the underside. But the tire treads are there. I wave my hand. Charlie comes running back.

"Lift the other end," I tell him. "We need it in one piece."

"Roger."

We set the plaster back inside the litter box.

"This is so high tech," he says.

"And not," I add.

Charlie carries the box back to the Jeep, which the man is now inspecting. And finding problems. I hop in, Charlie sets the evidence on my lap.

The man points his newspaper. "I demand to know who you are!"

"And I will tell you," Charlie hops in, turns the key, "as soon as I find out!"

He squeals back in Reverse. I grip the box with both hands. He peels rubber down Cary Street.

He's singing again.

CHAPTER THIRTY-SEVEN

E VEN UNDER GLOOMY gray skies, Monument Avenue looks like a postcard.

I direct Charlie onto Allen Street, to the edge of our back alley.

Charlie lifts his goggles. "I'm kinda surprised you live here."

"Me, too." I climb out of the jeep, balancing the heavy cat box.

"Want some help?" he asks.

Yes. But then I'd spend the rest of Christmas break answering my mom's paranoid questions about the strange guy dressed like the Red Baron who showed up on Christmas Eve.

"Thanks, I've got it."

"Roger that." He replaces the goggles.

"I really appreciate this, Charlie."

"Aw, it's nothing." He gives that bashful smile. "But promise you'll tell me if something happens with that impression?"

"Roger that."

He grins, whips that white scarf over his shoulder, and cranks up the engine. I stand by the high gate, waiting for his jeep to rumble away, watching his tires bump over the uneven cobblestones with a sound like distant thunder. When he's gone, I set the box on the ground and wait another five minutes, in case the engine noise brought my mom to any window.

With freezing fingers, I manage to open the back gate and carry the cat box across the patio. Frost dusts the slate, and the house looks so quiet I'm already congratulating myself on another stealthy arrival.

But I see my dad.

Sitting at the kitchen table, reading the morning newspaper. His eyebrows are raised in that skeptical expression that means the paper, once again, doesn't have all the facts right. Maybe the story's about that emergency commitment yesterday. Or the murder trial.

I suck in a deep breath. Then I utter that familiar two-word prayer.

Help me.

When I press my elbow into handle of the French door, my dad hurries over to open it.

"How's Drew?" He sees the plastic box. "What is that?"

Lying is wrong.

I know that.

But looking into his tired blue eyes, the dark circles underneath, I decide the truth is only more torture for him.

"I'm fine, Drew's sleeping, and this is a geology project."

Technically, all true.

Still, I change the subject. "What's that smell?"

"Brunch. Your mother's putting on quite the spread for Christmas Eve."

"For us?"

He shifts his head, evaluating me. "You want to invite someone?"

Oh, God, no. "It's that word 'spread.' It means more than the usual quantity." Of my mother's inedible food.

"That's right."

My stomach lurches.

"I'll be in my room, call me when it's time to eat."

I carry the box up the servant stairs. Maybe I'm just tired but our house feels weird. Too quiet. A silence different from the holiday quiet outside, different from any joyful anticipation of something great. This silence feels weighted. Sad and desperate, like I'm back in the waiting room at the hospital, only no doctors are coming to help.

I set the box on my desk and take out my cell phone. No incoming calls, and the battery's almost dead. I plug it in, phone the hospital, get connected to Drew's room. Jayne sounds groggy. Hung over. She manages to tell me Drew hasn't woken up.

"I'll be there soon," I tell her.

When I hang up, I want to boot up my computer, start an Internet search on Michael Turner and Bettina Collingworth.

But the silence takes over. And it feels like it's never going away.

I shuffle to my unmade bed and sit. So tired my legs feel heavy as boulders. I try to breathe. But the air stops at my throat. I push it down, and something hits a trip wire in my chest.

A sob rises.

I choke it back.

But it's no use.

I grab my pillow, burying my face in it, and tell myself one more lie.

It's going to be alright.

CHAPTER THIRTY-EIGHT

"W AKE UP."

I open my eyes. Blink. My eyeballs feel like they're coated in sand.

"Are you awake?" Helen stands beside my bed. She holds two cans of Coke. She offers me one. "I spike mine."

I glance out the window. Gray clouds continue to smother the sky, only they're even darker now. That eerie slate-blue that whispers of snow.

I snap open the Coke. "Did I miss brunch?"

"Yes. But she wouldn't stop cooking. So now it's dinner."

Helen lifts her soda, and guzzles.

WE WALK DOWN the servant stairs like wordless inmates heading to their final death row meal.

And a surprise.

The formal dining room is usually encased in dust and clutter. But now four gold chargers wait on the polished mahogany table, bearing white china with the swirling monogram H.

The good Harmon china.

With cut-crystal goblets. And real silver, also monogrammed.

It all gleams under the dust-free crystal chandelier.

My dad stands in the wide doorway. His face looks so expectant, the warm blue eyes darting from me to Helen and back to me.

"Wow, Dad," I tell him. "This looks amazing."

"I'm glad you like it." He smiles. It almost overpowers the dark circles under his eyes. "Please have a seat. Your servers will be with you momentarily."

He walks through the butler's pantry into the kitchen. I can hear him talking to my mom, offering every glad tiding.

"God help us." Helen swigs the last of her spiked can. "If God even exists."

"Try to be nice." I pour my Coke into the crystal goblet and take my seat. "For him?"

She sits down with a heavy sigh.

When my dad walks back into the room, he's practically levitating, even though he's carrying what is surely the world's most lumpen casserole.

"Thank you," he whispers to us.

My mother trails behind him. She carries a basket of rolls that actually look delicious but will probably taste like Charlie Judisch's clay.

With everyone's seated, we bow our four heads and say grace. I feel a pinch on my arm. *Helen.* We used to play a game as little kids, seeing who could make the other bust up during grace. I ignore her. No way am I ruining this. My dad looks too dang happy.

". . . and we lift up those in need, those who are suffering."

Drew. My mom.

"We thank you for this food," he continues, "and for the beautiful hands that prepared it. But above all, we thank you for gathering this family together on Christmas Eve. May the bright light of this season shine through the darkness all year long, and forevermore. Amen."

"Amen." I open my eyes.

Helen's gazing up at the ceiling. She points. "Spider webs."

I kick her under the table, pick up my white china plate, and walk over to the buffet, which—like the table—is cleared and polished and now groaning with food. I know my dad means well, but here in this room with its twelve-foot ceilings, our foursome feels abandoned. Like more people were supposed to be here but they all had somewhere better to go. The loaded buffet doesn't help. Three casseroles. An entire ham. Green beans, potatoes, sweet potatoes, succotash. Fruit salad, rolls.

I fill my plate, while the sadness fills me.

My dad packs his plate, too. Helen stays at the table.

My mom walks over to the record player, drops the needle.

The first no-el—

"No," Helen says. "Turn it off."

I open my red linen napkin, also monogrammed, and place it in my lap. But my dad stands by his chair, waiting for my mom to sit down first. But she picks up the needle, starts the song again.

"This is insane," Helen says.

"Helen, I will not warn you again," he says. "Raleigh, go ahead and eat."

The polished silver fork weighs two hundred pounds.

The first no-el—

"What part of this do you think this is normal?" Helen asks him. "Because it's not normal. It's actually totally crazy. Insane. Nuts."

My dad clasps his hands together. He might be still praying. But he's definitely waiting for my mom. A gentleman doesn't sit down before the lady of the house. We're also supposed to wait for her to take the first bite, but that rule got thrown out because of her paranoia. We eat first, so she can know the food's not poisoned. Food she made herself.

If that's not paranoid, tell me what is.

I swallow a bite of ham. It must've come from the most dehydrated pig on the planet. I gulp the Coke.

My mother, still over by the old record player, watches me. "Do you like the ham, Ray?"

I don't get a chance to answer, because Helen says, "Ray?"

"Let it go," I whisper.

"Who the hell's *Ray*?" She looks around at us. Nobody answers. "Oh, I get it. Because Raleigh's not her real daughter."

I whisper, "Stop."

She doesn't. "What if I don't think this is my real family?"

My mom says, "Maybe it's not."

We all turn toward her.

She stands beside the old wooden box where the vinyl record goes round and round, 78 revolutions per minute. The Christmas carol plays and plays, and every word expands the size of this room until none of us is near the other, and my mother looks like a delicate figurine trapped inside an grand old dollhouse.

"Honey." My dad steps toward her. "Honey?"

"That's not Helen," she says. "I knew it the minute she supposedly came home. The train, wasn't it? That didn't fool me either."

Helen laughs. "You don't think I took that stupid train?" She upends the empty can, draining it for all it's worth.

"What did you do with Helen?"

"I set her free."

"Please, you two." My dad moves toward my mom, but once again he stops. She's looking at Helen like any sudden movements will trigger a land mine.

"Helen," my sister says, "went to spend Christmas with her real family. They're normal. The kind of family where the mother doesn't disown her own children."

The fork is still in my hand, but it's shaking. A wave is cresting over me. I can feel it coming, one of those gigantic ocean waves that bend over your head and sweep your feet out from under you, tumbling you through churning sand and saltwater until you know you will never breathe again. I want to reach out, touch Helen, signal her. *Stop right now.* But I can't move. I've wished Helen knew what it was like to get disowned by our mother. I've wished for that maybe a million times.

Now my wish is coming true.

And I wish I'd never wished it.

"Leave," my mother tells her. "Leave so the real Helen can come home."

"Only she's not that stupid." Helen shoves back her chair. It topples to the floor. She stomps out of the room.

I still can't move.

My dad walks around the big table and picks up the chair.

I stare down at my plate, afraid to look up. When I finally get enough courage, I regret it.

Victory. That's the look on my mom's face. Demented victory.

"I knew that was not Helen." She lifts the needle, killing the song, and walks out of the room.

My dad gazes at the table. I force my fork into the food, lift it to my mouth. I can't taste anything.

"Raleigh. You don't have to eat."

But I don't see another way out of this churning wave, spinning me through a cold winter's night that was so deep.

CHAPTER THIRTY-NINE

A FTER CLEANING MY plate, I shower, find some clean clothes, and head back downstairs with my coat.

My mom is in the kitchen, washing all the china and crystal that wasn't used. My dad's drying the dishes with a towel. Like nothing's wrong.

"I'm going for a walk," I tell him.

"It's supposed to snow," he says. "Dress warm."

My mom says nothing.

I lift my coat, showing my preparation, and step outside.

Helen sits in one of the wrought iron patio chairs, wrapped tightly into her down jacket. Her teeth are chattering. "W-w-want a smoke?" she asks.

I want to run. Run until my mind clears and my heart snaps open. But my stomach's full of ballast.

"I'm heading over to the hospital."

"How is she?"

"I'm about to find out."

But as I'm walking toward the back gate, my dad opens the kitchen door.

"Raleigh, telephone."

He must read the look on my face—the hospital?—because he adds, "DeMott Fielding."

I'd tell my dad to take a message. But he looks almost happy again. So I walk back inside. My mother doesn't even look at me.

I take the phone. "Hello?"

"I'm sorry," DeMott says.

My mother leans back, peering out the window.

"That's what I should've said." He pauses. "I'm sorry."

I follow my mother's gaze to Helen. She is still hunkered down in the patio chair, puffing away. The ever-confident troublemaker looks uncertain, almost scared. But my mom? Still wearing that sick look of victory.

"Raleigh?"

"I'm fine."

"Okay." Another pause. "Does that mean I've ruined any chance of seeing you tonight."

"What?"

My dad glances over, mouthing the word.

"Pardon?" I add.

"Your dad said you didn't have plans tonight. You and your sister."

"He did?"

"He said he's got plans with your mom. But you could, maybe, come out, to . . ." His voice trails off.

So many things are wrong with this scenario, I don't know where to begin. My mom's freaking nuts. My dad's the white knight, bearing unconditional love. And my sister's just been dealt the maternal death blow of rejection. Meanwhile I'm still trying to get to the hospital to see if Drew's conscious, unlike her drunken mother and doped-up dad.

Seriously? This might be the worst Christmas ever.

"It's casual." DeMott says, trying again. "Friends and neighbors. Nothing fancy."

I keep my gaze on Helen. *Why didn't she leave?* "DeMott, I don't think—"

"Please?" It's the voice of a guy asking for a second chance. But not begging. Just asking, with all his heart. Maybe his Christmas is less than perfect, too.

"What time?" I ask.

HELEN DRIVES ME to Stuart Circle Hospital and waits in the car.

The highlights are that Drew's been moved to a private room. Some of the plastic tubes are gone.

But within ten minutes, the low-lights begin to play.

Jayne sways.

Rusty paces.

Drew vegetates.

Sitting in the chair beside the bed, I hold the hand that feels chilled and describe how snowflakes form ice crystals. How they are like rock crystals. But not.

"Raleigh," Jayne interrupts. "I need to run an errand. Will you stay awhile?"

Rusty watches her leave the room. "Time for another drink," he mutters.

But what does he do?

Leaves. Without even saying a word to me.

I stare at Drew's face. The blank expression makes my heart accelerate. Her dark eyebrows are usually in constant motion— frowning, leaping with surprise. Now they rest above her closed eyes like dead caterpillars.

"Drew." My voice sounds rough. "Were you going to the counselor or coming back from seeing the counselor? I really want to know. Because I think that matters. I think whoever hit you knew it was you." I stare at her blank face. "Squeeze my hand if you got hit *after* you talked to her."

The machine beeps. But her fingers don't move.

I tell her about Mr. Turner and Charlie Judisch—"name sounds like 'jewish,' doesn't it? You'll like him." And I tell her about the tire tracks and how I got this idea for making impression of them with Charlie's clay. "Without Teddy's help. Cool, huh?"

Beep.

"The dried clay is my room. Aren't you impressed. Get it, impressed?"

She just lays there. Stone cold. Not yet dead.

"Drew, please. Wake up. I'm not a genius. I can't figure this out unless you help. Please explain Sloane's journal. I don't understand why you highlighted those parts."

Rusty walks back into the room, eyes bloodshot, sleepy-looking.

"Hey, Raleigh, thanks for sitting with her." His voice sounds airy, loose. Drew calls it *cannabis communication.* "Super cool you're here. But you can take off."

I squeeze her hand.

There's no response.

THE VEHICULAR ASHTRAY is waiting at the curb.

I climb in and the dome light flashes, just long enough for me to see what my sister is wearing.

"Helen."

"He said, casual."

"Casual doesn't mean pajamas."

"They're comfy."

"Go change."

"I'll go naked."

"It's Weyanoke."

"Don't worry." She punches the lighter and shakes out a Marlboro. "I'm not going in."

"What."

"I'm dropping you off."

"Where are you going?"

"Biker bar. In New Kent."

Red flannel. My sister's wearing red flannel *pajamas.* To a biker bar. On Christmas Eve. I start to argue. But personal experience has taught me rejection does strange things to people.

We drive full-throttle through downtown Richmond, the streets empty and waiting. As we cross into Shockoe Bottom she suddenly says, "Dad needs to wake up, get her some help."

"He's doing his best."

"Denial, that's what he's doing."

"He's not in denial." I roll down my window, letting out the smoke. "He's totally aware of what's wrong."

She cranks the volume on the music. Some whiny pretentious garbage that's probably the rage at Yale. The city lights disappear on New Market Road. Forests gather on either side. Clouds block the moon and stars. All that's visible is the road, winding alongside the river. Every turn reminds me of what Drew said, that if Sloane wanted to die, this road gave her plenty of chances. But she was racing into downtown. *Why?*

Helen turns into the wide gate for Weyanoke. "Be careful hanging out with these people."

"What people?"

"The rich."

"Dad's rich."

"*Was* rich. Big difference."

Her car rattles down the long driveway.

"See what I mean?" She points. There's a flashlight waving at us. "When these people say 'casual,' it still means valets."

She rolls down her window, blows smoke, and says to the guy, "Just dropping off."

I step out of her car. After all that cigarette smoke, the fresh air tastes like ice water on a hot day.

"Raleigh." Helen leans across the passenger seat, looking up at me through the open door. "Get into some trouble tonight, will you."

"I'd say the same to you, but you're already wearing pajamas."

She laughs, and drives away.

CHAPTER FORTY

A S SOON AS the butler takes my coat, I realize coming here was a mistake. My black pants are covered with ash from Helen's many cigarettes, and when I brush off the stuff, it smears gray galaxies into the fabric.

Casual party?

"Would you like someone to accompany you to the ballroom, miss?" asks the butler.

"Oh, no, thank you. I'm fine."

I drift through the historic foyer, following the piano music playing somewhere down the long hallway. A maid passes, carrying a round tray of empty high-ball glasses. I wave her down.

"Coca-Cola, please?"

"Certainly."

She gives me a small bow, and an excuse to stay right there, far from the chattering crowd. I lean against the wood-paneled wall. Above me brass sconces hold flickering white candles. Farther on, the piano player lilts into the holly and the ivy, the running of the deer, and the murmur of many fine voices that makes me want to run all the way home.

The maid returns with my Coke, plus a silver platter of cheese straws, tiny tarts and yucky caviar. Even though my mom's ballast filled my stomach, my mouth waters.

The maid hands me a napkin. I fill it and stay right there, sucking down my Coke and scarfing appetizers.

Casual?

Perfect.

My party of one is going very well, when DeMott steps from the ballroom. He glances down the hall. I stop chewing.

"How long have you been here?" he asks.

And then they're here, too. Trailing behind him. That whole coven of St. Cat's classmates.

MacKenna, his sister.

Mary Vale, looking pale and nervous.

Norwood, trussed up in some holiday dress that doesn't fit.

And leader of them all, strung tight as guitar sting in winter-white, the girl who looks—I hate admitting it—perfect: Tinsley.

I drop my gaze. Not only are my pants ashen, but the toes of my black suede boots look blue from heavy wear.

Why. Why did I even come here?

DeMott walks toward me. "Are you here alone?"

I nod, grasping for words.

"May I get you another drink?" he asks.

I hand him my glass.

He smiles. "Coke, no crushed ice. Right?"

I nod again.

The second he leaves, the coven swarms. They head toward me, crossing an oriental rug that's probably been here since Jefferson was president.

"Did you hear?" Tinsley purrs. "It's going to snow. You should've brought Drew. We could watch her count all the snowflakes. Bless her heart."

I fix my eyes on Mary Vale. "What did you say to her?"

"Who?" Mary Vale glances around, checking with the group.

"Drew. When she called you yesterday."

"Called you?" Tinsley spins, her white-hot hair flashing. "Mary Vale, you said she came to your house."

"She did. Before." Mary Vale keeps glancing around. She reminds me of liars on the witness stand in my dad's courtroom. "She called later. She called a lot—ten times!"

I step closer. "You told me she only called six times."

"*Only* six!" Tinsley laughs. "Drew really is getting better. Nice job, Raleigh."

I want to clock her with my clenched fist. But my focus stays on Mary Vale. "Drew must've had a good reason to keep calling. I'm betting you know who the counselor is."

Those Victorian eyes. They're so wide right now that the white shows all the way around the blue.

Mary Vale takes a temperature read of the group. But everyone's waiting now.

She says, "I don't know *what* she's talking about."

"Baloney. You know exactly what I'm talking about. And if you don't tell me who the counsel—"

"Here you go." DeMott reappears with my drink. But he doesn't even pause, taking my hand, leading me away from them. "Dance?"

"*What?* No! No, I don't—"

He sets my drink on a sideboard that probably held Martha Washington's punch and puts his right hand on the small of my back, turning me in one smooth motion, walking me backwards into the ballroom. I glance over my shoulder, the coven is staring. I glance at my feet—*can I do this?*—and look into his eyes.

The world falls away.

He pulls me close.

We pass the piano player sitting at the big black grand. DeMott nods at him and the notes change, slipping into the air and building that white Christmas, just like the one I used to know. Hand on my hip, he turns me where treetops glisten and children listen, and the whole horrible disaster of St. Catherine's is gone. I breathe in his scent, warm and clean, and lean my head on his chest. Another breath. My eyes sting. *Is this love?*

He whispers into my hair.

"Merry Christmas, Raleigh Harmon."

CHAPTER FORTY-ONE

THE NIGHT IS perfect, until snow starts to falls.

It's like a high-pitched dog whistle goes off. Everyone rushes down the hallway to the foyer.

"Roads are getting bad."

DeMott kisses my forehead. "I'll see you outside."

Casual to these people includes a receiving line. So DeMott and his family step out the front door and line up on the wide covered porch, saying goodbye to all the people hurrying home to beat the worst of the snow.

I wait for my coat.

"Having a good time?"

I turn around.

Tinsley stands in line behind me. Her smile is ice. Mary Vale's next to her, but studiously avoiding my gaze. Mrs. Stillman, dressed in black, looks heroic. A mourner refusing to give up on life. Behind her, the white-haired lawyer, Mr. McNeill, is talking. They both act like I'm not here.

"Actually." I smile right back at Tinsley. "I wasn't enjoying myself. I was enjoying DeMott. How about you?"

The blow hits the target. She flinches.

I decide this is my Christmas present from God.

But the snake slithers back.

She turns to Mary Vale, "Drew called you *ten* times?"

Mary Vale stares at the floor. I lean toward her. "By the way, Drew's in the hospital."

She looks up. That small perfect mouth falls open. Her surprise seems genuine.

"She was riding her bike, after talking to you on the phone. A car hit her, and took off." I gaze into those scared eyes. "You need to tell me why she was calling you."

"I—I—" Mary Vale glances at Tinsley, then her mother, then back at me. "I don't know."

"Mary Vale." Tinsley waves her hand, shooing me. "Raleigh's manipulating you. It's not *your* fault that freak got hit by a car."

"*Freak?*" My fist clenches.

"Oh, pardon me." Tinsley places a hand where most people actually have a heart. "Mentally challenged, bless her heart. That's the right term, isn't it Raleigh? You should know."

Mary Vale stammers. "Is—she—Drew's not going to die or anything, is she?"

Maybe it's the word "die." But our conversation catches Mrs. Stillman's attention. She looks fragile, clad in black, but there's no mistaking her steel glare. She hates me. When her gaze shifts to McNeill, however, it's pleading. He reaches forward and lightly touches Mary Vale's shoulder. Her beautiful face drops, and she turns away from me.

But Tinsley is beyond reach. In every way.

"Raleigh, how *dare* you burden poor Mary Vale. You should be *ashamed* of yourself. It's *your* fault Drew's hurt. The two of you won't even let cousin Sloane rest in peace."

My fist tightens. *A right hook—is that too casual?*

"Miss?" The butler holds up my coat.

Of course he remembers my coat. Cheap wool with a torn lining. I shrug into it but my mind's flashing images of Tinsley. At Sloane's funeral. In the cafeteria. At her own house. Constantly goading Drew. Something happened to Sloane in that car, but Tinsley's setting us up.

She wants DeMott back.

I grit my teeth, and turn around.

"Tinsley, leave Drew alone."

"My God, Raleigh, you need professional help."

"Uh, Miss?" The butler again.

The line in front of me is already outside. I step out into the cold air and see Mrs. Fielding. She shakes the hand of somebody wearing a fur coat.

"Thank you for coming," she says. "Careful on the drive home."

I glance out at the huge front lawn. It's white.

Snow.

Falling soft and silent as feathers.

I dig my cell phone from my coat pocket. A message is waiting. But before I can listen, Mrs. Fielding's handing me a tiny crinoline bag. Inside, red and white candied almonds are stamped with a silver W.

Casual. *Right.*

"Thank you for coming," she says.

Her smile is automatic. She turns to the person behind me. And a real smile appears.

"Tinsley, sweetie, always so lovely to see you. You'll stop by tomorrow, won't you?"

"Of course, Mrs. Fielding," Tinsley purrs. "I can't imagine Christmas without it. Y'all are like family to me."

My hand is out to the next Fielding, MacKenna. Her shake is the same temperature as snow. The next sister, Jillian, actually speaks to me, not that I can hear a word she's saying because Mr. Fielding's next and he's looking at me like I should be with the butler and maids.

I hold out my hand.

He reaches out. But at the last second, he raises his arm.

"Tinsley." He shakes her hand. "Could you look more beautiful?"

I look up into the tan chiseled face. I can't breathe.

Mr. Fielding tells her, "Make sure DeMott picks you up for the wedding. Promise?"

"Yes, sir."

Something bitter sits at the back of my throat. In front of me, the fur coat wishes DeMott a very Merry Christmas.

I force myself to smile.

He takes my hand, giving a light squeeze. "Is your ride here?"

"My sister's coming."

Mr. Fielding is hugging Tinsley but he makes sure to say, "Remember, son, Tinsley's your date for the wedding."

DeMott's face turns to stone.

"See you around," I tell him.

I step off the porch.

Snow drifts from the sky, falling as lightly as ash on the bare trees, the cars, the valets waiting among Audis and Cadillacs and even an antique car with running boards and pop-up headlights. A car for Bonnie and Clyde.

But the Hippiemobile? Nowhere in sight.

I lift my phone.

"Aw, gee." Tinsley rushes past me. "Nobody cares enough to come get you?"

I press my finger into the phone, so hard it hurts. Helen's message starts. "It's nine o'clock and snowing. I'm driving back to Richmond. You want a ride, call me. Now."

More than an hour ago.

Great.

Mary Vale walks past me, head still bowed. She's followed by Mrs. Stillman who is taking teeny-tiny steps and gripping the attorney's arm like she expects to fall and break a hip. I feel nothing but sympathy for her. Obligated to attend a party after her daughter dies?

I pretend to look around for my ride. Mr. Fielding watches me from the porch. So I turn back around and see the Stillmans. They're climbing into that antique car, the Bonnie-and-Clyde-mobile. Maybe it's one of Mr. Stillman's classic cars. Like the Cherrymobile. Mary Vale sits in the back seat. Face turned away. She knows something. Or maybe she's just sad. My Christmas sucks, but hers is much, much worse.

The white-haired lawyer gives the valet a tip, then helps Mrs. Stillman onto the running board, into the car. He walks around the front. He has really long legs. His stride seems to scissor the beams from the pop-up headlights. Suddenly, Mary Vale glances up. Those wide Victorian eyes gaze right at me.

She knows something alright.

DeMott wraps an arm around my waist. "Where's your sister?"

I take a deep breath. "She already drove back to town."

"Excellent!" He waves goodbye to the Stillmans. "So that means I get to drive you home?"

Get to.

Not, *have to.*

He brushes flakes of snow from my forehead and walks me back toward the big house. The snow falls in thick clumps. Falling on my eyelashes. I blink it away. And see Mr. Fielding standing at the top of the porch stairs.

"Where's her transportation?" he asks.

"I'm driving her home."

"What for?"

"Because . . . I want to."

I watch the snowflakes. They falls softly, then spiral in slow motion through the cold black air. It's like gravity hardly exists.

But it does.

"If you really have to take her home," Mr. Fielding says, "clear the road while you're out there."

CHAPTER FORTY-TWO

DeMott attaches a snow plow to one of the estate's work trucks and scrapes our way down New Market Road.

Mr. Fielding is an evil genius. The ceaseless scraping of the metal blade against the pavement makes it impossible for us to talk without yelling.

"You okay?" he hollers.

I nod.

But, *no,* I'm not okay. And not just because of this amplified version of nails-on-a-chalkboard. Mr. Fielding's contempt has lodged deep down in my bones. That same contempt I've seen a million times. But it's usually directed at my mother.

And something else. It bothers me even more.

I take a deep breath, and yell over the scraper.

"Wedding, huh?"

He leans over, keeping his eyes on the road. "Excuse me?"

I raise my voice even further. "Your dad said something about a wedding?" *The wedding you're taking Tinsley to?*

"Oh." He straightens. Outside the bright headlights hit the falling snow, pulling a white curtain in front of the truck. "No big deal. It's on New Year's."

I wait. But I can't stand it. *Why are you taking Tinsley?* "Who's getting married?"

"Mrs. Stillman."

My jaw drops. One word leaps out—*"What!"*

"You're surprised?"

"*Yeah!* Who's she marrying?"

"Mr. McNeill. It's been in the works for a while, they've been dating for years. I thought maybe it would get postponed, when Sloan . . ." He doesn't finish that thought. "But I think it'll help Mrs. Stillman and Mary Vale. Stability, you know?"

No, I don't know. In front of me, that white curtain of snow hangs like a movie screen playing images of Mrs. Stillman. At Sloane's funeral. In my dad's office. Clinging to the lawyer's arm tonight. *Wow, am I dense.* I look over at him. *No wonder he's taking Tinsley instead of me.*

"How does Mary Vale feel about it?" I ask.

"I think she's glad." He glances over, his eyes even brighter in the snowlight. "She was a toddler when her real dad died. Mr. McNeill's been a father figure all these years."

"And Sloane, she was happy about it?"

"Sloane appreciated McNeill. I'll put it that way. But Sloane was devoted to her real dad. Like how she cherished his Chevy."

That steady scraping sound fills the cab. I think about Sloane's journal, trying to remember if she mentioned any of this. But Drew didn't highlight those sections. And I think about Michael Turner, crying in the science library. The same Michael Turner in the NCIC database. Is that why Sloane went on antidepressants?

Did she confess all this to Collingworth, tell the counselor she was pregnant?

And what's Collingworth's connection to Turner?

I dig out my cell phone and call the hospital, asking to be connected to Drew's room. I clamp one hand over my other ear so I can hear the receptionist. She puts me on hold.

"Yel-lo," Jayne answers.

"It's Raleigh. Is she awake?"

"A-wake." Jayne mulls over the word. "Awake. No. Not awake. She is not awake."

My next question would be rhetorical—*Are you drunk?*—so I just tell her, "I'll stop by as soon as possible."

I end the call. DeMott keeps glancing over, I can feel it. But my mind wants to go elsewhere, especially as we come to the junction where New Market Road meets downtown Richmond. Where Sloane's car rocketed off the pavement and struck that tree.

"Raleigh, is she okay?"

"Fine."

The falling snow haloes the city streetlights and glitters frozenly from the ground.

I call Helen. She picks up on the fifth ring.

"Hull-lo?" She yells so loudly I can hear her over the snow blades.

The Christmas of drunks.

"Where are you?"

"Raleigh, that you?" She laughs. And riotous laugher echoes behind her. "How're all those stuffed shirts?"

I repeat my question.

"Buddy's," she says. "I'm at Buddy's."

"Stay there." I cut off the call then tap in the number for my dad's cell phone. He picks up before the first ring ends.

"Raleigh, honey, are you okay?"

I explain that DeMott's driving me home.

But then, God forgive me, I lie.

"Helen's waiting at a nice restaurant." I steal a glance at De-Mott, lowering my voice so he can't hear my words over the scraping blade. "How's Mom?"

"She . . ." His tone shifts. "I got her to take a muscle relaxer."

Uh-oh.

I glance over at DeMott again. He looks calm. Like nothing could go wrong. Maybe that's how life is when you don't have to worry about your parents. Or your sister. Or your best friend. Or yourself.

"Dad, I'll take care of Helen."

There's another pause. He knows what I'm saying. "Thanks, kiddo. Love you."

I hang up. My ears ring all the way to Buddy's.

DeMott double parks beside the Hippiemobile. "Guess I'll see you tomorrow," he says.

"Not another party!"

He laughs. "Church. The Christmas service? I'm assuming you'll be there."

"Oh. Right." I unbuckle my seat belt. It's questionable whether my family will make it to church tomorrow, given my mother's psychotic delusions, the muscle relaxer my dad gave her, and Helen's sure-to-be-wicked hangover.

"See you there," I say cheerfully.

Technically, not a lie. It could happen.

He leans over. "Just in case you're not there."

He kisses me. Another wonderful tender delicious kiss. I reach up, hold his face in my hands, drinking in all his goodness, his utter certainty that the world is fine-fine-fine.

He draws back, staring into my eyes.

"I know it's not a perfect Christmas," he says. "But it's still Christmas."

CHAPTER FORTY-THREE

STAND AT the edge of Buddy's bar, trying not to gag.

The place smells of stale beer and grilled cheese and all the forced laugher from people who have nowhere else to go on Christmas Eve.

Not that I'm in any place to judge.

A crowd's gathered around the bright neon jukebox in the corner, crooning off-key about rocking around the Christmas tree.

I search the faces for Helen.

The bartender behind the long bar walks over to me, wiping his hands on a rag. "No minors allowed, sorry. It's the law."

"I'm looking for my sister." I scan the room, find Helen, and point at the beautiful girl wearing red pajamas. "She's over there."

"Helen?" he says, with clear admiration. "You're her sister?"

She's sitting in a back booth with three guys and two pitchers of beer. She doesn't look over at me. "Can I just grab her and leave?"

The bartender looks at me for a long moment, then glances at a nearby table. Four men are talking over empty pitchers, their ties loosened, shirt sleeves rolled up. The bartender calls out, "Yo, Mike."

The guy who looks over has short black hair that sticks up like porcupine quills. "We're good," he tells the bartender. "Just need the check."

"Right, but." The bartender chucks his chin toward me. "She needs to grab her sister. It's Helen."

Now I get evaluated by the guy named Mike.

"She's just going to grab Helen and take off."

Mike smiles. "I never saw a thing."

"Make it quick," the bartender tells me.

I work my way through the crowded room. Faces flushed with alcohol, the moist heat of the loud room. By the jukebox, a couple dances in a new-old-fashioned way.

I wave at Helen.

"Raleigh!" she yells. "Come sit with us!"

I cringe and glance over my shoulder. The guy named Mike is watching me. But his eyes are really on Helen. The face that launched a thousand drunks.

I stand beside her table. "Come on, we gotta go."

She lifts a pitcher of beer. "Wanna drink?"

"Home. Now."

She plunks down the pitcher. Beer sloshes onto the table. She looks at the guys across the table. "Meet my sister."

"Helen, give me your keys." I hold out my hand.

"She-za one woman police force," Helen slurs.

"Keys. Please."

"Sure, youbetcha." She makes a big production of digging through her gigantic bucket bag—lifting out paint brushes and charcoal pencils—until she finally finds her car keys. But then she flings them away, laughing as they jingle through the air and land somewhere behind me. She giggles. The scruffy guys laugh.

I turn around, searching for the keys.

Oh, great.

The guy named "Mike" is picking them up.

I walk over to his table, my face enflamed. But the closer I get, the more he looks familiar. Neighbor? That spiky hair. I've seen it before. There's also a dark suit jacket draped over his chair. He hands me the keys.

"Thanks," I say.

"Glad you're the one driving. She'd be looking at a really expensive ticket. Or jail."

Lawyer. That's how I know him. From my dad's courtroom. That hair, who could forget it? I glance at the bartender. Of course, he asked a lawyer, because normally me being in here is a Class 1 misdemeanor. I glance at the other men at the table. They have that weary-pasty complexion of courtroom lawyers.

"You want some help getting her to the car?" asks Lawyer Mike.

"No. Thanks." I spin around.

My dad.

Like his wife's behavior isn't embarrassing enough. Here's his oldest daughter bombed in public with a fake ID—another Class 1 Misdemeanor plus a potential year in jail because Helen used the ID to buy alcohol.

And the other daughter? She's about to drive the drunk daughter home, even though she doesn't have a driver's license.

Quite the family, judge.

It takes an eternity to walk back to Helen. And when I get there, she's blithely telling these guys about Vincent Van Gogh. And they're listening. Because even drunk, Helen is still stunning.

"Time to go," I tell her. "Right. Now."

"Raleigh, give it a rest."

"I mean it. Now."

"I think she means it," one guy says. They all laugh.

But something in my expression penetrates the fog of alcohol because Helen squints at me. Then nods, like some clear thought rolled across her inebriated skull.

"Well, boys." She gathers her purse and belongings, stands, and falls back into the booth. "I meant to do that!"

I turn around. The attorneys toss dollar bills on the table, paying their check.

"I got it." Helen gets up, spreads out her arms for balance. "Everyone, outta my way."

But I block her. I don't want the lawyers to see her.

She pushes right past me. I grab her purse, yank her back.

"Hey!"

"Hang on a second."

"You said—time to go!"

The lawyers are waving to the bartender.

"Taking off?" he asks.

"Gotta beat the Christmas rush."

The bartender laughs. "Be careful out there, counselor. Roads are pretty bad."

The lawyers step outside.

Helen's talking to me. Something, she's saying something. But suddenly even the noise of this place is a million miles away.

And one word rings clear as a bell.

CHAPTER FORTY-FOUR

I SHOVE HELEN into the Hippiemobile's passenger seat and dash through the snow to hop into this ash-stinking sleigh.

"Did you hear what he said?" I turn the key, pop the clutch, and lurch the car into the road.

"I kin drive," Helen slurs.

"Tomorrow." I stay in first gear all the way to The Boulevard. Then I look both ways and roll right through the stop sign. "That bartender said *counselor*."

"Should go, you." Helen stabs the seat belt buckle at the clip, missing each time. "Not so bad.

"Helen, what does Dad call all those lawyers?"

"Liars."

"No. In the courtroom. He says, 'Counselor, please approach the bench.' "

Helen squints at me, like my face is out of focus. "What."

"The bartender called that lawyer '*counselor*.' "

"There!" She slams the buckle into the clip, beaming like a two-year-old who just tied her own shoes. "Did it."

I wipe the moist condensation off the windshield. Snow falls in fist-sized clumps now, like all the flakes joined hands. Helen's wipers are almost useless.

"I dun wanna go home," she says. "You?"

"We're not going home."

"Really?" She sits up. "Can we get beer?"

"Absolutely."

Not.

Drew's taught me how to deal with drunks—say whatever they want to hear, because tomorrow they won't remember one word. "We'll be there soon."

Another lie.

It takes an hour to drive back out New Market Road. And the only way we don't slide off the pavement is because these old VW bugs keep their engines in back.

And when I turn into Still Waters, Helen's fallen asleep. Or passed out.

Some serf has salted the driveway. The wet black pavement shines like onyx. At the far end, the picture-perfect white plantation house sparkles with Christmas lights.

I cut the engine and drift into the keyhole driveway, where DeMott dropped off us off Sunday afternoon. Another car is parked here, too. That Bonnie-and-Clyde vehicle that was at Weyanoke.

I slowly pull the emergency hand brake. Helen doesn't wake up. Shaking off my coat, I lay it over her like a blanket.

And step outside.

Black night above. White earth below. I trudge across the front lawn, the new snow crunching under my blue-black suede boots.

Counselor.

The word pounds through my heart.

That's why Drew highlighted those sections. She figured it out.

Sloane wrote about being depressed. *My counselor is helping me with that.*

It was sarcasm.

And I missed it.

I stand next to the sliding glass door that leads into Sloane's closet. The smooth dark surface reflects the twinkling Christmas lights. I listen and stare at my reflection. Snow in my hair. Eyes too wide.

But the only sound is that muffled silence of heavy snow.

And my own shallow breathing.

The second I slide back the door, the stink pours out.

I turn my head, gulp fresh air and lunge over the cat box. When I'm inside, I leave the door cracked two inches so the stench doesn't kill me.

Blindly, I fumble across the closet, and open the door to Sloane's bedroom. My eyes adjust to the dark. Outlines appear. Her bed, still unmade. Desk. I walk over, patting down the computer until I find the On button. The monitor lights up. But it's dim. I pat down the base of a gooseneck lamp on the shelf above, find the switch, but push too hard. The lamp falls, hits the desk, spins sideways, and lands on the floor.

I stand frozen.

The lamp lays there, bulb shining straight into my eyes.

I kneel down. Purple orbs swim cross the backs of my eye lids. I blink, pat around for the lamp's neck, and twist it so the light shines away from me, under the desk.

But somebody's at the door that leads to the outer hall.

I hold my breath.

Not knocking. Just rubbing the wood, quietly, enough to get my attention.

Mary Vale?

I tiptoe over, whispering her name.

But she doesn't answer.

I crack the door.

The cat shoots into the room.

And stops. He sees the gooseneck lamp on the floor. Arching his back, he hisses.

I quietly close the door and curse the cat.

He circles the lamp. His ginger fur poofs with danger. The lamp does look vaguely alive, with the gooseneck and head.

I creep forward, kneel down, and pick him up just like Mary Vale did.

Only he leaps out of my arms and lands on the computer keyboard. Frantically, his paws clatter across the plastic keys. He yowls. And jumps off the desk to Sloane's bed.

My heart slams into my chest, so hard it hurts.

I hold my breath.

Silence.

Still kneeling, I lay one hand on my chest. I'm having a heart attack. I take a breath, slowly blow it out, gazing at the floor.

Breathe in.

Breathe out.

Stare at the floor.

I see a shadow under desk. But it's bumpy. My gaze fixes on it, my heart slowing. I pick up the lamp and turn it so the light shines all the way under the desk.

Dirt.

I crawl under the desk. The spot's about the size of my hand, but all the way up against the wall.

I pinch the grains.

Gray.

Kitty litter.

But the other stuff . . . I pinch the other grains, rubbing them between my fingers. The scared sweat on my skin moistens the soil. I hold my fingers under the light. The whorls in my finger prints are orange. That weird orange. A color like iodine. And Teddy's voice is in my head. *Pamunkey soil.*

That soil I checked at the school lab.

The soil taken from the crash site.

I lean in closer, tilting the lamp. The splotch has a shape. Part of a shoe? A large shoe. But if Sloane died at the crash site, how could soil from the site get here, on her rug.

Under her desk.

A chill runs up my back. Deposits. They run in sequences. Chronological sequences. I pull out my cellphone and click open the camera. But my body's casting a shadow over the soil print. I reach back for the lamp.

My sudden movement startles the cat.

He rips across the bed, jumps to the floor, and bangs into the door.

My heart will break my ribs.

Holding so still I can count the pulses in my neck, I watch the cat.

He paces across the bedroom making some kind of feline whine. When he turns to cross a second time, I lunge. He puts up a good fight, but I hang on tight and race to the closet, throw him inside, and push the door closed.

Back on the floor, I focus the camera on the partial shoe print. *Click.* I check the image. Take two more for safety, then inspect the rest of the rug. No more prints. I press down, dividing the fine silk fibers. More orange grains are lodged deeper in the weave. Somebody cleaned the carpet.

Or thought they did.

I scoot out from under the desk, replace the lamp, and type Sloane's password. My fingers are shaky. It takes three tries to get BIOLOGYISLIFE.

I stare at the files. What's the journal called? I should've paid more attention to what Drew did. I type keywords. Then click open the History.

It's blank.

Not one file.

Not even Drew's search from Sunday.

I sit there, staring at the blinking cursor, ignoring the mewing on the other side of the closet door.

All those passages in Sloane's journal. She was unhappy. She didn't like being in this house alone. She wanted to take Mary Vale with her to Harvard. She said her mother's "big news" made Mary Vale happy.

Counselor.

It's all so clear I want to puke.

I know how Sloane got pregnant.

And I know what she meant in her journal, why she wanted Mary Vale out of the house.

Sloane was being molested. By the man who was about to become her stepfather.

Counselor. Lawyer.

The cat is scratching loudly at the closet door.

I type the word "counselor" into the computer. The software replies: "No matches found."

The blinking cursor matches my heartbeat.

Sloane driving into town. Fast.

No more hiding.

She was speeding.

Was she going to tell someone, the truth?

Collingworth?

My heart keeps pounding. But it's no longer fear. It's the ache of a stabbing knife. It nearly doubles me over.

I glance at the unmade bed. *In this room?*

Her grades were plummeting.

My God.

I stare at the photographs next to her bed.

None of Mrs. Stillman.

None of McNeill.

But Mary Vale—I push away from the desk.

Tonight, in that receiving line. The lawyer reached forward, touching her. Mary Vale dropped her head. Turned away. Sloane called Mary Vale "oblivious."

Not anymore.

I stand up. My hands shake as I turn off the computer. I reach up, clicking off the lamp. I can't feel my arms.

The bedroom door opens.

I look up.

His white hair glows.

CHAPTER FORTY-FIVE

BOLT ACROSS the bedroom and whip open the closet door.

The cat flies out, straight at me.

Except he sees two people, rushing toward him. He screeches like a wild animal and leaps. I jump to the side.

The cat hits McNeill.

I run through the closet. Behind me, the cat yowls and McNeill lets out his own cry. I shove my fingers into that two-inch gap I left for fresh air, and lunge over the cat box.

My boots hit the snow.

Slipping, I try to run for the Hippiemobile. It's more like a stagger, but I get to the car, fling open the door, and look back.

Once.

He stands in the doorway.

I expected him to chase me.

But he stays there, the twinkling Christmas lights throwing haloes on his white hair.

I drop into the driver's seat and shove in the clutch, twisting the key. The car's first lurch throws Helen awake. She groans. I push the gas pedal into the floor.

"Where's the beer?" she mutters.

So much for forgetting.

At the end of the drive, I hang a hard left. Helen slides into the passenger door. The Hippiemobile fishtails across the snow. Back and forth. I manage to keep us on the road. Barely.

"What the hell are you doing!" Helen yells.

I glance into the rearview mirror. Waiting for headlights. I shove the gear into second and wipe off the windshield. Helen's breath clouded the glass. The wipers flap back and forth. The pace matches my frantic heart. I want to stomp on the gas pedal and fly down the road—

Sloane.

I glance up again. There's nothing outside but snow and road.

But I see can see the whole picture. All of it.

He was chasing her.

That's why she was driving eighty-eight miles an hour. To get away. From him.

I look over at Helen. She's still holding her forehead, staring at me in a strange way. Half-drunk and half-sober.

She frowns. "What'd you just do?"

"Nothing." I shift into Third—*outta here!*—but the car slides across the road. I downshift to second.

"Cops. Is that it? The cops are after us?"

"No."

"Then why—you only get like this when we're in trouble."

"We're not in—"

"Don't lie to me."

I look over. Drew is the person who knows me better than anyone. But my sister's a close second.

"If I tell you, you have to promise—swear to God—do not call me crazy."

"Mom's crazy. You're not. But hang on, before you start." She fishes out her cigarettes, lights one, takes a deep drag. "Okay. Tell me."

So I tell her everything. From the memorial service when I thought Drew was insane, to the crash site and the junkyard, to the visit with Mrs. Stillman and Joe McNeill in Dad's office. "They told me Sloane was pregnant."

"Sloane?" She says it softly.

"Sloane." I describe the sheep experiment, and how the miscarriage affected Sloane. "So I didn't think she'd commit suicide.

240

Maybe give the baby up for adoption. But then Drew found a copy of Sloane's journal. It mentioned a 'counselor.' Mary Vale insisted the Stillmans don't believe in therapy. I thought she was lying. When that bartender in Buddy's said 'counselor'—meaning, lawyer—it hit me that Sloane meant counselor-lawyer. But she didn't want to write his name because he was about to become her stepfather. And I think she let him do it so he wouldn't prey on Mary Vale."

"Wait—a lawyer was molesting Sloane?"

"And pregnant, remember."

"What did I tell you, these rich people are *sick*."

"Helen, *pay attention*. I was just on Sloane's computer. I wanted to be sure. She had a crush on Michael Turner—"

"The Latin teacher?"

"And biology. I wanted to make sure before I jumped to any conclusions. But the journal's gone. Erased. And then he walked in while I was there."

"He—who?"

"The lawyer!"

Her cigarette smolders, but she's not even puffing it. "What happened?"

"I ran." My breath comes in frantic gasps. I'm trying to go as fast as we can without sliding off the road. And I keep watching the rearview, expecting McNeill to run us down. Or send the cops.

Helen lights another cigarette. We pass through a deserted downtown blanketed with snow, then into the Fan. The white-edged row houses look like the inside of a snow globe.

"Sloane Stillman was really pregnant?"

"And I think she was planning to keep the baby. Which, of course, would be a huge problem. I really think she was fleeing him the night she died. And she wanted to protect Mary Vale. So Drew was right. It was an accident that killed her. Not suicide."

Helen blows smoke. "What a freaking Christmas."

I have to park the Hippiemobile two blocks away, because only one street's been cleared of snow. As we head toward Allen Street,

Helen links her arm into mine. She smells like a wet ashtray.

And I'm so grateful she's here.

"What about Drew?" she asks. "Do you think it was an accident?"

We turn down Strawberry Street.

"Drew called Mary Vale a bunch of times, pestering her for information about the 'counselor.' I think Drew had figured out the whole thing."

These deserted roads, pillowy with fresh snow. Any other time this would seem like some perfect dream. Where all is calm, all is bright. But my chest feels like somebody's been punching it from the inside.

"I just thought Mary Vale was hiding the counselor's name. But now I think Drew connected the lawyer to Sloane's pregnancy."

"Wait a second." Helen stops. Her ashy breath puffs soft clouds into the cold air. "I heard there was a suicide note."

"Typed." I recall the sight of McNeill's long legs, scissoring across the headlights tonight. So tall that his legs went way under that desk. He cleaned the carpet. But missed half a shoe print all the way in the back. "I think he typed it after the accident. I found a shoe print under Sloane's desk."

We turn on Allen Street. I tell her about soil deposits. That he must've stepped in the dirt near the crash site. "If he was chasing her in his own car, he would be first on the scene."

"Maybe he got out, to make sure she was dead." Helen shivers. "I'm getting as paranoid as Mom."

I know what she means. McNeill didn't chase me. What if I'm wrong? What if this is crazy? "Michael Turner could be the baby's father," I tell Helen. "There's an outstanding statutory rape charge on him. From Louisiana."

"Why does that school have to get interesting as soon as I leave?"

At Monument Avenue, I pull out my phone and call the hospital, listening to Jayne's report. Nothing's changed. I want to run over there, shake Drew awake, tell her I finally figured out what she already knew.

But all that adrenaline bursting through my system in Sloane's room has drained me. I tell myself I'll visit first thing in the morning.

The alley behind our house looks pristine. Not one footprint, not one tire track. Just a bumpy white blanket over the uneven cobblestones.

"Van Gogh could paint that," Helen says.

We hold onto each other, carefully making our way to the back wall, slipping every other step on the stones. I reach over the gate, working the iron latch.

"One more question," Helen says. "What about Dad?"

We crunch over the snow on the slate patio. "What about him?"

"You said this lawyer came to his office. So they're friends?"

"Dad's got enough problems right now."

"So you're not going to tell him?"

"Not tonight."

"That's a mistake." She opens the kitchen door.

He is standing right there, arms crossed, blue eyes full of strange fire.

Helen immediately gets defensive. "Okay, so I went drinking. Big deal. You heard her. She said I'm not her daughter. Raleigh can take it. I can't."

"Raleigh," he says to me. His tone is hostile. "Go to my office."

I glance at Helen, suddenly confused. "What did I do?"

"Helen, I'll talk to you later. Raleigh. In my office."

"It's not her fault," Helen says.

"Quiet!"

I walk down the hall. Something settles in my gut, a feeling between pain and confusion. I step into his office. But I don't sit down. He closes the door, turns to face me. The feeling solidifies. Fear.

"Is Mom alright?"

"I just got off the phone."

"What's wrong?"

"Mr. McNeill called."

Adrenaline surges back into my bloodstream. "Dad, he's not who you think—"

"You broke into the Stillman's house?!!"

"I can explain."

"He already did. He should've had you arrested."

"*Me?* He's the one who belongs in jail!"

"Raleigh, I was right there when he asked you to leave that family alone. And you apologized. Now I find out you trespassed into their house—on Christmas Eve! What is wrong with you?"

"Please, let me explain."

"You *lied.*"

"Can you listen for a minute? McNeill is not who you think he is."

"Neither are you."

His words slice deep. I feel something rip inside my heart. All that scar tissue, torn away. All that protects me from pain, from my mom. But my dad? Looking into his angry blue eyes, I can't believe it's him.

"Do you want to hear my side?" I ask.

"No. I don't want to hear *anything* from you."

"Fine." My heart goes cold. I am stone. I can play dead with him now, too. "Be that way."

"Go to your room," he says. "And don't come out until I tell you."

CHAPTER FORTY-SIX

I GO TO my room alright.

I go to my room, tear off my clothes, throw them in the closet, yank on sweats.

And grab my running shoes.

When I crack open my bedroom door, there's a rumble of voices downstairs. My dad, reading Helen the riot act. My sister, throwing it right back. That muscle relaxer he gave my mom must be really strong. Otherwise he'd never risk raising his voice like this.

I tiptoe down the servant stairs. Helen's voice sounds far enough away to tell me they're not in the kitchen.

I leap off the final landing and run out the door.

Goodbye. All of you.

The first quarter mile is painful. And perfect.

My fingers sting from cold. My feet slip on the road. Snow freezes into ice.

I glance at my watch. Midnight.

Christmas.

Every breath rips down my chest, rakes my lungs. I pull in more. Again and again and again and the tears start coming, hot on my cold skin, as I pass Stonewall Jackson. The next mile, I can't tell where the pain's coming from. But all I see is my dad's face, looking at me just like my mom does.

Like I betrayed him. Deceived him. On purpose.

I run down the middle of the Boulevard and dart into the property for the Daughters of the Confederacy. Icicles drip from the iron cannons. Snow claws the skin on my ankles.

I run until my feet are numb.

As I'm leaving of the property, the light changes. I check my watch. Thirty-three minutes past midnight on Christmas Day. The world is luminous. Endorphins must be kicking in. Ice sparkles like diamonds.

I look both ways out of habit before crossing Grove Avenue. A car is down the street.

I jog to Strawberry Street. The road's half-cleared. More light. I glance back.

A single car, closer now.

On Park Avenue, I pick up speed. But my shoes are frozen, the soles slipping on the snow and ice. More light. I glance back. The car passes under a street light.

I check. Twice.

Pop-up headlights.

It's the Bonnie-and-Clyde-mobile.

My heart thuds. I tell my legs to move faster. But they refuse. And suddenly it's like Sloane is here beside me, pressing the gas pedal into the floor of the Cherrymobile. And Drew is pedaling madly, trying to get away.

I look back again.

The car follows me to Allen Street, closing in.

Every pore in my body breaks into sweat.

The row houses are dark.

I look up. One block. I can do it. One block to Monument.

At the corner, the road's four lanes glisten with ice. I turn right, running parallel to Monument. Behind me, the car turns.

I pivot, sliding, and race in the other direction.

The car fishtails. I run with everything left inside. The car's engine roars. I look back.

He's in reverse.

I cross the first lane of Monument. The car slides into a half-turn. Comes up behind me. I lean forward, sprinting across the second lane. Third. One more—I can do it. I stretch out my hands but everything falls away. My knees smack the ground. Ice cuts into my palms.

I look up.

Headlights burn into my eyes.

I scramble into a crouch. Those purple orbs, they're back, floating across my vision. I can hear the car, coming closer.

I race across the last lane but slip at the curb. I slide down the snow between parked cars. Pain shudders through my leg. I stumble to a stand.

The car is backing up. I stand between the two cars, afraid to move. The engine revs but he stays out there, motor racing. Wheels spinning. Then I hear the catch. The car comes forward.

He's going to crush me. Between the cars.

I throw myself on the parked car's hood. My fingers scream, ice under my nails, as I grasp for the wipers. I draw my legs up onto the hood. Close my eyes. Hang on.

The car shudders forward. The wipers lift off, I slide forward. Can't hold on. I look up, some desperate hope surging through me. Somebody will hear this, won't they? Only he's not slamming into the car. He's pushing forward, patiently grinding, trying to crush whatever's between the cars. I lift my head. My fingers so cold I can't hang on. I roll sideways, sliding off the car, hitting the sidewalk. Air punches from my lungs.

Get up.

But my legs. They don't work right. I crouch beside the car. He's out there, I can hear him. I scramble to the corner.

The alley. Just ahead.

I stagger for it. Our footprints are still there. Mine and Helen's. Sunk deep into the unplowed snow. He can't drive through that—

But as soon as my feet hit the cobblestones, I know this is wrong. So very wrong. My legs are gone. And the uneven stones, covered with snow, it's like running in place. I fall to my knees. Our wall. On my right.

The headlight hits my back.

I stand up.

He will run right over my body.

And nobody will see it happen.

My mouth opens to scream. But nothing comes out. I see my flailing hands, my fingers flickering in the headlight. I get up, stumble forward, look back. The chrome grill is bashed in. But the wheels chew through the snow. A scream tears up my throat.

He accelerates.

I stagger to the gate. The latch. *I'll never*—my scream is not human.

"RALEIGH!"

The gate opens. My dad steps out. His eyes flash white, hypnotized by that one headlight.

"No, don't!" I scream. "Get back!"

But he opens his arms. I push my legs, forcing them to move, and suddenly I am six years old, running down the diving board while he waits below promising, *Trust me, jump, I will catch you.*

I jump.

He grabs me, spins into the gate.

"Dad!" I look up into his face.

But he's watching the car. It rumbles down our alley, and turns at the corner, fading from view.

"Dad, you don't understan—"

"I do." He looks down at me. "Helen just told me. I came out here to find you."

"You saw him, right? McNeill?"

He squeezes me tighter.

"Dad, I didn't tell you what was going on, because you'd only worry. And you've got so much—"

"Oh, God, Raleigh." He pulls me close, so close I almost can't breathe. "You carry too much."

I want to say something. But my throat's closed.

"Will you forgive me?" he asks.

"Yes." It takes me a while to finish. "On one condition."

"Anything," he says. "*Anything.*"

"Call the police."

CHAPTER FORTY-SEVEN

NINE HOURS AND thirteen minutes later, it's still Christmas.
But I'm wondering about it.

Not just the gifts and the garlands and all the tiny white lights. Not just the parties and presents and evergreen trees.

I'm wondering about the pain.

In our family pew at St. John's Church, I hurt in ways I've never hurt before. But I'm singing that glorious song of old—how it came upon that midnight clear.

Standing beside me, Helen smells like a brewery, her face as gray as cigarette ash with a wicked hangover. But she is here, with her stubborn refusal to stuff all her emotions deep down inside. A refusal that last night saved my life.

She groans through the part about peace on earth, goodwill to men.

And we take our seats. Pain shoots through my shoulders, my knees. I close my eyes and breathe in the pine scents.

Reverend Burkhardt takes the pulpit.

"God sent a baby. To save us from our sins. If that's not ridiculous, I don't know what is. Even worse, this baby was marked for death."

He looks out at us, that fierce expression he wore at Sloane's memorial.

"People wanted a king. A ruler. Somebody to crush those cruel Roman overlords. But we get an infant born with a bunch of farm animals—to an unwed teenage mother. How does any of this make sense?

Helen leans into me. "What?"

"Just listen."

"We bake cookies," he says, "and gussy up our houses and throw parties because that's a whole lot nicer than remembering that God sent a baby to save my sick soul and your sick soul and every sick soul that's walked this earth."

Helen leans into me again. Pain shoots through my entire body. "What in the hell is he talking about?"

"Listen."

Because for once, I think Reverend Burkhardt is making sense.

Six days ago I walked into this same space to say goodbye to Sloane Stillman. Today, their family pew is empty. Over to the right, the Teagers all face forward. Maybe it's my imagination, but Tinsley's hair looks really bad.

"Face it, if God always gave us what we wanted, we'd mess it up."

My mother rests her head on my dad's shoulder. She woke up this morning looking slightly broken. Like somebody whose dreams were sad. But she slept through the night. Through everything. My dad calling the police. My dad helping Detective Holmgren draft a search warrant for the Stillman's house, Mac-Neill's car. My dad listening as I gave my statement to Officer Lande.

"We believe we have all the answers," Reverend Burkhardt says. "But we don't. So God has to keep doing the unexpected to snap us out of ourselves."

When Sloane collided with that tree, MacNeill was right behind her. He walked to her car, getting Pamunkey soil on his shoes. Before the ambulances got there, or the police, or the EMTs, he made sure she was dead. Then he drove back to Still Waters.

In her journal, Sloane wrote about how Mary Vale and Mrs. Stillman were "doing the Eloise thing" at the Plaza in New York City. They weren't home. McNeill went through the glass door into Sloane's room, unseen by Otto the butler, and at Sloane's desk, he typed out a suicide note. Officer Lande said the forensics team can find the deleted note on Sloane' computer's hard drive, time stamped *after* her death.

"Is this Christmas not what you expected?" Reverend Burkhardt looks out at us. "Good. That's how God wants it."

Early this morning, Officer Lande took Mary Vale's statement. She described how Drew kept calling, wanting to know if Sloane writing "counselor" referred to an attorney, not a psychologist.

Mary Vale wouldn't answer. Because McNeill listened to their calls on another line in the house.

Drew told Mary Vale that if she didn't answer, Drew would go tell the school counselor the truth. Right away. That night. Drew called four more times. By then McNeill was already in the car, driving to Drew's house. Her address is in the St. Catherine's phone book.

But he made some serious mistakes.

He drove on the shoulder of the road, for one thing. That's why I was able to get the impression of his tires. Which aren't like other tires, because they're on an antique car.

And when he snuck into Sloane's bedroom to type the suicide note, he forgot to remove his muddy shoes. He thought he cleaned the carpet. But long legs stretch far—far under a desk. He missed that one crucial shadow.

I look over at my dad. Last night, when I showed him the cell phone photos of the shoe print, he stared at them a long time.

"Raleigh, do you realize what this is?"

"What?"

He didn't even correct me with "pardon."

"This is the difference between circumstantial evidence and forensics."

He turns now, looking over my mom's head, and winks at me.

But his eyes are moist.

Reverend Burkhardt is talking about how heaven and nature sing. But I believe they also weep. For Sloane. And the baby she carried. For Drew. For me. Even for a man so twisted he covered up his disgusting abuse by killing his victim and typing out a fake suicide note.

Heaven and nature weep.

"You see," says Reverend Burkhardt, "after you take away every other possibility, you're left with a very strange truth. Improbable. But it's the truth. God sent a baby—a baby—to save the world."

My dad whispers, "Amen."

I feel that burn in my eyes.

Six days ago I was mad at God because my best friend was crazy. Everything Drew said was improbable. Totally improbable. But it was true. And when I called the hospital this morning, Rusty said the doctors might bring her out of the coma tomorrow.

What her personality will be like after this, I have no idea.

Helen leans into me. Once again pain shoots through my body.

"When does this end?" she asks.

"Never," I whisper. "Christmas never ends."

I blink away the burn in my eyes and stare at the row of heads up front. DeMott sits with his family. Mr. Fielding faces forward.

And then we are all standing. The organ bellows the opening bars. Hymnals flutter open. People sing, they sing so loudly that the plaster walls echo with joy. My voice is breaking, fracturing over the words that, maybe for the first time ever, make sense to me. Words about peace. And mercy mild. Words about God and sinners.

Reconciled.

ACKNOWLEDGMENT

Have you ever woken up from a dream and tried to describe it to someone? It's really hard. They can't see what you saw, or feel what you felt.

Writing a novel's a lot like that. Every writer needs help re-telling their dream. Here's who helped me with this dream:

My editor, Lora Doncea. She is steadfast, kind, and detail-focused, Lora holds me accountable. And I'm fortunate—not lucky!—to call her my friend. Without her, this book might not exist.

It also wouldn't exist without the guys in my house—Joe, Daniel, and Nico. They let me serve them frozen pizza more nights than I care to admit, and accept with good humor all the times I can't find my phone, car keys, or clean clothes. I love them with all my heart.

And I'm grateful to you, the reader, for coming on this journey with Raleigh Harmon.

As W.H. Auden once wrote: "Let your last thinks all be thanks."

If you'd like to know about new Raleigh Harmon mysteries, sign up for Sibella's newsletter.

To sign up, please go to http://eepurl.com/oe3wX.

Read the first chapter of Book 3 of the next Raleigh Harmon
mystery, *Stone and Sand*

I AM NOT ready for this.

Not for my aunt's car dying.

Nor for me to be hitchhiking down Ocracoke Island on some two-lane strip pavement named the Irwin S. Garrish Highway. Not my aunt trudging behind me, explaining between panting breaths how the universe *really* works.

"Everything is connected." She wheezes. "Karma."

I jab my thumb higher. A shiny black Audi is heading our way. "There's no such thing as karma."

"Oh, yes, there is."

I try to make eye contact with the Audi's driver. But the driver wears huge bug-eyed sunglasses. I jab my thumb way out into the road, waving it up and down.

The Audi almost amputates it.

In the blur that passes, I see a blonde girl in the back seat. She sneers at me with pity.

"The only reason you don't believe in karma," Aunt Charlotte says between more wheezing breaths, "is you don't think it's scientific."

I hold down the deepest sigh known to humanity and walk back ten paces, picking up her suitcases. Two gigantic suitcases. For one short stay. On a tiny island. Just a speck of the Outer Banks off North Carolina's coast. Carrying the bags forward, I listen to my Converse tennis shoes crunch the gravel shoulder. The dark granite rocks sound like snickering.

"Didn't you tell me science is cause and effect?" she continues.

I drop my head. *I am not ready.*

"Raleigh." My aunt comes unequipped for hints. "Karma is where each thing causes another thing to happen."

I grit my teeth. "Great."

"You mark my words, everything's connected."

And unfortunately I am connected to Aunt Charlotte, my dad's sister, who is completely crazy about New Age stuff. But not as crazy as my mother. Which is why Aunt Charlotte brought me to Ocracoke instead of my parents.

I glance back. The local car mechanic—a guy named Merk—drives his tow truck off the ferry, my aunt's decrepit black Volvo hooked to the back. I should be grateful. The car got us here from Virginia before dying.

But now the last vehicle is coming off the ferry. A truck. It makes its way around Merk's tow truck.

Our last chance.

I drop her luggage and stab my thumb into the air. Sixteen miles separate us from our bed-and-breakfast. The B&B that doesn't offer pickups from the island's ferry. Which wasn't going to be a problem, since Aunt Charlotte was driving her car. Only she forgot to mention that her Volvo is so old it was built by Vikings and the last time she put oil in the engine, Jefferson was building Monticello.

The truck isn't slowing down.

I step into the road. Right in the middle of the Irwin S. Garrish Highway. I wave my arms.

"Raleigh, look out!"

I wave my arms like I'm drowning at sea.

"He's not slowing down!"

Hit me.

I squeeze my eyes shut.

Put me out of my misery.

I hear brakes squealing. Rubber skidding.

I open my eyes.

"You've got some great karma," Aunt Charlotte says.

I walk over to the driver's side. The window is already lowering. Mirrored sunglasses shield his eyes. Longish salt-and-pepper hair sprouts from under a faded baseball hat. Philadelphia Pirates.

He says, "You're either really brave or really stupid."

"Or both."

"I take it you need a ride?" He glances over at Aunt Charlotte. She is a large woman. Wind billows her burgundy caftan, revealing Birkenstock sandals and white socks. In the afternoon sun, her hair look like an orange wig.

"We're not dangerous," I say.

"Throw your gear in back."

I drop my duffel bag off my shoulder, grab my aunt's tonnage, and toss it all into the dented truck bed. A work truck. I slam the gate and open the passenger door.

"Honey, you better go'n first," she says. "Could get a little tight for me."

I climb in. She follows. And we head down the Irwin S. Garrish highway.

"Where y'all staying?" the man asks.

Aunt Charlotte leans forward, speaking across me. "Blackbeard's Inn. Do you know where that is?"

"Sure." He nods. "Right fine place."

"I'm glad to hear that. When nobody was picking us up, I thought, *Either this place isn't all that nice or this is what I get for chewing out my husband before I left home.* You know, karma."

"Most locals would've picked you up," the man says. "But this week the island's sort of empty. Everyone's taking vacation before the tourist season kicks off next week."

"I don't blame people for not picking us up," she says. "I blame karma. Cause-and-effect, like I was explaining to my niece here. She doesn't believe in it, but the whole universe operates on karma. Lately mine's sinking me like a stone tied around my own neck. But Raleigh's got excellent karma. She's the whole reason we're here."

He glances over at me. I see my reflection in his mirrored shades. "You're the reason?"

"She's the reason," Aunt Charlotte says. "Won a big science contest. A man down here named Bill Brogan chose five teenagers from across the whole country. They're going to compete for a college scholarship. And Raleigh's going to win. Mark my words."

"Brogan, huh."

She leans forward. "Do you know him?"

"Everyone knows him." He doesn't sound the least bit interested.

"Well, after this contest, everyone will know her, too. Raleigh's going to be famous."

I want to throw up.

"In that case," he says, smiling, "I should know your full name. For when you're famous."

"I'm Charlotte Kittle. But she's Raleigh Harmon."

"Raleigh. Like the city?"

"Uh huh." I change the subject. "How much farther is the inn?"

"Right up ahead."

He turns left, toward the ocean, and follows a narrow road until it ends at a large white colonial structure. The black shutters match a pirate flag waving skull and crossbones by the front steps.

"Blackbeard's Inn," he says. "Enjoy your stay."

My aunt's already out the door.

"Thank you," I tell him. "You saved the day."

He smiles again. A nice smile. White, straight, kind. "Good luck with your contest, Raleigh."

Normally, I might say something to that. But we've done enough damage here. So I climb out of the truck without telling this guy that—like karma—luck doesn't exist.

I'm living proof of it.

Stone and Sand Now Available

ABOUT THE AUTHOR

S ibella Giorello is the fourth generation of her family to grow up in Alaska. After riding a motorcycle across the country, she wrote feature stories for the *Richmond Times-Dispatch*. Her stories won state and national awards, including two nominations for the Pulitzer Prize. She now lives in Washington state with her husband, sons, a large dog, a sweet parakeet, and a Russian tortoise that could've worked for the KGB.

Made in the USA
Lexington, KY
28 April 2018